FLIPPED INSIDE OUT

Flipped Inside Out

A Life Unraveled and Reawakened in the Sixties

Zoë West

LIBRARY OF CONGRESS CONTROL NUMBER: 2025921994
PAPERBACK ISBN: 979-8-218-78568-0
EBOOK ISBN: 979-8-218-83843-0

PRINTED IN THE US

Where there's a will, there's a way.

— OLD ENGLISH PROVERB

I

RIDING THE RAILS

"You want me to do what?"

My long-limbed friend nudged my arm with his elbow. "Come ride the rails with me. To Oakland and back."

I shifted my view, from searching the sky for the giant condors that swooped down from the Santa Ynez Mountains, and took a better look at Gil, who was my good friend. Soft spoken and unassuming, he had a unique way of looking at life that never failed to surprise me. We were sitting in my favorite place, a eucalyptus grove overlooking the magnificent Pacific Ocean, sharing a joint of excellent Mexican weed. Being high on really good marijuana made me slow to respond.

"I've been to the train yard in Santa Barbara to consider the possibility of hopping a free ride. I know when the freight trains head north, which cars could carry us, and when the bulls are roaming the yard."

"Cows wander around on the train tracks?" I stared at my friend, trying to figure out the joke.

Gil's smile spread across his face and lingered. "No, Kimmy. Bulls are the security guys who patrol the trainyard. They're big, mean brutes. All brawn and no brains. They enjoy beating up the hobos who try to catch rides."

Cautiously I asked, "And you want to do this?"

"Yup. I think you will too 'cause you have a sense of adventure. Come with me to the trainyard. We'll check it out after dark when the bulls won't be there. I'll show you what I've learned."

Now I was curious. I thought only hobos rode the rails, and that was during the Great Depression of the Thirties. This was the Sixties. But, I could dig it. "Okay...Sure. Why not? " I nodded twice to make sure I got the info right. "I'll pick you up tonight at eleven. In the meantime, let's get some ice cream."

Eleven p.m. arrived. I dressed all in black, so I could blend into the shadows. Driving us to the trainyard, we left my car a couple of blocks away and walked without talking. My stomach felt like I had swallowed a bunch of butterflies. Gil wove us through the parked boxcars that towered above me, as big as houses.

Wrapping an arm around my shoulders to pull me close, Gil whispered, "We'll catch a ride at night, when no bulls are here. We'll bring our sleeping bags, get comfortable in one of the reefer cars and wake up the next morning in Oakland."

Scoffing in disbelief, I clenched my hands on my hips. This time I was sure he was kidding me. I whispered back, "A reefer car, Gil? Reefer is an old term for marijuana. Does that mean this train transports pot?" This time I was sure he was teasing me.

He pressed a hand over his mouth to stifle a laugh, but his shoulders shook. "No, no. Reefer is short for refrigerator. It's for food, to keep it cold so it doesn't perish during transport. The cooling system's turned off when the car's not being used. C'mon. I'll show you."

He led me between more cars until he found what he was looking for. We climbed up the outside attached ladder. Lifting open the roof door for me, I peeked into the internal darkness. I couldn't really see anything. It was like looking into a cave. Spooky.

"There are metal shelves that fold down. They'll be our beds."

I trusted Gil. He sounded sure about hopping a free ride to Oakland. His plan seemed reasonable and thought out. Mostly I just didn't want him to think I was a sissy. So I said, "OK. I'll do it."

The next night we drove into Santa Barbara and again parked the car on a side street. We walked quietly. All my senses were on alert. When we passed the last row of train cars, he turned and, with catlike agility, climbed an attached ladder on the nearest car. He motioned for me to follow. When I got to the roof he had already pulled open the hatch. It was definitely dark inside, but enough distant street light allowed me to see the wide metal shelves. Gil had released two of them.

"Put your sleeping bag here. I'll be right next to you. We'll be rocked to sleep by the motion of the train. Tomorrow we'll wake up in Oakland and go exploring."

I heard the delight in his voice.

The metal was cold, so I quickly unrolled my bag, took off my hiking boots and climbed into my makeshift bed. It was definitely weird, like being in a tomb. I wondered if bats ever lived in here, but I didn't want to sound stupid so I didn't ask Gil. Instead, lying on my back, I decided to focus on the view through the hatch. I could see all the way to Orion and the Big Dipper. There was even a shooting star.

Suddenly I heard banging sounds that got closer and closer. "Gil, what's going on?" I grabbed his hand.

"It's OK, Kimmy. The train's beginning to move. We got here just in time."

The banging got louder and there was a jerk, and another, and another. The engine was moving our car forward as each preceding car joined the momentum. The rough start became a relaxing rhythm. Discordant clanging sounds announced the beginning of my new adventure. Butterflies again filled my stomach. Yet in a few moments I fell asleep to the gentle jostling of our giant metal bedchamber on wheels .

Morning arrived. Sunlight poked through the open hatch and warmed my face. When I opened my eyes, Gil was rolling up his sleeping bag. "It looks like a good day out there." Enthusiasm filled his voice.

I squirmed my way loose from my cozy nest, rolled up my bag, shoved my feet into my boots and followed my trusted friend through the roof's hole. I couldn't begin to imagine what awaited us.

The train had stopped. I clambered down the ladder and effortlessly jumped to the ground. The cool morning air persuaded me to pull my knit cap from my jacket pocket and tuck my hair up inside it. Dressed all in black again, I felt incognito. I was ready for more of our adventure.

Gil motioned for me to follow him away from the tracks, and the possibility of the bulls spotting us. When I looked to see where we were going, I realized that there were several rough appearing men just beyond the tracks who seemed to be waiting for us. The four of them wore battered looking clothes with rips, or dark smudges. Beards covered their faces, long and bushy, or somewhat trimmed. The men with the long beards didn't seem as scary to me. They reminded me of Santa Claus.

All the men's eyes focused intently on Gil as we walked towards them. Feeling intimidated by them, I walked as discreetly as I could behind my tall, lanky shield, trying to fade into obscurity. I held onto the back of his jacket.

Over his shoulder Gil whispered to me, "We have to introduce ourselves to the Hobo King and ask his permission to be in his territory. This is how it goes in all the trainyards. Each yard has its king. Walk beside me Kimmy. You're safe with me."

I certainly didn't feel safe, but I wasn't about to show that. My self admonished me, *Toughen up, Kimmy.* Then pulling back my shoulders, I yanked off my knit cap, stuck it back into my jacket pocket and ran my fingers through my hair. My hands fluffed it up with the hope that maybe I wouldn't look so much like Gil's kid brother. I thought I looked like a floor mop, because I was tall and skinny, with a flat chest and lots of thick dark hair, which was definitely my best feature. Then completely faking how I really felt, I boldly stepped out from behind my friend.

Those rough, scary looking men's faces suddenly blossomed into huge grins that revealed some missing, or cigarette stained, teeth. They closed the distance between us with their strong strides. Still focused on Gil, the closest man grabbed his right hand and pumped it up and down. Two other men slapped him on his back. They were all saying, "Welcome, brother, welcome."

Gil had slipped his left arm around my shoulders and drawn me closer to him. He said, "My name's Gil, and this is....." He didn't get to finish.

Those men finished for him, "Yer woman. This is yer woman. Nobody ever brings ther woman. You're welcome. Come eat with us." They all grinned big time.

So that's what we did. Gil, the hero, and me, the woman, joined those hobos for breakfast in the middle of their camp. It was behind a tumbled down building, and really wasn't much more than a fire pit with a few upturned crates around it to sit on. I guessed they slept beneath the ragged tarps that were stretched out and nailed to the old building's wall.

I didn't need to say a word. They were only interested in "my man." Lots of questions popped out of those craggy faces, "Where ya from? How long ya been riding the rails? Where ya headin' next? Are ya takin' good care of yer woman?"

Gil responded with his usual good nature to answer every question. Then stretching his long limbs he asked, "Will you take care of our sleeping bags while Kimmy and I check out the sights of Oakland?"

"Sure. Sure," the King responded with one of those strong, manly handshakes of assurance that guys give each other. "I don't know what yer gonna find out there that's interestin'. Just beware of them angels from hell. They're an ornery bunch."

We thanked them and headed in the direction of the city. When we were out of earshot, I tugged on Gil's sleeve. "Angels from hell? What do you think he meant by that? Satan and devils?"

Gil drew in a deep breath and rubbed his chin. "I have no idea. Maybe living by the rails for so long made him superstitious about what goes on in cities."

"Like dragons lurking around castles?"

Gil laughed and stuck his hands in the pockets of his jean jacket. "Maybe. Let's go see if we can find an art gallery that's got fire breathing dragons in it."

We walked until we found a couple of cool galleries, a huge old bookstore, and a dingy little market. But we spotted no dragons. After a few hours, when our stomachs began growling, Gil suggested we join the crowd we saw outside a pizza place. "A crowd is a definite sign of good food. C'mon. My treat."

While waiting for our slices of yummy thick crust pepperoni and pineapple pizza, we chatted with the other customers. There was a cross section of workers in suits or overalls. They came from nearby offices and construction sites. It was lunch break for them and this was a favorite spot.

All of a sudden there was a really loud rumbling noise that kept getting louder. "Gil, is this an earthquake? We're right across the bay from where that gnarly earthquake and fire destroyed San Francisco a hundred years ago."

Before he could answer, some of the people around us said, "No no. Don't worry."

"Don't we wish it was."

"That would be so much easier to take."

A guy in paint splattered overalls, who had been standing behind us, spoke up, "Yeah, this is show off time for them. Their headquarters is on Foothill Boulevard, which is just a few blocks away, which means we see way too much of them here."

Then from around the corner came at least a dozen hopped up motorcycles with burly looking men in black leather jackets. Two of the bikers brought their girlfriends, who looked like they wouldn't let anyone give them a hard time.

"Ohhhhhh, these Hells Angels." I was awestruck. These men, and women, were real life dragon slayers. They tried to stand up to wrong actions by our government. They wanted changes for our society. I didn't agree with how they acted all the time, but they certainly brought attention to situations.

Gil nudged me. "Shush, Kimmy. I think the crowd we're in doesn't appreciate these guys."

The paint splattered guy raised his voice. "You're damn right we don't appreciate these assholes. Who do they think they are?"

A woman in a dark suit and hair pulled back into a tight bun said, "They're just on a power trip. They think they don't have to follow any rules. They're no better than those so-called Flower Children, who have been crowding our streets with their peace and oneness nonsense."

Paint splattered guy stepped in front of Gil and me. "You look like Flower Children. Are you? Is free love yer thing?" He looked me up and down. "OK, girly. Let's see you do it right here, right now."

Someone shoved Gil while someone else tried to grab me. But my friend was quick to respond. He slid between me and the angry talking men. He didn't say anything to them. Instead he backed us out of there. The roar of the motorcycles was still loud enough to drown out whatever was being yelled at us. We didn't look back.

After Gil bought candy bars and four pouches of rolling tobacco from a tiny hole in the wall market, we safely returned to the hobo camp. He shared our adventure with the craggy faced men, whom we counted as our friends. "We saw the Hells Angels, but they weren't a problem. It was the people on the sidewalk who got riled up and wanted to hurt us. They really didn't like the idea of citizens wanting to make changes with society, especially citizens who rode Harley Davidson motorcycles."

The hobos told us that they didn't know what the Hells Angels wanted to do, or why. They weren't interested. They just wanted to be left alone. They didn't want any changes with their lives either.

Gil and I thanked them for their hospitality and for keeping our sleeping bags safe. He handed them each a pouch of tobacco that he had bought for them.

In unison they responded, "Thank ya. Thank ya," while busily rolling up their smokes.

We sat around a campfire for a while, eating hot dogs on sticks and listening to their stories of railroad rides in different places.

Eventually we laid down our bags and climbed inside. I fell asleep to another view of Orien and the Big Dipper with Gil saying, "Tomorrow let's hop on a flatbed to go back to Santa Barbara. That way we'll be able to see all that we missed on the way here." That sounded exciting to me, to see where we were going, and have the full experience of riding the rails.

Maybe we got a late start that next morning. Maybe the hobos told Gil that the southbound train was ready to leave. All I knew was that after rolling up our sleeping bags and eating bean and spam-filled burritos that the hobos offered us, Gil said, "Grab your bag, Kimmy. We've got to hustle."

He took off trotting towards the tracks and darted past a chain of parked railroad cars. After crossing a couple more empty tracks, he kept going until he reached the farthest ones. His long legs definitely had the advantage over mine, but I kept up with him. He increased his pace a bit until he was jogging, and then picked up even more speed.

I was still right behind him when I realized we were running alongside a moving train. The blood pounded in my ears. My lungs began to burn. My vision shrunk to the immediate view of Gil's back and his arms pumping up and down. Then holy moly! He tossed his bag onto a flatbed and fairly leaped aboard. He turned around and shouted to me, "C'mon, Kimmy. You can do it!"

I liked to run. As a kid I ran all over the place and often won races. I also climbed trees and swam. Now I smoked pot and ate psychedelics. I had an adventurous nature. However, at that moment I felt body numbing fear. My ears rang and I began to gasp for air. It was no easy feat I was being encouraged to perform. The top of the flatbed was level with my chest. I couldn't just leap aboard like long legged Gil did. There was nothing really to grab on to. If I tried and missed getting myself launched far enough onto the flatbed to keep from slipping backwards, I could fall under the train's metal wheels and be killed. That was a fact.

Gil reached towards me. "Toss me your bag." I flung it at him. "Now jump. I'll grab you. I promise."

I couldn't think clearly and breathe at the same time. I just ran, feeling my feet pound the ground. I seemed to be in a very bad dream and I desperately wanted to wake up. I knew I had to do something impossible and I really didn't have a choice. If I didn't act immediately I could be left behind, stranded by railroad tracks in unfamiliar surroundings. I didn't think I had the strength to follow Gil. It truly became a leap of faith that I needed. In my mind I screamed for help. Then flinging out my arms with a desperate hope, I lunged for Gil and felt the space between heaven and earth.

He grabbed and quickly pulled me all the way onto the flatbed. I lay there, shaken to the core of my being. Then I fiercely threw my arms around his waist. I was beyond talking, or even crying. I just wanted to be held.

"You're safe Kimmy. You made it." Gil's strong arms encircled me, and his calm words reached deeply inside me. They gave me relief and settled me. The pounding of blood in my ears gave way to the sounds of the train click clacking on the metal rails. Gil directed my gaze to the middle of the flatbed, where I saw a trough. We both rolled over to it, pulling our sleeping bags behind us. It was about a foot and a half wide and maybe two feet deep. We dropped in our sleeping bags and sat down on them. Gil was behind me. I leaned against him, closed my eyes and breathed deeply. I told myself to shake off my fear. A moment later I opened my eyes to check out my new reality.

There wasn't much to see because we passed fenced backyards. The rickety wooden structure separated the ramshackle homes from the tracks. Kids had climbed that fence and watched the train pass by. We waved at them and they waved at us. Then they threw rocks at us. I guessed we were their daily sport. We ducked down into our trough to retreat from the battering.

Exhaustion from my narrow escape with death caused me to seek release. Gil rolled a fat joint, lit it, took a couple of hits and offered it to me. I smoked and tried to calm my mind. *Gil saved my life. But what if he hadn't?* Perhaps that possibility weighed heavily on him too. Both of us rode deep in our own thoughts. The pot helped me to relax. I again leaned back into him, thankful for his strength, protection and friendship.

The ride to Santa Barbara lasted all day. There must have been beautiful countryside that we traveled through. California had lots of that. But I wasn't able to see any of it. My focus was all internal. Scenes and sounds kept occurring in my head as I tried to grasp and process what I had so profoundly experienced.

Running. Running. Running. Stretching to keep up with Gil. My heart was pounding. Afraid of being left behind or stranded in an unknown place. Running. Running. Running. Next to a powerful machine. Metal that could easily crush me, without even noticing, and keep on going.

Who am I to think I could compete with that? What am I trying to prove? Why did Gil ask me to go with him? He has a girlfriend. Did he ask her and she turned him down? I trust him like a big brother. He's really smart. He knew how to talk to those men, those hobos. He said he'd keep me safe, and he did, I guess. But did he know how dangerous it all would be, before we left? Did he know? Why didn't I know? Why didn't I ask?

I must have fallen asleep because I don't remember anything else except for Gil whispering in my ear that we had returned to Santa Barbara. My car was where we had left it, and it was an uneventful ride to our homes in Isla Vista. The familiar ocean air greeted us. I dropped my friend off at his place with a faint kiss on his cheek, because I was home again.

My roommates were home and wanted to know where I had been with my sleeping bag. There was so much that I could tell them, but I needed the oblivion of sleep. I'd save my tale for another time, perhaps tomorrow. I went to my room, pulled off my coat and boots, and fell across my bed. Visions flickered across my inner eye. Trains, hobos, children on a rickety fence, Gil's long, powerful legs leaping easily onto the flatbed. The fear of that moment returned. My heart began to pound. I wanted to scream. Instead, I lay still, willing my breathing to calm down. Gil's words, "I'll grab you. I promise," pierced my consciousness. I had ridden the rails.

2

SCORING POT

A couple of weeks later Bob showed up on my doorstep and talked me into going to Tijuana with him to score pot. Most likely I agreed to do that because he was cute. He possessed a magnetic aura and I wanted to drape myself all over him, in spite of the fact that his sweet girlfriend, Suzanne, was my dear friend. That was really all I knew about him. I had no clue where he grew up, or if he took classes at nearby UCSB, or if he had a job. He was cute and he asked me to go to Tijuana with him for the weekend.

"So why are you asking me?"

Bob shrugged his shoulders. "Oh, I don't know, Kimmy. I thought this is just something that would interest you....And you have a car."

It took five hours to drive from Isla Vista, California to Tijuana, Mexico. I drove my 1949 Chevy Fleetline. My dad gave it to me when I graduated high school. The back seat was its best feature because it was so comfortable. I would let my friends drive while I viewed the world from there. However, on this trip to Tijuana, or TJ as we often called it, I drove because Bob did not have a driver's license.

The trip revolved around Bob's plan: drive to Tijuana, find a taxi cab driver who knew how and where to get marijuana, make contact, collect it, and drive back to Isla Vista. All of that would be accomplished during the weekend jaunt. He never mentioned Tijuana being in a country with really strict laws against possessing marijuana, or that the prisons there were hideous, rat-infested places where people died in agony. Bob was not the talkative sort, which meant I had lots of time to think on our drive.

"Care to join me?" Bob asked as he passed me a lit joint.

I took one tiny hit, because any more than that would cause me to be a very distracted driver. I contented myself with smelling the wonderful smoke's aroma, while humming Buddy Holly songs. The lack of communication allowed me to ponder the meaning of this trip. *Why am I doing this? I was raised by parents who love me and taught me to be a well-behaved person. I score above average on intelligence tests, I'm healthy, and I have friends. Although I dropped out of UCSB after my first year, I have a job on campus working for the portrait photographer, and I pay my bills. All of this points to me being a level headed young woman.* I nodded to myself in agreement.

On the other hand, *I really like smoking pot, getting stoned, and looking at life from different perspectives. All the ice cream I devour when I'm high is totally groovy too. So, during the week I work, but on weekends I dig new scenes. Although I barely know Bob, his plan is totally cool with me.*

We had no trouble passing through the border security checkpoint. The Mexican guards didn't ask for ID, or anything. They were happy to see us. Afterall, we resembled college kids looking for the drunken, lurid excitement of that south of the border city with the assured reputation for sin. We were good for business.

I didn't pay attention to where we drove because Bob just told me to turn here, or turn there. But I saw that this city was dirty, noisy, ugly. It overflowed with open garbage cans. Some of them had skinny, dead dogs tossed on top. Also, there were small, filthy children chasing each other around without an adult in sight. They ran up to our car when we stopped at a traffic light, stuck out their grubby fists that held packs of gum and jabbered, "Cheeklets, Meester? Only one peso." I kept my window rolled up. Broken down cars seemed to be everywhere, with missing wheels, smashed windows and headlights. The smells that filled the air were bad too.

Bob picked out a hotel and pointed to a parking lot.

I locked my car and followed him inside. "This is so spooky and weird." I grabbed his arm. "It feels like that Hitchcock movie, 'Psycho.' "

He glanced over his shoulder at me. "Yeah, I can see how you might think that." Then he walked straight to the short bald man with a gigantic mustache who stood behind a counter, and spoke to him in Spanish. The bald dude turned towards me, looked me up and down, and said, "Si, si." Bob gave him money and received a key. We walked up creaky stairs to the second floor. I was careful not to touch the walls that looked like maybe the holes were from bullets and the spots were bloodstains. Ugh!

The room had no bathroom. It was at the end of the hall and was shared by the other lodgers. The bedcover was torn in several places. The table and two chairs could be better used for firewood, and the sink turned out to be plugged up. At least the one grimy window let in a bit of sunlight.

With his usual low-key presentation Bob explained, "Kimmy, you stay here. I need to find a taxi driver who can score for us. It won't be safe for you to go with me. I'll show you some sights when I get back. Lock the door."

I sighed and said, "OK."

There hadn't been anything for me to do while he was away, except look out the dingy window and wonder how anyone could live in such a forlorn, filthy and noisy city. Every car that drove by had the need to blast its horn. I hummed more songs. Good ol" Buddy Holly. But my mind kept intruding with its own song. *What if Bob doesn't come back? What if he gets mugged, or kidnapped and held for ransom? How will I get back to Isla Vista, or even find my way out of here? At least I have my car."*

Fortunately for me Bob wasn't gone long, maybe an hour. "I found a driver who agreed to make the deal for us. We'll go with him in the morning to get the package. Now let's eat and go to a bar." He pulled money out of his pant's pocket and counted it.

"A bar? Neither one of us is twenty-one." I reached for my jacket.

"Don't worry, Kimmy. That doesn't matter here." He held the door open for me.

I soon learned that a lot of things didn't matter here.

We stuffed ourselves on big, fat burritos from a nearby cafe. Bob had a beer, and I had a Dr Pepper. Afterwards we walked another block. He held my arm so I was pulled close to him. He whispered, "It's better if you don't look at anyone. Sort of keep your eyes down. OK?"

The building we entered was dark and stuffed with people, mostly men. I might have been the only female person there. No, wait, I saw two or three others, but they looked so old and worn out. I mean, they couldn't have been anyone's girlfriends. Could they?

Bob pushed his way through the crowd, still holding my arm. He approached a table near an open space and gave money to the two men who sat there. They got up and gave us their seats. The open space looked like a dance floor.

I didn't know Bob liked to dance. He's full of surprises.

He ordered two bottles of Dos Equis beer for us and settled back in his chair. We were just in time for the show to start. Lively Mexican music poured from a speaker on the wall. The star performer appeared. She looked younger than me, maybe sixteen years old.

"Bob, how old do you think she is?"

He didn't respond.

Is this part of the show, pretending to be a young girl? Then I realized she was wearing a short nightie. It was see-through. It didn't even cover her bottom. That was all she was wearing, except for very high heels and tons of makeup which gave her a play doll appearance. She pranced around in her seriously too high stilettos like she'd been born wearing them. Waving her arms back and forth over her head, she swayed her hips as she danced around with a radiant smile and beguiling eyes. She glowed with pleasure. She was the center of attention. All the men's eyes were glued to her, including Bob's. Obviously she knew what she was doing.

I tried to imagine her reason for this performance. *Does she have a desperately sick mother, or baby brother, at home who needs medicine, and this is the only way she can get money to buy it? Or has she been forced into this activity by a drug dealing boyfriend?* I had no way of knowing.

She was radiant. She looked like she really enjoyed herself. When she began pointing first at one man, and then at another, beckoning them to her, I saw Bob's body jerk and his face and ears burned crimson. Maybe that's how all the men in the room responded. But they didn't budge from their seats. At least the Mexican men didn't. Then, suddenly, a young white dude with a blond crew cut and tight muscles sprang up and charged towards her. He had been sitting a few rows back from the open floor. I could see his biceps flex below the sleeves of his bright red tee shirt as he swiveled through the few tables that separated him from his desire. He stopped within inches of the young temptress. He jerked open his Levis, forcefully stepped out of them and his briefs, and kicked them aside. WIth his manly sword extended, he also was fully and unabashedly ready to perform.

The crowd cheered enthusiastically, "Ole,ole, el toro"

The girl coyly turned her back to him and leaned over.

Bob quietly concentrated on the action as he too leaned forward.

I looked for a way out. I started to stand up, but Bob firmly pulled me back down and whispered into my ear, "Remember Kimmy, it's not safe for you to be alone on the street. We'll leave soon." He smoothly returned his attention back to the dance floor.

I turned my chair around to face away from the wretched performance. I slumped over in shame and disbelief. I thought to myself, *Is this what people my age willingly do? They come to TJ to see this show? This is certainly not part of my plan.*

The cheering stopped, but the crowd asked for more. The disgusting creep in the red shirt put his pants back on. I didn't see the girl anywhere. Bob took my arm again and guided us out of there. We walked back towards the hotel. In his ultra calm manner, without even looking at me, he said, "There are other bars in Tijuana that feature women with donkeys. Would that be more to your liking.?" He chuckled.

"Shut up, Bob. Does your girlfriend know you come to these places?"

He gave me a shocked look. "Of course not."

Back at our hotel room I was only interested in the oblivion of sleep. Bob's sex appeal completely diminished for me. All I wanted was to get the pot and go home. I trusted that the next day would offer a better reality. Tomorrow was Sunday, the holy day of the week.

After a quick breakfast of mini tacos from a food stall on the corner by the hotel, Bob found the taxi driver with whom he had made the arrangement. The man didn't look old, nor young. I didn't see anything about him that would distinguish him, so I don't know why Bob picked him.

Off we went. Bob sat with me in the back seat. He concentrated on where we were going, as we drove out of the city and traveled a few more miles into the countryside. The driver pulled over by a narrow dirt road, parked, and turned off the engine. He turned to Bob and said something. I sort of wished I knew how to speak Spanish. Bob seemed to understand him and that's all that really mattered.

"Wait here, Kimmy. This will only take a few minutes."

They both left the taxi and walked down that dirt road, where they disappeared around a bushy corner. I again felt like I was in that 'Psycho' movie and something weird would happen any second. I twiddled my thumbs to calm myself. That didn't really work. However, they returned shortly. Another Mexican man, in a ragged shirt and faded pants walked between them. He wore beat up sandals and an old straw hat, and carried a package wrapped in newspaper. Everyone smiled and shook hands. I couldn't see how much money Bob gave the dude when he received the package.

During the Sixties, marijuana was incredibly cheap. We purchased a kilo (2.2 lbs) of high grade weed (also referred to as a brick) from the farmer for five dollars. On the other hand, Acapulco Gold, supposedly the finest marijuana in the western hemisphere, sold for a lot more. In the next few years it climbed to $500.00 per kilo.

Bob and our driver slipped into the taxi. We headed back to Tijuana.

"How much did you pay him?"

As Bob pulled out his rolling papers and matches, he responded, "The price you and I agreed upon."

"How do you know if it's any good?"

He ripped open a small hole in the package and pulled out a pinch of the weed. "Smell this," he said as he passed it below my nose.

"Oh my goodness gracious! I do declare. And what are we waiting for?"

In seconds Bob's nimble fingers had rolled up the grooviest smelling pot into two fat doobies. He lit one and gave it to the driver. He lit the second one, took a giant sized hit and passed it to me. With the three of us toking away, the cab soon filled with smoke and I became very high. I don't remember what Bob talked about, but whatever he said was hilarious to me. I laughed my fool head off. That's how I usually got when I was stoned. All fluff and no substance.

When I felt the taxi slow down, pull over and come to a stop, I tried to peer through the haze of pot smoke to see where we were. Our driver left the cab. He spoke to an older man in a tan suit. They stood by a shiny car which we had parked behind. Then our driver came back to the taxi, sat down and spoke over his shoulder to Bob. I didn't understand a word, but he sounded upset. He rolled down his window and tried fanning the smoke away with his hands. That was really funny to me. I bellowed out laughter and flopped around on the seat, not at all trying to contain myself.

"For God's sake, Kimmy, stop." Bob, not so gently, grabbed my shoulders and shook me. He actually appeared a bit ruffled.

"Listen to me. You've got to stop laughing. Act normal. Sit up straight and be quiet."

I hadn't a clue that there was a problem. I saw the man in the tan suit walk towards our taxi. He looked different from any other Mexican men I had seen in the last twenty four hours. I mean, he wore a nice suit. He even wore a tie. And he had a very shiny car. I liked his shiny car. I wished my car was that shiny. I wondered what kind of wax he used on it. I could see there were other people still in that shiny car.

As the man got closer to us, our driver, whose face had turned white, pounded his palms against the steering wheel while saying, "Caca, caca, caca." That word I knew. It meant 'shit.'

That's when I noticed Bob had a firm grip on my arm. I thought of asking him what was going on. However, my mouth didn't want to do anything but laugh. Bob squeezed tighter and leaned towards me. He whispered, "That's the Chief of Police for Tijuana. He was taking his family home from church, when his car ran out of gas. Our driver had to stop, to offer assistance, or else he would lose his taxi permit, and who knows what else could happen to him. We're in serious trouble." He released my arm and tucked in his shirt, making sure he got it just right in the back.

I wondered if I needed to tuck anything in. With this new information, I semi-sobered up. I padded my hair to make sure it was in place. I sat up straight and tried to look my best proper girl self. But the situation still rocked me with hilarity because it was so outrageous. Truly I was a full blown pothead. An all-too-clear picture formed in my mind. *Here I am in Mexico. My friend and I just scored an illegal drug from a scruffy looking farmer, on a dirt road off the main highway to Tijuana. We or, at least, I am obviously stoned out of my mind. The cab billows and reeks with pungent smoke. Undoubtedly Bob and I will soon be arrested and thrown into prison. Our families will never know what happened to us. We'll rot in prison. I'll spend the rest of my life being raped daily and having only rats to eat.*

When the Chief of Police got into the front seat of the taxi, he did not look happy. He grunted something to the driver and waved to his family, who were peering out of every window of his nice, shiny car. He turned around to look at Bob and me. It was more of a glare, than a look. I wanted to apologize. I took a deep breath and opened my mouth. As the Chief turned back around, Bob slapped his hand over my mouth. I got the message to shut up.

The closer we came to Tijuana, the more I sobered. What a bummer. Nobody talked. We just all looked straight ahead into our separate futures. However, as we neared the city, the three men started talking in rapid-fire Spanish. Bob had let go of me. He was nodding his head up and down. Up and down. He very clearly said, "Si, Señor. Si. Si. Gracias. Muchas gracias." Then he turned to give me a penetrating look while nodding his head.

I mimicked him and nodded my head. My mouth even uttered the words, "Si. Si."

The taxi stopped. We arrived at my car. Bob opened his door and again grabbed my arm, pulling me out behind him. He maneuvered me directly behind him and kept me close. Just before the Chief had gotten into the car, when Bob was frantically tucking in his shirt, he was actually shoving our illegal 2.2 pounds of very good marijuana behind his back and under his shirt. He held me close hoping the bulge wouldn't be noticed.

"What do you say, Kimmy? Let's high tail it out of here and get back to the good ol' USA. How about I drive us home?" He nudged me towards the back door and opened it for me.

That sounded like a great idea, since I was still really high. "OK. Sure. Works for me." I handed my keys to him. I waved to the men in the taxi, the way a proper girl would do. The driver had already turned the cab around. I watched it fade into the background of noisy, filthy Tijuana. Then I settled into the backseat of my car with its beckoning comfort and safety. *Whew. What a weird day.*

During the quiet, uneventful drive back to familiar surroundings and friends, I pondered the rotten day experienced by Tijuana's Chief of Police. "Hey, Bob, simply because the Chief forgot to fill the gas tank of his nice, shiny car, his day went miserably wrong."

Bob barked out a laugh. "Yeah, it sure did. He was just a regular dude taking his family to church. Except on their way home his car ran out of gas and he had to ask for help."

I tried to imagine myself in his shoes.

Bob laughed harder and spit out his words. "This was the man who brought law and order to wild Tijuana. He had to leave his family by the side of the main highway, for all to see, because he screwed up. But I bet the worst part was having to accept help from a stupid taxi cab driver who scored pot for two equally stupid Americans." He almost choked on his laughter.

I took the moment to voice my opinion. "I see the Chief as a decent man. He excused the driver's illegal involvement, in exchange for helping him get gas for his car. He needed to get his family safely home."

"Yeah, maybe. So what?"

Leaning forward to rest my folded arms on the back of Bob's seat, I said, "I think he let us go because we don't look much older than his own children. Instead, he told us, or told you, 'cause I didn't understand a word he said, exactly what would happen if we ever tried that again."

"Well, OK, you're right, Kimmy. He must not have seen our package." Bob patted the newspaper wrapped brick that nestled close to him on the front seat. "Otherwise, he might have thought differently about us. We got away with scoring a kilo of primo marijuana." Bob showed me his big grin in the rearview mirror.

I leaned back into the comfort of my car and watched the scenery go by. We were lucky, no doubt about that. I vowed to myself that there was no sane reason that could bring me to Tijuana ever again.

3

SHOEBOXES

Maybe a month after riding the rails to Oakland with Gil, I pulled out the tree pruning ladder from behind the garage and climbed onto the roof of my house. There I sat, on the edge, holding a shoebox of peyote on my lap.

Peyote was sacred to me and my friends. The psychedelic experiences it brought gave us glimpses into a mystical world full of creativity, harmony and spiritual insights. Gil had taken a bus to Arizona and found an Indian medicine man who showed him how, and where, to gather their ritual plant from the desert. Then he mailed them to me in an old shoebox wrapped in plain brown paper with no return address. He didn't have enough money for a bus ticket back here, and it wouldn't be safe hitch-hiking with an illegal substance. So he mailed them to me. I hadn't been told to expect any unusual packages. I didn't know it was coming until it arrived.

Carefully I placed each spineless cactus, about the size of a peach, onto its own spot in the lovely California sunshine. I wondered how many days it would take for them to dry into the hard little buttons that my friends and I would then chew to release the mescaline.

A week later Gil showed up on my doorstep and asked, "Hey, Kimmy, did you get my package? I figured you'd know what to do with it."

I did know what to do with it. Also I knew that possession of peyote was illegal. If anyone were to get busted for these amazing plants, it would be me, because they were on my roof, where I put them.

After showing Gil where to find the ladder, I hunkered down beneath the apple tree to assess my reality of partaking in this criminal activity. *How did I get here? Not only am I doing something illegal, I'm happy to be doing it. This is surely not the shoebox of life that I had been raised in. Why have I so profoundly veered from my parents' guidance?*

Mostly my friends and I smoked marijuana. We usually called it pot, weed, or grass. Getting high was a major occupation in the Sixties. It could have been viewed as a religion for us. We definitely adored it and indulged in ceremonies, such as gathering together and sitting in a circle. We passed around a joint (with the various names of doobie, blunt, fatty, J) and took a puff (toke, hit) or two while someone else rolled up another. Toke. Toke Toke. Sometimes cough, cough, cough.

Rolling a joint by hand was a skill. I practiced diligently to be able to hold the tiny cigarette paper, add an accurate amount of pot to cause a good high, tuck the remaining paper in and around the loose leaf bits, twisting gently, then licking the flap and pressing it in place.

"C,mon, Kimmy. What's holdin' you up?"

"I'm getting there. Whoops. OK. OK. Just ummm a minute... Got it!"

We smoked joyously. We laughed vigorously. That's what it was all about. Enjoying each other's company and having a good time. We were delighted to be together, sharing an experience that allowed us to feel good about ourselves. Feeling safe together, we wore a sense of pride in daring to do what our society deemed harmful and illegal. Marijuana was our friend. It could cause no harm, even when it gave us the 'munchies'. That was the all-compelling desire to eat, especially ice cream, which often meant a journey to the ice cream parlor.

We piled into my 1949 Chevy and headed to Baskin Robbins 31 Flavors in nearby Santa Barbara. I focused on keeping the car going the speed limit. I don't mean that I drove too fast. No. Just the opposite. Being stoned slowed everything down. There was just so much that caught my attention. "Wow. Do you see that old lady with her gigantic dog? What kind of hat is that guy wearing? Where does that street go?"

"The stop sign, Kimmy. You've got to stop at the stop sign."

"Go faster. The speed limit is thirty-five."

"Let that car pass you."

"Are we there yet?"

We always arrived safely. The real problem came when we each had to decide what flavor to get, and was one scoop enough, which of course it wasn't. Then how could anyone choose between burgundy cherry, butterscotch ribbon, or choco-late mint? My absolute favorite was peach. Our friend, who worked there, had tried all the flavors. She gained twenty pounds.

That's how it was with us potheads. The peyote trip was a bit different.

"Kimmy. Hey Kimmy, what world are you in?" Gil stood over me nudging my foot. "The peyote's looking good. Another week, or two, and they should be dry enough to use." He sat down beside me and passed a lit joint my way.

After a couple of tokes I said, "I remember my first time with peyote. We were at Matt's apartment. You were there, Gil. You,

Eddy, Nancy and Bob, who had scored it from somewhere. But he didn't know any more about it than the rest of us."

Gil nodded, took a hefty hit on the well-rolled doobie and replied, "Yeah, he thought it could be chopped up and put into soup to drown out its horrible taste. Imagine thinking a can of vegetable soup could do that." He shook his head and took another hit of pot, holding in the smoke for maybe half a minute to heighten its effect.

Just the memory of the taste made me gag and clutch my stomach. "I couldn't just swallow them, like pills, to avoid the hideous taste. They had to be chewed. Those dried buttons were so darn tough. Eventually I got them down, but then the nausea and vomiting happened." A laugh rolled over my lips. " In order to connect with the gods we had to have no taste buds and cast iron guts."

"But there was a period of calm before the show started. Right?"

"Right," I said as I took a deep toke on the joint and recalled the memory.

Gil spoke softly. "We all hoped to gain spiritual access. We wanted to see beyond the veil of our society's concepts and enter different dimensions. We wanted a mystical experience like the Indian shamans had."

" And wow....what an experience it was!" I exclaimed as I clapped my hands for emphasis. "When I was indoors, everything became surreal. The walls oozed and dripped. The ceiling sprouted faces and incredible patterns. And for some reason my body only moved slowly, like a sloth in the jungle trying to climb up her tree."

Gil grinned and nudged my ribs with his elbow.

The memories started pouring out of me. " At some point I decided to take a shower. I struggled to get my clothes off. My jeans had a button and zipper. How absurd. I wondered why on earth I even bothered wearing clothes. I tugged and pulled until I peeled them off and dropped them in a heap just outside the bathroom door. They looked so lonely there that I brought them into the bathroom with me. Can you believe that? I just stood there, holding my clothes, feeling sorry for them until I remembered that I wanted to take a shower."

I massaged my forehead as I recalled more of that event. "Somehow I figured out how to make the shower work, at least the cold water. It created the loveliest sounds, like raindrops falling from an angel's fingertips. I listened and watched the water mingle with different parts of my body, which changed colors and slipped away down the drain. That kept me raptly occupied, until some kind person found me and turned off the water. He told me something, but I couldn't understand what sounded to me like a language from outer space. Instead I heard music that came from the living room and headed for that, dripping wet and wiggling my hips."

"I definitely remember that day, Kimmy," Gil responded as he gently laid his arm around my shoulders.

I relaxed and leaned against him. The warmth of the sunshine soothed me. "I never did figure out who had helped me out of the shower and put clothes on me. Hopefully it was Nancy."

Gil spoke softly, but clearly. "Whenever we bowed to peyote, there would be one of us who stayed straight to watch over everyone else to keep them safe."

" Of course."

" Well, that time I was the straight one. And let me assure you, it was a delight to be of assistance to you."

"Oh......" Shocked by his admission, my face blushed with intense heat and I quickly shifted to sitting up very straight.

If my friend noticed my discomfort, he didn't draw attention to it. Instead he said, "So a month later, after Bob had scored more buttons, he was sure that ice cream would drown out the unbearable taste. Of course that didn't work. How could he even have thought of defiling ice cream? But we were devoted to the mystical experience, so we once again chewed, vomited and emerged into an altered state of consciousness."

I nodded my head in agreement. "That was almost the ruination of ice cream for me, but it was one of my favorite peyote trips. Eddy watched over us that time. In fact he drove us to the bluffs that rose above the ocean. The grove of eucalyptus trees there smelled so wonderful. It was a beautiful blending with Mother Nature. I was barefoot, as usual. The warm powdered dirt, the soft ocean air, the open space created a magical palace of earthly harmony. I wanted to be there forever. "

"Yup, " Gil agreed. "We just wandered around, being a part of all that beauty and amazement. And you kept your clothes on."

"Shut up, you big meany!"

Gil laughed and stood up. "Thanks for knowing what to do with the peyote package. I'll take them back to my shack and let you know when they are ready."

I relaxed against the apple tree. *This life is so much better than the one my parents planned for me.*

The truth of the matter is, I was not prepared. My parents loved me but they did not lay the groundwork for me to step into my future. After high school they sent me to college to find a husband. They expected me to find a man there who would marry me, in exchange for complete devotion to him, which included being an excellent mother and a competent homemaker. Of course I was to remain a virgin until my wedding night. That was the prevalent ideology of middle class, white America during the Fifties. So, the summer of 1960, before I was sent to UCSB, I pondered how I would accomplish that goal.

My parents' relationship didn't offer any clues. I had seen my dad kiss my mom one time. They hardly ever talked to each other. They just seemed to be in agreement about everything.

My mom rarely talked to me either. She didn't tell me anything about anything. I didn't even know why I had a menstrual period. "That's just something that happens to girls. Wear this giant pad between your legs and that will take care of the problem." She spent most of her time being that competent homemaker. That was her domain which she wasn't about to share with me, except how to iron pillowcases, dust the furniture, or make Jello. All the cooking, shopping and budgeting know-how she kept to herself.

Then there was my dad, who read the funny papers to me on Sunday mornings when I was little. He also taught me to bowl, play tennis and use correct grammar. However, as for me going out into the world and being a successful adult who could take care of herself and possibly be a benefit to the human race, none of those skills were passed on to me. Even though he gave me a weekly allowance, I didn't have to do anything to earn it. And the only encouragement to work was through a job he arranged for me at a men's clothing store during Christmas break of my senior year. He knew the owner.

My parents didn't talk with me about what major I wanted to pursue in college or what my aspirations were, or even that they were proud of me and I could succeed at whatever I chose. Besides all that nonexistent moral support, I had no opportunities to speak up for myself, because no arguing was allowed in our home. If my older brother and I had any disagreements, we didn't get to work them out because my mom always stepped in to make sure I wasn't being a burden to him. Therefore, I also had no access to him, who happened to be one of our high school's football heroes and a renowned heart throb. He would undoubtedly have had all the information I was looking for.

I asked my girlfriends what they knew about men and how I

could get me a husband. But most of those girls didn't date, or have boyfriends, and the ones who did only shared their info with other girls who did.

Although I had been well liked in high school, holding class offices all three years, being in the popular girls' club, and having lots of friends, I never had a boyfriend. And I'd only been on one date. That was with another couple to see the Rose Parade in Pasadena on a very cold winter morning. *What was wrong with me? Why wasn't I desirable?*

The 1949 Chevy Fleetline, that my dad gave me for graduation, was filled to the brim with everything my girlfriend, Pam, and I knew we would need to be successful college coeds—our clothes and a bit of bedding. The compact dorm room came with twin beds, desks, chairs and dressers. With the boys' dormitory only a few yards away, what more could we possibly need?

Pam and I eagerly explored our new surroundings, learning to use our campus ID cards to order meals in the cafeteria. We jostled with the throng of other students at open class registration, when we scrambled to sign up for the classes we wanted. It was 'first come, first served." We both got into the same biology and history classes.

Those first two weeks were fun and engaging for me, with the newness of campus life. Then it wasn't. Classes and studying became drudgery for me. I reread assignments three and four time, but the words just bounced off my brain. Instead, I wanted to know what went on at that boys' dorm. I soon found out that it was not the happening place I had hoped for. So, I got to know a few girls who lived in the sorority houses. They told me about the honor of being a sorority sister, plus all the rules and codes that went with that. Would I like to join? Maybe.

A date was arranged for me to attend a combined sorority and fraternity party. It was supposed to be a big deal. The guy was really cute. Learning to dance the Twist was sort of fun. But all the booze, crude jokes and innuendos turned me off. Instead, Pam and I drove into Santa Barbara to look for regular guys that we could get to know. Mostly we sat in their cars, talked about not much, and wondered when they would try to kiss us, which they didn't. Boring.

The second semester we moved off campus, to the tiny beach community of Isla Vista, and into the gated and supervised college apartments. There we gained another roommate, Becky from Buttonwillow. The three of us were a good match, along with our next door neighbors, Linda and Susan.

My horizon began to expand, with beer that we somehow acquired and smuggled in. It's first time effect caused me to roll around on the floor giggling with gay abandon. Weekend visits to my new friends' homes broadened my perspective even more. Becky grew up in a tiny town in the middle of nowhere. Her parents scraped together every penny they could to send her to college. That was my first look at people who struggled to make a living. On the other hand, Susan and Linda were "army brats" who lived at the Presidio in San Francisco, which was a totally cool place to visit with nearby Coit Tower, a bustling waterfront, and people in uniform. I was intrigued.

In the meantime, Pam had acquired a boyfriend, who took up most of her time. I roamed Isla Vista, meeting groovy people who had interests that didn't only involve getting good grades. I also became aware of the sexual realm of life and found young men willing to introduce me.

By the end of the school year, both Pam and I dropped out of UCSB. She would enroll in secretarial school in San Francisco. I didn't know what I wanted to do, but I had summer at home to try to figure it out.

My parents were disappointed that I quit college (and finding a husband to take care of me). I realized that I had not at any time questioned how I had been raised. Instead, since I believed they loved me, and took good care of me, I automatically accepted their values and viewpoints. "Be a proper girl, and do as you are told." I was at a turning point.

By the end of summer I knew I had to return to Isla Vista. I wanted more of the new, compelling scene that had nuzzled up against me. My parents didn't know what to do with me. But after I assured them that I knew a girl who I could move in with, and that I would find a job, they let me go.

I felt a deep void looming before me. There was something missing from the picture of my life. Something very large, and I intended to find out what it was.

4

THE DRAFT

The draft for the Vietnam War came to Isla Vista. It did not matter that the United States government never formally declared war on North Vietnam. The peacetime draft registration was put into effect.

There were ways to be exempt, but they didn't always work. My friend Gary was a full time student at UCSB. He was in his senior year, when his number was called. Majoring in literature didn't apparently qualify as an endeavor worthwhile enough to keep him from fulfilling his patriotic duty. A month earlier he received the official letter that informed him when the bus would arrive to gather the draftees for the medical exam and induction.

Gary did not want to be a soldier. He did not want to be trained and expected to commit murder. He formed a plan of resistance. For that ensuing month, whenever he defecated he did not clean himself. The physical exam would reveal his intention of appearing mentally and emotionally unbalanced. Furthermore, when he and the other young men had to load onto the bus, he acted out. "I won't go! You can't make me. Fuck the government. I'm a free citizen." Gary screamed. He flung himself on the ground and rolled around like a crazed animal.

I was there to see his tormented performance. I hoped my presence supported his desperate need. My heart broke for him. I stood shocked to witness the effect of the belligerent act my government imposed on this gentle, sensitive and intelligent soul.

The other draftees dutifully entered the open door of the bus. Most of them looked proud, with their shoulders thrown back and their brotherly punches on each others' arms. As for Gary, the two army officers who were in charge of this ride grabbed him and shoved him aboard. He landed in one of the seats by an open window. I thought he was going to climb through it, but someone held him from behind. That didn't stop him from hanging out as far as he could with his arms flung wide. He continued to writhe and scream, "Help me! Save me! I am not a killer." The door closed and the bus drove away.

Gary returned to Isla Vista later that day, an altered man. His humiliation hung on him like the rotting flesh of a road killed animal. He had succeeded in being declared unfit for military duty. I rarely saw him after that. He stopped going to his beloved literature classes. He didn't graduate. I don't know what happened to him.

His roommate, Dennis, was also not soldier material. I knew that because we had dated for a short while, before he got involved with a male professor. Dennis could have received a military exemption for being bisexual, but he did not want to expose the professor, who would have lost his job. Although homosexuality had recently been decriminalized, it was still generally considered to be repugnant and abnormal.

Other young men, who were opposed to war, were placed into non-combatant roles such as medic or chaplin, or they fled to Canada as Conscientious Objectors. If they remained in the USA they would be fined and imprisoned for being draft dodgers.

Not all of us were eager to be sent halfway around the world to kill people who didn't look, or talk, like we did. And our homeland certainly did not need to be defended. No one was bombing Isla Vista! My friends and I believed in brotherly love and the Golden Rule of being kind to others.

We weren't the only ones who objected. Muhammad Ali, who had been born Cassius Clay, and "danced like a butterfly, but stung like a bee," when he was in the boxing ring, became the heavyweight champion of the world. He fought a court battle for four years, to claim his right to avoid the draft. During all those years he was not allowed to box, and he was stripped of his title. He had changed his name when he accepted the Muslim faith of Islam, which was non-violent. Maybe boxing was OK because there was no intention of killing anyone. At any rate, he became one of our heroes.

Another way not to be drafted was to have an important job that contributed to the defense of democracy, like being a scientist, or maker of weapons and battle ships. Or you could be married and have a family to take care of. That's what my roommate, Karen, did. She married Dennis, to make sure he was safe.

5

THE WEDDING

I married my friend Don, who wasn't exempt. He wasn't a student, nor was he married with a family to support. He qualified for active duty. Also, he had no intention of fleeing to Canada, nor of being a 'Conscientious Objector.' He was a hard working auto mechanic, with a solid life that he didn't want to be forced out of. In his spare time, Don restored a MG TD, which he painted scarlet red. It was totally cool. I looked forward to a ride in it. I knew it had a 'souped up' engine. His biceps were souped up too.

I hung out with him a few days after the draft bus had done its dirty work. Don and I relaxed on his couch after work. He drank a beer and I smoked a doobie. Our feet were stretched out on his coffee table. A stack of car magazines and Popular Mechanics lay scattered underneath. Playboy was sort of hidden amongst them.

We'd been talking about the draft bus. I explained that I went to work late so I could be there. I gave him a full account of the young men who dutifully came and obeyed instructions. Then I told him about Gary's supreme effort of voicing his objection. "You should have seen what he went through. It made me gag. I did all that I could to keep quiet and not interfere."

Don was silent. I imagined he was wondering when he would receive his letter ordering him to comply. I took another hit from my doobie and offered it to him.

Don shrugged it off. "No thanks." He got up and went into the kitchen. I heard banging sounds from cupboards being slammed shut. He returned carrying a plate with sandwich and chips in one hand and a bowl of rocky road ice cream in the other. The bowl went to me. Yum.

After a couple of big bites of his sandwich, Don looked up and stared at nothing. "I don't have anything like that going for me. I'm definitely able-bodied meat. I mean, look at these muscles."

"Are you worried?"

"Of course I am. I don't have it in me to make a fool of myself like Gary did. He's a ruined man."

I concentrated on my bowl of ice cream. "My roommate, Karen, is going to marry Gary's roommate, Dennis." I lay my spoon aside, as an obvious and simple idea came to me. "Why don't I marry you?"

Don didn't respond. He put his plate on the table, and cleared his throat a few times. I could hear him breathing deeply. Oh oh, I hoped I hadn't insulted him, or something. I began to feel stupid and thought I should go back to my house. I had left a sink full of dirty dishes and my roommates were probably not too happy about that. I stood up and turned towards the door.

"Don't go, Kimmy. I mean," Don seemed to have trouble talking. "I mean," he began again. "You'd do that for me?" He gently held my arm to stop me from leaving.

"Well, gosh Don. We wouldn't be married for real. You just have to have the paper that says we are, right?" I turned around to look directly at this man who faced a reality that I couldn't comprehend. "Of course I'll marry you."

The hug he gave me infused me with joy. His relief lifted my spirit. My friend would be able to walk an honorable path to avoid this abhorrent possibility of being drafted into an insane war. Sure, it wasn't a real marriage of man and wife. But it was a marriage of like-minded souls. The purpose was to protect Don from being harmed and committing harm to others.

"How about this weekend? Will you marry me this weekend?"

"So soon? Don't you have to make an appointment, or sign up, or book a church. Or stuff like that?"

"No. We can go to Las Vegas. It's completely legal." He rubbed his hands together like he was creating a plan.

"Las Vegas? Sure. Why not? I've never been there. Bright lights, big city, here we come. Do we go in your MG?"

"No, sorry. I've got to do more work on it. We'll take the Chevy. I'll pick you up Saturday after breakfast. It's a long drive."

"I should probably wear a dress. You can look fancy too, like with a cute little bow tie." His look told me that was not likely to happen.

My friend arrived in his big baby blue Chevy Bel Air convertible. He no longer looked sad or worried like he did a couple of days ago. The top was down on his car and it was shiny clean. His attitude sparkled like his car's exterior. The grill gleamed and the fins stood at attention. The back seat was stuffed full of bags with empty beer and soda bottles.

I nodded towards them and asked, "What's this all about?"

"Insurance. I don't know if I have enough cash for gas, food, motel room and the wedding. If necessary I can get my deposit money back on these."

We headed south on the freeway from Santa Barbara and picked up Route 66 at the Santa Monica Pier. It wouldn't take us all the way to Vegas, but it was a good start. Don turned on the radio and let me pick a station. Happily I found one that belted out Buddy Holly, Chuck Berry, and Elvis. He brought sandwiches and apples, so we only needed to stop for pee breaks.

I enjoyed the scenery, especially the Mojave Desert. Its serenity and vastness caused me to reflect on how I knew Don. He wasn't part of my regular circle of friends. In fact, he didn't live near us. His little house sat on the outskirts of Goleta, which was the gateway to Isla Vista.

During my senior year of high school, my friend, Pam, and I realized we'd chosen the same college and agreed to be roommates. When we moved off campus for our second semester, I met Don through our next door neighbors.

The story behind that move involved the discovery that college was so much more than studying and going to classes. As a consequence, neither of us pulled in great grades, especially in the history class that we shared. Since that particular instructor graded on the curve, which meant that most of the students received the average grade of C, only the two very best students received the A. That left the two worst students to receive the failing grades of F. She got the F and I got the F minus. We burst out laughing when the notices arrived. There was only one thing to do—destroy the evidence.

We put our report cards in the metal waste paper basket in our dorm room, and lit them on fire. Our dorm room was small and there was other trash already in the basket. The fire created enough smoke to escape out the partly opened window, under our closed door and into the hallway. Pam and I didn't notice because we were too busy laughing our fool heads off. But somebody noticed, because soon the dorm mother pounded on our door and a fire truck siren could be heard in the distance heading our way.

There was no damage done to anything. Also there was no

sympathy for us having an old fossil of a history teacher who graded on the curve. Fortunately the letter each of our parents received explained there was off campus housing that might be available. The outlook on my life took a definite turn from there with new people and events to encounter.

Now I was on my way to Las Vegas, the City of Lights, to marry my friend to keep him from being drafted into the Vietnam War. Don got us a motel room on the edge of town. We ate at a little diner next to it. Afterwards we returned to the room and changed into our wedding clothes. He wore a regular tie with his short sleeved white shirt. His biceps looked good. My dress was not what anyone would call a wedding dress, but my fiance seemed to like it.

"Don, is that a lecherous look I'm seeing from you? If so, you'd better cool it right now, Daddy-O."

It was early evening when we drove around trying to decide on a wedding chapel. There were so many to choose from, and each one had a different theme. Chapel of Flowers, Chapel of Bells, Hitching Post. We decided on one with a white picket fence in front. It looked sweet and homey.

I was a bit nervous. I needed to have a good story, because I had no intention of giving my real name and being legally married. I just wanted to get his name on a marriage license. I hadn't told Don that, since I just thought of it as we walked through the front door. What we were about to do started to become very real to me.

An older woman, with short permed curls tinted silvery blue, rushed towards us. Her arms reached out like she wanted a hug. "Welcome, welcome."

We were the only customers. I saw a man in a black suit in the background waving us forward. They looked like anyone's parents. Middle aged, slightly plump, with forced smiles.

Piped music came from somewhere. The Temptations were

telling us how wondrous love could be. I noticed bouquets of calla lilies, baby's breath, sweet peas and a few red roses in glass vases that rested on pedestals along the sides of the tiny pink chapel.

The minister guy got right down to business and told us the rules. "This will be a legally binding marriage. I am authorized by the State of Nevada to perform this ceremony. You will receive a certificate."

Don showed his driver's license, signed a paper and produced money. I wasn't paying a whole bunch of attention to what transpired between them because I was thinking about what name I wanted to give. Suddenly I realized that giving my real name might not be such a good idea. I mean, how would I explain that to my parents?

Then the minister turned to me. "How old are you, young lady?"

"Nineteen."

"Do you willingly consent to this marriage?"

"Sure. I mean yes, sir."

"Do you have proof of your age and identity?"

"What?"

" Donald showed me his driver's license. What did you bring?" The smile was fading from his pasty face. He really needed more sunshine. A tan would do him some good. He cleared his throat and sighed. "Do you have proof of your age and identity? Do you have a driver's license?"

I could sense Don's energy changing from relief to worry. But he didn't twitch a muscle. Those biceps hung loose.

Lie number one bubbled to the surface. In my sweetest voice I responded, "No sir, Donny does the driving." I released a radiant smile as I visualized my driver license lying on top of my clothes in the motel room.

Another throat clearing, "And what do you have?"

"I have a pretty red bicycle that I ride."

From behind me the wife emitted a very faint, "O my."

"I mean," the minister continued through clenched teeth, "do you have any proof of your age or identity? A birth certificate perhaps?"

I included both the minister and his wife in my next smile and lie number two. " No, sir. Hopefully my mama has that..... But I am a student at UCSB in California."

This slowly smoldering man did his very best to be patient and supportive. Unbeknownst to him, he held Don's future in the balance. With a heavy sigh he tried once again. "So you have a student body card with your name and photo on it which would also offer a reasonable estimate of your age. That would certainly be acceptable proof. May I see that, please."

Don shifted his weight from one foot to the other. The minister's wife moved from behind me to stand right next to her husband.

I kept my properly respectful and innocent appearance as I released lie number three. "Oh golly gee, we were in such a hurry to come here, and Donny didn't say a word about me needing ID or anything. I....." Wringing my hands a bit, sniffling and trying to look like I would cry a bucket of tears at any moment, I looked at my friend. "Oh dear, Donny, what are we to do? You know how upset my daddy will be when he finds out."

Don did not budge. His eyes were getting bigger. His biceps began to flex.

But before he could say anything, the minister's wife stepped towards me and cushioned me in her doughy arms. "There, there, Honey. Don't you fret. You aren't the only couple who's come to us in their time of need." Her eyebrows raised expectantly at her husband. "Harold, surely we can make an exception for this nice young couple."

The minister's jaw tightened. He began to grind his teeth. His nostrils flared.

"Harold?" His wife's tone gained in force.

Harold's attitude instantly shifted. He cleared his throat once again and turned his attention to Don. "Did you at least bring a ring for your darling bride?"

"Yes sir, I certainly did." Don vaulted into action. His hand dove into his pants pocket and produced a ring that looked like it came out of a Cracker Jack box. But, hey, it was only going to be worn for ten minutes. That worked for me, and apparently for everyone else.

"And young student from UCSB, what is the name you will be using this evening?"

Oh my gosh, does the minister see through my lies? I can't break down and confess. What would happen to Don?

I looked at the floor. I bit my lower lip. I pulled back my shoulders and lifted my head. Then looking straight into the minister's eyes I declared, "Jennifer Rose Wainwright, your Honor."

A mere five minutes later, Don had his piece of paper that kept him from being drafted into the United States Army and fighting in a war that had not been declared. He took my hand, the one with the ring on it, and kissed it. Then we took a stroll around the City of Lights.

"Jennifer Rose Wainwright? How did you come up with that name?

" It was the most romantic name I could think of, like a damsel in distress would have. That's how I was feeling. If I didn't get that ring on my finger, you would be doomed."

6

TIJUANA AGAIN

There I was, once again, driving to Tijuana with Bob to score pot. This time, however, there were more of us. I invited my roommate, Nancy. Bob asked tall, dark hair and handsome Eddy to come along for the adventure.

Also I had a different car. My '49 Chevy Fleetline had bit the dust. It ended up in a junkyard with blown cylinders, or something like that. It had to do with needing oil. A mechanic, a guy with a German accent, declared my car was 'kaput.' He happened to have just finished working on another car, which he sold to me at a price I could afford. My new car had a funny name, Borgward Isabella. I never met anyone who had ever heard of it. I called her 'Old Reliable.' She was a sort of tomato red color. I didn't care. She took me where I wanted to go.

Bright and early on a Saturday morning my friends and I loaded up. Nancy sat up front with me and we chatted away as the time flew by. The guys both sat quietly in the back seat.

Again we had no trouble driving through the inspection line at the border. The officials seemed just as happy to see four of us as they had been when only Bob and I passed through a month ago. They still weren't interested in IDs. I guess we just looked like easy money to them. Dumb gringo kids who came to get drunk and spend their mountains of dough on disgusting shows with women performing unnatural sexual acts.

I had told Bob there was no way I would return to TJ if he had those intentions again, even if he just went alone to see those shows. No scoring of pot was going to get me to be a part of that indecent activity. But how would I know if he did, or didn't? He just popped in and out of my life. Apparently I was again trusting him to be a good guy.

How Bob found his way around Tijuana was a mystery to me. It was a big city that made no sense. All the dirty, smelly, noisy streets looked the same. So many of them were dead ends. And where were the street signs? However he nonchalantly directed us to a hotel. "Go straight, Kimmy. Turn right after that parked green van. Look out for the kid. They have no fear of cars. Keep going straight. Now turn left. We're going to that building with the big hotel sign on it."

Nancy and Eddy were as appalled with their first encounter of "Sin City" as I had been. He didn't say anything as he stared out the backseat window, but Nancy voiced her opinion, "My god, this place is filthy. There's garbage everywhere. The air literally stinks. And dirty little children are running around barefoot in the middle of it. Are you guys seeing this?" She pulled a tissue out of her jacket pocket and held it over her nose with one hand, while fanning the air with her other hand.

I responded with, "It doesn't seem so stinky to me this time. I hope that doesn't mean I'm getting used to it." I glanced in the rearview mirror to see if Eddy had a reaction. Instead, I saw Bob nudge and whisper to him. "For Pete's sake Bob, are you telling him about the bar you took me to? It was horrible, Eddy. Ignore him."

"Lighten up, Kimmy," Bob said as he leaned back to his side.

"That was our special time together." He chuckled a bit and continued. "I was telling Ed about what we'd do after we dropped you girls off at the hotel room. Turn left here. Park over there by that colorful van with the bullet holes on the side. Haha. Just kidding. C'mon. Let's go get a room."

We all trooped after him into the mangy looking building. I was surprised to see Eddy pull out money to pay for the room. I assumed that Bob would pay. They must have made an arrangement ahead of time, like everyone had given me a couple of dollars for gas before we left Isla Vista.

As we walked up the stairs, I was curious to see what our room would look like this time. Realizing we would need at least two beds, I wondered how that situation would unfold. None of us had talked about that. Were any of us curious, or worried? I wasn't going to let Bob near me since he showed me his true colors the last time we came here. On the other hand, there was something about Eddy that made me want to know him better.

This room was a bit of an upgrade from the other time Bob and I were here. This time there was a sturdy looking table with metal chairs, plus an almost clean window and sink, and two beds. I turned on the water to make sure the drain wasn't plugged. On one of the pale yellow walls hung a black velvet picture of a matador and charging bull.

Nancy had brought a suitcase. She plopped it down on the bed farthest from the door. It seemed silly to me to bring a suitcase for just one night. "I like to be prepared," she responded to our questioning looks.

"OK," Bob said. "You girls sit tight while Ed and I make the connection. We'll only be gone half an hour. When we get back, I have a treat for us. And don't worry, Kimmy. This will be an outdoor event.....Lock the door behind us."

I sat down on one of the metal chairs and watched Nancy open her suitcase. She rummaged around in it and then, lo and behold, she pulled out a can of disinfectant spray and went to work on the room. Under the beds. On top of the beds. All along the floor and the walls. I was impressed, even though I soon had my head hanging out the window (it didn't have a screen) to breathe fresh air. Fresh air? Not here in Tijuana, but at least I wasn't gagging on the disinfectant spray that filled our room.

"Do you feel better now, Nancy"?

"Yes, somewhat." She looked around the room trying to determine if she had missed anyplace. She put the can back in her suitcase, closed it and sat down on the other chair. "What are we doing here? I mean, I know we came to score pot. You and Bob did that once before, so supposedly you know what you are doing. But why are 'we' here? Why didn't he just bring Eddy, or his girlfriend?"

That was the grand question. I had asked it myself and I couldn't give Nancy a quick answer. Instead I sucked on my bottom lip, and chewed my tongue a bit. I wiggled my nose like I was trying not to sneeze. I glanced around the disinfectant smelling room, looking for the answer. I had learned that Nancy always tried to face her life head on. She'd grown up with a lot of responsibility. No father that I ever heard about and a younger sister to guide and comfort because her mother was depressed most of the time. Nancy carried a load and she was determined to make changes with her life for the better. She was a student on scholarship at UCSB who worked hard to get good grades.

I was a dropout. I lasted one year before I made the decision to explore other avenues of life. My best answer to Nancy's question sounded mighty weak. "I guess I'm here because I have a car and Bob doesn't. He probably asked Eddy to come because he wants two bricks of weed this time. Eddy might have to hide one of them under his shirt, like Bob did before when the Chief of Police had us cornered." I paused and squeezed the bridge of my nose because I could feel a headache coming on. "I figure he asked you along to keep me in line so I don't become a stoned lunatic again."

Nancy stared at me and folded her arms across her chest. "Honestly, Kimmy, I hope this plan works. We're all taking a big risk. I think the only reason I came is that I was burned out from studying so hard, and I wanted a break. Now I'm not sure I made a good choice." She slumped over and covered her face with her hands.

I got up, walked over and pulled the other chair beside her. "It'll be OK. It has to be. Bob is this mysterious guy who comes up with all these crazy plans, but they always seem to work. He knows where and how to score pot, LSD, peyote, and all that kind of stuff. He speaks Spanish. And he has a sweet girlfriend. So he can't be all bad."

Nancy lifted her head and looked at me. "Yeah, but that's all you know about him. And I know even less." She swept invisible dust off her clothes with the flick of her fingers. "Maybe he's a gangster from L.A."

We both burst out laughing. When she finally caught her breath she said, "But Eddy's not. He's more like an innocent lamb. I think his dad might be a preacher."

I added on to that thought, "And what a gorgeous lamb he is. That dark curly hair and beautiful body. Do you know he's on the college track team? I've heard he runs high hurdles and usually wins his races. But his coach gets so mad at him because he doesn't go to practice. He just shows up for the events."

My roommate finally wore a smile. "So, how long do we wait here for the misfit pair? Do you want to play gin rummy?" Always prepared, Nancy pulled out a deck of cards from her suitcase.

We were finishing up a second game, when there was a knock on the door. I opened it a crack to see both of the guys standing there. Bob entered with a swagger as he announced, "Mission accomplished."

Eddy didn't say anything, but he was lit up like a Christmas tree. Nancy and I looked at each other. She put her cards down, stood up from her chair, and walked to Eddy. She took him by the hand and guided him to one of the beds, where she sat down. Patting the bed, she motioned for him to sit beside her.

She asked, "How did that go, Eddy? I want to hear from you."

He sat up straight and looked at each one of us. "Bob knew where to go to find the right taxi driver. We walked a couple of blocks and waited about half an hour for him to show up. The transaction went smoothly. They talked in Spanish, so I don't know what was said, but it wasn't much. Bob and the Mexican dude shook hands and that was it." He grinned from ear to ear. "I've never seen anything like that. We just stood on the street asking to score marijuana. Nobody seemed to pay us any attention."

Nancy spoke up in her straightforward manner, " You were gone way longer than half an hour."

Eddy clarified, "Yeah, right. We stepped into a bar and got shots of tequila. I didn't have to show an ID. Boy, was it strong!" He shook his shoulders like a dog shaking off wet fur. "Do you know that most bars here are for men only? And running along the foot of the bar is a narrow trough to pee in? Just stand there, drink and pee."

Nancy and I looked at each, at a loss for words.

Bob chuckled in the background. "OK. That's enough of that. Let's get something to eat and then we'll go to the main event. It starts at three."

We found a clean little taco place with delicious smells. Bob told us to pay for our own meals, because he would pay for the event. We decided what we wanted and he ordered for us speaking Spanish. That continued to impress me. After stuffing ourselves, Bob sent us to my car while he ducked into a dark little market. When he caught back up with us, he had a paper sack with bottles of beer, which he called 'cerveza,' and a bag of peanuts, still in their shells, that he called 'cacahuates." Hey, maybe we'd all be speaking Spanish by the time we went home.

In the car, Bob directed me to drive to the Plaza Monumental. "It's known as the Bullring by the Sea. It's practically brand new and it's bigger than any building in Spain or Mexico, except for in Mexico City."

"Nancy, we're gonna see a bullfight." I squeezed her arm and stifled the urge to bounce up and down. "Wow, Bob, this is so cool."

She got a big grin on her face too. "Kimmy, we'll see handsome matadors wearing super tight pants and shiny little jackets. They'll twirl flashing red capes at ferocious bulls, showing how brave they are."

"How can they get so close to the bulls without being scared?" I asked."

Nancy answered, "I think it's like a dance they learn and practice for several years. It's a really big deal here in Mexico."

Eddy glanced at Bob before he spoke up, "I'm pretty sure the matadors do more than just dance with the bulls."

Bob didn't add to that conversation, except to say, "Yeah, well, let's wait and see. C'mon, let's find a place to sit. I only had enough money for the sunny side." He led the way.

It was a huge arena. I didn't know what to compare it to. It was a big circle with wooden stadium benches. There were already quite a few people there.

"Look Nancy," I exclaimed. My head swiveled back and forth trying to take it all in, like at a tennis match. "So many people brought picnic lunches with them. See their baskets. What a fun event this will be." I was sure of it.

"Maybe, but I don't see any children here," she informed me with her usual astute observation. "It might not be like a circus."

Bob's clear voice interrupted. "This will be nothing like a circus." He sat down next to Nancy.

Eddy settled by me, which made me nervous and caused me to blurt out, "Hey you guys, we look like a sandwich with Nancy and me squeezed between you two. Nancy's definitely a tomato, and I'm probably a pickle. Do you think I'm sweet or dill?"

The guys both had blank looks on their faces, but Nancy quickly spoke up, "It doesn't really matter, as long as these two don't turn out to be heels." She grinned and knocked her shoulder against mine. We were true buddies.

"Look," Eddy said, "it's starting. See the band over there in the shaded side. That's an introductory march it's playing." He leaned forward to give his full attention. Then a trumpet sounded and a thick wooden gate opened at the far end of the arena.

Nancy squirmed in her seat and swept her hair out of her face. "Oh, look at those two men on their horses. Such pretty clothes. And their hats have big fluffy feathers. Do you think they're ostrich?"

None of us responded. We were raptly paying attention as the riders crossed the open space. Their horses pranced. When they reached the other side they stopped to talk to a man sitting in a boxed off space. They doffed their hats to him, and he doffed his back.

"Bob," I asked as I leaned forward to see him, "what's going on?"

"They're getting permission for the event. Don't ask me any more questions, Kimmy. Just watch."

The fancy riders returned to the gate they came from. Turning around they led out the matador and two other men on horses. Those second horses had thick padding that covered most of their bodies.

"Bob," I asked, "Why are the poor horses covered with that heavy padding?"

"To protect them from the bull's horns. Now hush."

The matador and riders all moved behind a big, thick wooden fence near the gate.

Another trumpet sounded. A different gate opened. Out rushed a huge black bull, snorting and pawing the ground. While he ran around the enclosure, one of the men on a padded horse came out from hiding. The rider (Bob called him a 'picador') jabbed the bull with a spear, just behind his head. Blood spurted everywhere.

Nancy and I both gasped. I felt Eddy stiffen beside me.

Bob said, "Don't worry. It's just to make the bull mad."

I leaned back and bent my head down. *What does Bob mean, 'don't worry' and 'it's just to make the bull mad?' Of course it's going to get mad. That's not fair.*

Again a trumpet sounded and the audience yelled " Ole. Ole." The matador came out of hiding and swung his cape around. I saw some people near us eating their lunches and drinking their beer.

A third trumpet sounded. A different rider came close to the bull. His horse was padded and blindfolded. That man thrust a spear into the bull's side. Two other matadors ran out there and jabbed sharp sticks in the bulls hump. The sticks flopped around and more blood spurted. All that mutilation happened in a few minutes.

A fourth trumpet blasted away. The main matador danced around with a small red cape. He did fancy things, like standing still and staring at the bull, while it charged right at him. Just when the bull almost ran into him, he turned sideways and the bull missed.

"Ole, ole, bravo," the people all around the stadium cheered.

Suddenly the matador had a sword.

Bob spoke up. " The matador wants to reach over the bull when it charges at him, to ram the sword down behind its head and into its heart. That's the goal, the whole object of the bull-fight. To get that close to the horns and kill the bull." Bob leaned forward, his fists clenched and unclenched.

I was aghast. My heart beat faster. The blood pounded in my ears as I saw blood spurt from the tortured, maddened bull. It charged at the little man in the shiny clothes, who twirled a crimson red cape and taunted him to come ever closer.

Eddy, Nancy and I were spellbound.

"Ole, ole."The shouts were almost deafening.

The bull thundered at his tormentor. The matador stretched up on his toes to reach over the horns of death. He was so grace-ful, so beautiful, so brave as he miscalculated. The bull's horns caught him, held tight and lifted him into the air. Then the mighty animal shook his head and dropped his enemy to the ground.

Silence everywhere. Profound silence. No more 'oles.'

The other matadores ran to their fallen hero, while the men on horses chased the enraged bull back into the opened gate and bolted it closed.

The matador on the ground stirred. He struggled to get to his feet. One hand was grasped over his gaping wound. His shiny golden pants were awash with his own blood. His other hand raised to the crowd, and raucous cheers broke loose.

Other matadors rushed to offer their support, but he refused. He would not be carried. No. He strode forth with the pride of his extreme effort. An ambulance waited for him beyond the arena wall. The brave, wounded matador was taken to the hospital.

Another bullfight began. The announcement of the mata-dor's death, from a loudspeaker, came in the middle of that performance. We were all so stunned by what we had just seen that we couldn't budge from our seats.

I gazed stupidly at the unfolding scene in the arena. Charging bull, red cape, padded horses, men with spears and sticks jabbing away at another innocent bull. A fancy dressed, beautiful little man danced for us with his blood thirsty cape. Then his sword appeared. But he was no good at trying to get it over the bulls horns, into its back to pierce its heart. He kept trying and trying. Stab, stab, stab. The poor bull staggered all over the place. Lots of "boos" from the audience. Finally another matador arrived and killed the poor animal with a knife cut across its throat. What a mess. What a sickening mess.

Nancy and I stood up at the same time. No one was going to stop us from getting out of there.

Eddy quickly followed. We waited for Bob in the car. He wasn't long in coming. "I'm sorry," he said. "That was worse than I expected."

We drove quietly back to the hotel. Nancy pulled out her deck of cards and asked if anyone wanted to play gin rummy. I joined her. Eddy stood by the window, staring out.

Later, when I thought about that sunny day with my friends, I realized that the brave matador had trained his whole life for that one moment. The moment when death came for him and he did not falter.

Bob had been fidgeting with his money. He handed ten dollars to Eddy. "Hang on to this. It's for tomorrow's score. I'm going out for a while. Unless you want to come with me."

Eddy shook his head. "No, I'll stay here to keep the girls company."

Bob grabbed his jacket and left.

The three of us had nothing to say. Nancy and I continued to focus on our card hands.

Eddy concentrated on the view through the window, until he turned around and said, "I don't know how to talk about what we saw. And talking probably wouldn't do any good."

Nancy and I looked at him.

Eddy said, "We went to a bullfight, and we saw what we saw. There's no way I can justify what happened. We have to set it aside. Let's just go find something to eat. If we stick together, we should be safe."

With my senses numbed, Nancy and I followed Eddy to the taco place. We pointed at pictures on the menu. The waitress showed us how much of our money to give her for payment. It was hardly anything, so I figured she didn't cheat us.

Back in the room, Nancy and I lay down on the bed farthest from the door. She didn't even pull out pajamas from her suitcase. We slept in our clothes. Eddy lay down on the other bed. He, too, slept in his clothes.

I don't know when Bob came back. Eddy must have let him in.

7

CROSSING THE BORDER

Bob didn't offer an explanation of where he spent last night, and we didn't ask.

Instead he started our day's conversation with, "Slip me each a dollar and I'll bring us breakfast. Come with me, Ed." They brought us mini tacos and fresh squeezed orange juice.

Bob told us his plan, "Ed and I are meeting the taxi driver at nine o'clock. We need to get going. You girls sit tight, OK? Nancy, be packed and ready to go."

When they returned, they looked like they'd each gained twenty pounds of belly fat. Actually it was 2.2 pounds of farm grown marijuana tightly wrapped in newspaper tucked under their shirts.

Glowing with pride, the guys set their packages on the bed.

Bob looked at me. "I want to put the kilos under the hood of your car."

Everyone looked at me as if I needed to give my approval.

Then Bob explained. "No one looks under the hood at the border inspection station." He straightened his shoulders with a new air of confidence. "They'll just wave us through, like they waved us in. Happy to have us spend our money in their country. Happy to see us go." He looked at me and continued. "So maybe it would be a good idea if we don't smoke until we get back to Isla Vista. We all need to act normal."

"Don't worry about me, Bob." I blurted out. "I have no intention of smoking any of this weed until we are safely home."

Nancy nodded in agreement and Eddy gave a 'thumbs up.' She grabbed her suitcase. The guys again stuffed their precious bundles under their shirts.

I held the door open for everyone.

At my car, Bob balanced the two kilos of pot under the hood, at the back of the engine. It was a perfect fit. Nancy's suitcase went into the trunk. We climbed aboard.

This time Bob was in the front passenger's seat so he could guide our departure. "To be extra safe, let's bypass Tijuana and exit through Tecate. It's the next border town, not far from here. Not much happens there, so the border guards won't be suspicious. We'll cruise right through."

I was relieved not to be driving all the way through Tijuana. A side trip suited me just fine. I relaxed into driver mode and let Bob tell me where to go.

When we got to the edge of Tijuana, the road to Tecate was not paved. In fact it was full of bumps and potholes. I had to slow down to ten mph. Bump. Jerk. Bump. Jerk. The jostling was sort of fun. Then it wasn't.

After one really big pot hole, that there was no way of missing, I glanced into the rear view mirror. I saw a little Mexican man hunched over, behind us, in the middle of the road. He had been walking by the side of the road when we drove by. Then, lo and behold, he witnessed a miracle. He ran onto the road and picked up one of our packages that had been jarred loose and slipped out through the engine.

"Look!" I cried out, nearly swallowing my tongue. I pointed to the back window. "Look, look, look!"

Nancy twisted around to find what freaked me out. "Oh my god," she wailed.

Eddy saw what we saw. His face turned pale.

"Holy shit," Bob gasped as he pounded on the dashboard.

All together we watched the little man open a bit of the package and sniff it. He looked up and around in all directions. Then, with the package clutched tightly to his chest, he scurried away as fast as his wobbly old legs would take him.

"What do we do now?" Nancy yelled, as her eyes bulged and her breathing came in gulps.

"Step on it, Kimmy," Bob shouted in my ear. "We've gotta get outta here."

Eddy's voice shook when he asked, "Do you think he'll call the police?"

"I don't know, Ed. But we can't take any chances. Kimmy, look for a place to turn off this road."

We all leaned forward, trying to see a safe side road. Bright eyed Nancy chirped, "Turn right," as she leaned over the front seat and pointed.

Fortunately this road curved and I drove until we were out of sight. There weren't houses or buildings anywhere. We were on a deserted road. I parked and we all got out. Eddy lifted the hood. Sure enough, one of the kilos was missing.

"Now what?" I asked.

Bob paced. Eddy kept his eyes on him. Nancy stared back down the road.

"How long before the police come after us," I shouted at Bob, trying to keep the tears from rolling down my face.

"Hopefully we have enough time," Bob answered. "Ed, help me," he said as he took the keys from the ignition and walked to the rear of the car. He opened the trunk, shoved Nancy's suitcase aside and yanked out the spare tire."Good girl, Kimmy, you've got a spare." To Eddy he said, "Open the package and break up the pot into fist sized chunks. Then help me stuff all of it into this tire."

Bob used the pry bar to separate the tire from its metal rim.

It took about ten more minutes for the guys to stuff the tire with the pot. Taking off his t-shirt, Bob wiped the tire clean from any residue. He put the tire back in the trunk and snuggled Nancy's suitcase on top.

I buried the newspaper wrapping in the dirt and under some rocks. I needed to feel useful.

"OK," Bob said as he brushed off his hands, shook out his shirt and put it on. "Now we have to beat it to the Tecate border station before the guards are alerted. We're halfway there. Let's go. Don't drive too fast, Kimmy. We don't want to draw any more attention to us."

On the road again, Bob told us the rest of his plan. I had no idea why Nancy and I agreed to it. Maybe we were too scared to think clearly. And Bob was so sure of himself.

About a mile before the border crossing, Bob told me to stop the car. He and Eddy got out. Nancy came to the passenger seat. The plan was for the guys to walk overland to the highway on the U.S. side of the border. Nancy and I would drive through the crossing. The theory, according to Bob, was that he and Ed were taking the risk, making a perilous journey across unknown desert.

"You girls should have no problem going through inspection," he gallantly offered. "The guards are always men, so they will be charmed by your beauty and sweet innocence. They will only wish for your safe journey home."

How could I have been so gullible to accept that hogwash? Yet the society that raised me had instilled those very notions into my trusting mind. I did what men told me to do, because I had been taught that they were superior to me, a mere girl. My duty was to accept their guidance, since they were smarter than I could ever be and therefore more capable of making decisions. Apparently Nancy had the same childhood indoctrination.

We bid farewell to our stalwart heroes. We continued with our mission of smuggling marijuana across the Mexican border. We rested in the confidence of Bob's words.

As fate would have it, when we reached the border crossing station at Tecate, it was noon. That was when the guards took a lunch break and a replacement stepped in. She, yes 'she' was stocky and square-shouldered. She looked like a person who could spot every lie imaginable.

Holy moly. What's going to happen to me and Nancy?

My head slowly swiveled right. My roommate's head swiveled left. Our eyes locked on each other with that look that said, "We can, and we will, do this."

I inched my car forward to where the don't-mess-with-me woman directed.

After looking at the license plate she marched straight to my rolled down window. She looked first at me and then at Nancy. "Please step out of the car. Both of you," she ordered in very good English. She pointed to the station building. "Stand over there." She followed us and took a parade rest stance. "Your license plate is from California. What are you doing here in Mexico?"

I produced what I hoped was a proper attitude of respect, helpfulness and innocence. "Ah, um," I stammered. "We're students at the university by Santa Barbara. We've been studying so hard. We needed a break. My roommate and I decided to go for a drive." I paused to wipe away the drop of sweat that had formed at my hairline.

Nancy took up the challenge of a convincing lie. "We'd heard so much about Mexico. How pretty it is and how nice all the people are." She held her hands in front of her, at chest level, like she was praying.

Square shoulders lady stared at us unblinking. I wondered how she was so good at it. "Did you shop in Tijuana?"

My response was quick, to persuade her that I had no time to think up a falsehood. "No, Ma'am, we never got out of the car."

Nancy chimed in, right on cue, "We just drove and drove. So many colorful streets and people. Then we found ourselves on this charming country road." Her smile was almost angelic. I was impressed.

I licked my quickly drying lips and said, "By then we were both hungry. We looked for a cafe. We had to drive and drive, and now we are here." I offered my best smile. Big smile. A Charming smile.

"Stay here. Don't move," barked our interrogator. She turned and walked to my car. First, she sat in the driver's seat, searched the glove compartment, flipped the visors down, and felt around the floor and under the seats. Second, she toured the back seat area, even running her hands deeply between the cushions. Third, she walked to the front of the car and lifted the hood.

I was so relieved that Bob knew to take the remaining kilo of pot out of there. Once again he proved to me that he knew what he was doing. I sighed and wiped away two more sweat drops that tried to roll down my face.

However, the determined woman in uniform did not stop there. Number four step in protocol was about to happen. She released the hood with a thud and firmly trod to the rear of the car. She was headed for the trunk.

Oh, oh. I wonder if I could request a bathroom break so I could throw up in private?

The trunk did not open at her command. It was locked. That competent woman did not ask me to bring her the key. She marched back to the driver's seat and plucked it from the ignition herself. With it firmly grasped in her fist, she returned to the rear of the car. Before opening the trunk she looked up and directed her penetrating eyes at Nancy and me. She then whistled a loud burst which caused a guard to stick his head outside the station. She motioned for him to guard us. He walked up to us, leaned against the building and finished eating a banana. She opened the trunk.

With our backs to the wall and our faces lifted to the noonday sun, my hand reached out to Nancy. She took hold. Together we breathed in the beauty of the day as we watched the decider of our fate lean into the depth of the trunk.

The border guard lady rifled through Nancy's suitcase. She appeared to examine every square inch of it. She stepped back with the can of disinfectant spray held at arm's length. She shook it and sprayed an arc into the air.

Nancy's voice sang out, "You're welcome to have that. It's really good at killing cockroaches."

The woman gave Nancy a startled look. A twinge of a smile leaked from her face. She set the can on the ground and commenced with her thorough inspection of the trunk. All that was left in there was the spare tire. She hefted it out, nudged it with her sturdy boot and set it next to the spray can.

I stopped breathing. My proper smile was frozen on my face. I couldn't look at my friend. But I could sense her desperation. She had to be worried about whether, or not, she would see her mother and sister again, or if she'd get to complete her education.

As for me, I just wanted to get back to my life of being a pothead and having adventures. I also wanted to find out more about Eddy.

The suspicious woman who was 'only doing her job,' nudged the tire again. Then she leaned into the trunk and pulled up the mat to see what could be hidden there. Finding nothing, she went back to the tire. She stood it up and felt its tread. She looked up at us. Then she placed it back in the trunk. Nancy's suitcase followed. The trunk lid was slapped down with a 'clunk. Taking the key in one hand and clutching the can of spray to her breast with the other, she approached us.

I quivered and tried so hard not to show it. Two drops of sweat were again at the starting line of my forehead. Quickly I brushed them away.

The border guard lady handed the key to me. "You may go."

She said it so simply. No big deal. Then walked away. The other guard joined her. They went into the station building and I heard laughter.

I let out the breath I had been holding.

Nancy and I bolted for the car. With my hand shaking, I started it up and latched onto the steering wheel. I backed out of there. As soon as we passed through the gate, both of us shouted with relief. "Yaaaaaaaaa!"

"We did it, Nancy! We just smuggled marijuana across the Mexican border."

"Wait until we tell the guys," she said "They'll be so amazed at what we did."

I tried laughing. That quickly faded into silence as I fought to catch my breath. My mind raced, alternating with what I had just experienced and visions of being home in Isla Vista surrounded by my friends. But first I had to find Bob and Eddy.

Nancy spotted them by the side of the road. We pulled over. I was eager to tell them what we had been through.

Before I, or Nancy, had a chance to say anything, the guys climbed into the back seat.

Eddy blathered away about how dangerous their trek across the desert was.

"The sun was so hot. It burned my forehead. And I got so thirsty. That was a really long walk." He jumped all over the place with his recounting. His words tumbled on top of each other. " There were lizards, horned toads, and scorpions. I had to watch every step I took. And I got so thirsty. But Bob had an orange that he shared with me. I think that's what saved us. And...he told me to save one seed to suck on to keep moisture in my mouth."

I looked in the rear view mirror at Bob. His head was leaned back on the seat. His hands rested limply in his lap. "So, Kimmy, stay on this road. It'll take us to San Diego. You and Nancy can follow the highway signs to get us back to Isla Vista. It should be just as easy as driving through the border crossing in Tecate." He closed his eyes and zoned out.

Nancy turned around to look at Eddy. "He's asleep too. They didn't ask about us."

"No, they sure didn't."

8

TINY PILLS

A few days after getting back from our smuggling escapade, my roommate, Nancy approached me. " I found a doctor who gives me a prescription for birth control pills. We don't have to be married. I'll take you there."

I was in the middle of a really good book, so I hadn't focused on her words. "What are you talking about?"

Nancy pulled off her fluffy pink sweater and tossed it on the coffee table where my feet resided. She sat down next to me on the couch. "You are a sexually active woman, Kimmy. Are you planning on getting pregnant?"

I closed the book. She had my full attention. "No, of course not."

"How are you keeping that from happening? Do you think that any of the guys you've been with, including Eddy, are going to prevent that? No matter how much you like them, and they seem to like you, they only want to have fun. They aren't interested in protecting you." She picked up a magazine from the coffee table, and casually read the cover while she waited for me to absorb what she said.

" Why do you say that? That's just not true. Eddy cares about me. He wouldn't let that happen."

"So, he uses a condom?"

"A what?"

"A condom. A rubber."

I sat back and crossed my arms over my chest. No words came out of my mouth, or even formed in my mind.

"You don't even know what I'm talking about, do you? Because no guy that you've had sex with used one. Gee, Kimmy, wake up. We have to protect ourselves. When I go to my doctor appointment tomorrow, you're coming with me."

The next afternoon, I drove us into Santa Barbara. The doctor's office was on a side street in a nondescript, one story building, with other business. I noticed a shoe repair and a family dentist signs. The doctor's door had a plaque with his name on it.

Nancy told the receptionist that she was bringing me to her appointment. Ten minutes later the receptionist led us into the examination room. Nancy didn't have to get undressed and put on one of those creepy gowns that open in the back. She explained that she only needed to talk to the doctor to get her prescription renewed.

The doctor looked like anyone's dad. He had gray hair and a bit of a pot belly. A stethoscope hung around his neck, and a little notepad and pen stuck out of the pocket of his white jacket. He glanced at me. "Who are you?"

Nancy spoke up. "She's my friend."

"Are you here for the same reason?" I nodded slightly. His abrupt question and harsh tone startled me. I definitely would not want him to be my dad.

He asked Nancy how she was feeling and if she had any side effects from the Ortho Novum pills he had prescribed. He didn't take her temperature, or check her pulse or heart rate. He didn't do any of those doctor things.

"I'm fine," she told him, "but I gained five pounds and I don't want to gain any more."

"You probably won't, as long as you eat healthy and get enough exercise, like walking."

He turned to me, looked me up and down. "How old are you?"

"Twenty one."

"Are you a student at UCSB also?

"Not right now."

The doctor wiped his hand over his mouth like he had food smeared there. "You both look like clean, nice girls. I don't see why you have to ruin your lives this way. But I am required by my profession to administer these pills. At least you are not going to bring unwanted children into the world." He handed me a sheet of paper. "Read this thoroughly. It explains why I'm telling you to take a pill daily. If you forget, don't engage in sexual activity, but do continue with the pills as directed. Do you have any questions?"

I shook my head.

The doctor asked my name and wrote the prescription for me. That was it. He ushered us out of the exam room and down the hall to the back door. We had to walk around the block to get to my car which was parked in front.

Nancy directed me to the pharmacy, where we got our prescriptions filled. Once we were back in the car, she showed me how to use the packet that the pills came in.

I couldn't drive yet. I had to find out something. So I asked my best friend, "Nancy, how do you know this stuff—-condoms and birth control pills?"

"My mom told me."

My mom never told me about this. She never told me what it means to be a woman, and how to take care of myself. She never told me I deserved to be respected and treated well by men.

"What about your dad? What did he tell you?"

"My dad left when I was three years old. My mom had to raise me and my little sister by herself. It was freakin' hard on her. She didn't do well. But she made sure I understood about men and how to take care of myself. That included going to college to get a degree in something other than being a waitress for the rest of my life."

On the drive back to Isla Vista, I thought about my mom and dad's guidance for my life. My parents sent me to college to find a husband. My mom had taught me how to iron my clothes and dust the furniture. She didn't tell me anything about protecting myself from pregnancy. She didn't tell me anything about sexual relations. I didn't even know sex happened until I dropped out of UCSB after my first year, and discovered marijuana and "free love." I didn't know that sex was the cause of pregnancy. I knew nothing! I was so not prepared for my future after high school.

"So Nancy," I asked quietly, "Why have you told me this stuff and helped me get these pills?"

Nancy turned in her seat to look at me. She patted me on my shoulder. "Because, Kimmy, you don't have a plan, and you need one. You're smart. But you need to see what's going on around you, and not trust everyone to care about you the way you care about them. It's obvious that you're a nice person. And I'm your friend."

9

MIDNIGHT MANEUVERS

Eddy was now my boyfriend. I could resist no longer. It was nearly impossible for me to keep my hands off him. Hurray for the "free love" of the Sixties.

Because I was so enamored by his attributes, I willingly accepted his suggestions. Most of which involved a bed. But there was one suggestion that circled around our friend, Ray. Actually it was all Ray's idea and Eddy went along for the ride. Literally. I was a minor character in the performance.

Ray's charm and sensuality flowed easily. Tall and slim, he moved with the grace of a big cat. Quiet and unobtrusive, his demeanor was beguiling. Also, he played the sitar in the manner of Ravi Shankar, the world renown master of classical Indian music.

Besides being gorgeous, and playing the sitar, Ray had a hankering to own a Porsche. Although he grew up in Hollywood with his father being a successful doctor, Ray was not spoiled with a rich kid allowance. His parents sent him to college to acquire an education that would enable him to support himself.

But, like I said, it was the Sixties, in California. Ray had the heart of a "Flower Child." Free love, psychedelics, exploring nature and playing his music did not leave him much room for serious scholastic studying. His focus was on driving his own Porsche.

He found one in a nearby junkyard. It was smashed up a bit from a car wreck. Mostly the body was damaged. Its engine still purred and the tires were good. Ray bought it "for a song." He drove it out of there, and did a few minor repairs. Although it was banged up, he didn't care about that, or bother with a new paint job. White it would be. Then he drove it to the DMV in Santa Barbara and received his very own title and registration. He was happy. For a while.

One night Ray showed up at Eddy's place. Of course I was there too. He entered with silent footsteps and joined us on the couch, by the glow of several candles on the coffee table. That was Eddy's idea of romance. He and I had been looking at a book about Glen Canyon in Southern Utah. The photographs caused me to hunger for a visit there.

"Hello. How's it going?" Ray offered.

Eddy responded, "It's all cool here, Ray. I didn't even hear you drive up. You sure got lucky with that Porsche you found."

I nodded in agreement.

"Uh huh," Ray responded. He rubbed his hand along his chin and said, "I've been thinking."He paused to give us time to place our full attention on him. "What if I found another Porsche? One in better shape, newer, maybe black instead of white, that I could swap for this one?"

Eddy turned to get a better look at our friend. "Perhaps you'd care to explain?"

"Yeah, well, I've been checking out the Porsche dealership in Santa Barbara."

"What do mean," Eddy's voice cracked, "you've been checking out the dealership? Ray, what are you scheming?"

Ray licked his lips and pulled on his right ear. That was his trademark for whenever he thought he had a good idea. "I spotted a black Porsche there that's the same year and model of my white car. It looks great. Probably a trade-in on a new one. And....."

When he didn't say anymore, I piped up, "And what, Ray? What else?"

"OK, I know that the keys for all the cars are kept in a little shed at the back of the lot. And sometimes it's not locked up at night. I mean, this is Santa Barbara. There is no crime here. Ever. And...."

Another pause that Eddy wasn't going for, "And?"

"And the lot is on the north end of town, which means we wouldn't have to drive across town. It'll be so easy to get in and out. We'll fade into the night."

Not a pause this time. Instead it was silence, because Eddy and I didn't know what to say or ask. We just turned to look at each other, then at Ray. I got up and went to the bathroom. Eddy moved to the kitchen for a glass of milk. He left that light on and blew out the candles on the coffee table when he returned.

After we both settled back onto the couch, Ray rubbed his hands on his thighs like he was smoothing them out. He leaned forward a bit to look at both of us and said, "All I would have to do is switch the VIN and license plates."

That statement definitely created another pause. It was Eddy who had the sensibility to ask the next question. "Why are you telling all of this to Kimmy and me?"

With wonderful sincerity, Ray had his response ready, "Because you've got the perfect place to hide the new Porsche for a week or so, and Kimmy can drive us to the car lot." He looked like he just came out of a confessional booth, washed spanking clean from any and all impurity.

Eddy wasn't done asking questions. He needed more clarity,

now that the light had been turned on. "What do you mean, 'the perfect place'? There's no garage here."

"We don't need a garage. Your backyard is covered with lilac bushes and you have no close neighbors." Ray's face began to shine with serenity. It was like he knew the gods were gonna smile on him big time.

I shook myself loose from watching this act unfold, to also voicing my concern. "When are you thinking of engaging in this activity?"

" This Saturday at midnight."

"And why might this be?"

"Because this is a God-fearing town. The lot is closed on Sunday. The absence won't even be noticed until sometime Monday. So....will you join me?"

There was such sweetness and positivity in Ray's voice that I felt like he was asking us to join him at the river for a baptism. I almost said, "Of course, brother. Praise God and Hallelujah." But I refrained.

I don't know what made Eddy agree to do Ray's plan. Maybe he just had to go along with it to see if it could really happen. I don't know. But because he agreed, I agreed.

Saturday, ten minutes before midnight, when Ray arrived, Eddy and I were dressed in our darkest colored clothes. The guys climbed into my tomato red Borgward Isabella. We were at the dealership lot in fifteen minutes.

I parked across the street and watched it all happen.

Ray casually walked to the shed at the back of the lot. He simply opened the door. The flash light he brought caused the shed to glow eerily. He reached in his hand, pulled it back out. The light was turned off and the door was closed. Ray motioned for Eddy to join him as he sauntered to a pretty little black Porsche in the back row of cars. Spellbound, I watched Ray unlock its door and slide into the driver's seat. Eddy slid into the passenger seat.

I didn't hear the Porsche engine start up, but I saw it back out and head onto the street. Eddy signaled me to follow them. He had the goofiest grin on his face as they drove off the dealership lot to make their getaway.

By the time I got to Eddy's place, they were already in the backyard. The black Porsche was in the far corner and they were piling some of the bush limbs around and on top of it that they had cut down earlier in the day.

After that, the only thing left to do was to go inside and smoke up a big fat joint of ever-lovin' grass to calm ourselves from the adrenaline rush. We all slept really well. Ray had conked out on the couch.

The next morning Ray pulled the white Porsche into the backyard and went to work removing the license plates. The VIN plate took more effort to remove, but he got it off. After breakfast Eddy helped put them on the black Porsche. The guys stood back to admire their work. I wondered if they considered themselves to be criminals. *Was I an accessory to a crime?.*

Since the white car no longer had license plates, Ray could no longer drive it around. I gave him a ride to his place.

Eddy and I didn't see Ray for a week. We didn't hear, or read in the local newspaper, about a car being stolen. So when he showed up, it was to discuss making the white car disappear. I had no ideas on that subject, but the guys easily made a decision.

In fact, that night, at a little before midnight, Ray and Eddy took their positions in the white Porsche and I got into my trustworthy car. I followed them out of Isla Vista and up the coast highway. The guys had agreed on a particular section of the bluff overlooking the Pacific Ocean. Eddy had discovered it on one of his countryside explorations. The narrow dirt road that led there from the highway was almost non-existent. Since the moon was full, we were able to turn off our headlights and still see well enough to drive on that road. We were being careful not to draw any attention to us.

Ray stopped the white Porsche a few feet from the edge of the bluff. He put the gear into neutral. Then without any kind of ceremony, or words of farewell, he and Eddy pushed it over the edge. Its banged up body shone in the moonlight to reveal its new wounds. A cloud passed in front of the heavenly glow. The shadow fell on the faithful, white iron steed that had served its purpose.

I drove us back to Isla Vista.

Ray enjoyed that shiny black Porsche for a long time. He graduated from the university, too.

IO

FRIENDSHIP

Eddy and his roommate Howard lived in a little house. It had no bedrooms, just a big living room with a kitchen and bathroom. They hung curtains around their beds for a sense of privacy.

In the backyard, the same yard that hid the stolen Porsche for a week, there was a six by ten foot cement slab. On that slab was a covered stack of redwood boards. Eddy built a room for himself there with those boards. It had a door and a window. It created enough space for a single bed, a rod to hang his clothes, and shelves under the window. He made an electrical connection for his hotplate and clock with a long cord from the house. My boyfriend hadn't asked the homeowner for permission to do that. Yet when the owner made a visit, he was pleasantly surprised with the achievement. There was no problem.

Since Eddy was basically living in the backyard, he and Howard agreed they'd take on another roommate, who could fill the vacated spot in the main house. The rent and electric bill would then be split three ways.

Howard found Dwayne, the new roommate. They met at

Nebi's, the little cafe in Isla Vista. Dwayne was from out of town and happy to have discovered our community. He'd been looking for a place to call home.

I first met him when I was hanging out with Eddy in his cozy abode. I needed to use the bathroom in the main house. Howard introduced me to Dwayne. This new guy seemed nice enough, although maybe a bit overly friendly. I supposed he was anxious to make friends. He didn't make much of an impression on me, so I didn't pay any more attention to him.

Over the course of the next month we (Eddy, Howard and I) learned three things about Dwayne: 1) he found a dishwashing job in nearby Goleta 2); he liked to smoke marijuana; and 3) he had always wanted to be a police officer, but he didn't pass the required tests. No 'red flags' waved in our fields of concern. We were potheads. We trustingly saw only goodness in the people who came across our paths, especially if they smoked marijuana with us. We learned our foolishness the hard way.

I had introduced Dwayne to two of our other friends, Matt and Will, roommates who shared an apartment a block over from Eddy's place. Sometimes in the evenings, when Eddy had to go to his job cleaning one of the local churches, Dwayne and I would walk to Matt and Will's. There we'd all relax and pass around a joint or two.

Lately I had been hoping to run into Bob, my friend who knew where and how to score pot, because I had run out. I figured he'd either have it, or know where to get it. Since I didn't know where he lived, our encounters usually happened when he found me. I bumped into him at the little market in the middle of Isla Vista. Since we were in a public place, we talked in code.

" Hi Bob. I've been hoping to find you, because my lawn needs attention. The grass is not right. Can you fix that for me?"

"Sure thing, Kimmy. Grass is my specialty. Ten dollars will take care of that. I'll come by tomorrow."

"Thanks, Bob."

We had so many names for marijuana. 'Grass' was currently my favorite. If it was a clean ounce of grass that I bought, without a bunch of stems or seeds, forty joints could be rolled from it. That made for a lot of good smoking. I decided I would like to have it all rolled up at once. However, that was precision work that required patience and fortitude. I knew just the man for the job.

I asked Matt if he'd be interested, with the understanding that he would receive ten of those joints in exchange for his rolling skills. There was no hesitation. Matt agreed. I joined him in his bedroom where he settled down to business. The first rolled joint, of course, we lit to find out how good it was. Superb. He took his time, and was done in half an hour. He separated his ten from the rest of mine, which I stuck into my purse. He slipped his into the inside pocket of his suit coat that hung in his closet. I thought that was a smart move.

I don't know how Dwayne knew where Matt stashed those doobies. Maybe he showed up later that day for a friendly visit, and he, Matt and Will all got high. That's the most likely scenario. However it happened, the narcs knew exactly where to look when they raided Matt and Will's apartment two days later. My dear friends were arrested for possession of an illegal drug. Dwayne left town the day after the arrest.

Eddy, Howard and I were panic stricken for weeks after that. Even with Dwayne gone, we feared that we, or other friends, would be arrested. But that didn't happen. I don't know why. Dwayne could have mentioned quite a few of us.

I went to the courthouse for the sentencing. It was simple and straightforward. Will was sentenced to six months in jail for being the roommate and smoking marijuana. Matt was sentenced to two years in Tehachapi State Prison for smoking and for possession of a controlled substance.

What I was never able to understand was that Matt didn't tell the cops where he got the pot. He could have made a deal with them and received a lighter sentence for his cooperation. Instead he protected me and paid a heavy price for doing so. I was spared because Matt was my true friend.

II

COLORADO, HERE WE COME

Christmas vacation for UCSB students was a week away. Campus would be closed. No classes for Eddy and no work for me at the photography shop. He wanted us to go to his folks' place in southwestern Colorado. Of course I agreed. It meant I would finally have this man that I adored all to myself. I was stoked.

I had to figure out what clothes would keep me warm enough. I particularly needed a hat of some kind. The main thrift store in Santa Barbara had the best possibilities. I ended up with a small fur stole, sort of like a short scarf. At home I sewed it together by overlapping it part of the way, which created a fat tube. One of the open ends I sewed closed. It looked like a Russian Cossack hat. Perfect. The overlapped space allowed me to stuff in a plastic baggy with a few joints. *I wonder if I should tell Eddy, or surprise him?* Combined with Levi's, hiking boots and my big brother's old Navy pea coat, I was ready for an adventure with my boyfriend.

The night before we left, I fell asleep thinking about how I met Eddy, which happened before he joined Bob, Nancy and me for our crazy trip to Tijuana to score pot.

It was on a night I had gone to a friend's apartment to hang out with whomever was there, and of course smoke a joint or two. I walked through the front door and straight into the kitchen because I was thirsty after jogging four blocks to get there. I liked to run. I drank a glass of water then turned around to head back into the living room where the action was. That's when I first saw him.

He sat on the couch between Matt and Will. This was Carol's apartment and she was in the kitchen making two big bowls of popcorn to share with everyone. I sidled up to her and with bumbling hesitancy whispered, "Who is that?" as I nodded towards the gorgeous, pale skinned, black haired, grinning man on the couch. For me it was 'love at first sight.'

Our trip to Colorado began with easily catching several rides, to go short distances through the towns along the way. Everyone wanted to pick us up. We were an enticing novelty, being young hitchhikers and me a girl. Maybe we became stories for the drivers to tell their families and drinking buddies. "I picked up two of those Flower Children we've been hearing about. One of them was a girl. Can you believe that? She wore a funny fur hat like a Communist. They had sleeping bags with them. Said they was goin' to Colorado 'cause it was Christmas break. Just 'cause that's what they wanted to do. They didn't smell bad."

When our ride crossed California, almost to Nevada, that driver dropped us off outside a little town. This was ok with Eddy and me. We were both antsy from sitting so long. Walking a bit suited us. We didn't get very far, however, before a police car pulled up alongside and stopped. The officer got out of his cop car and ambled towards us, with Billy club swing in one hand. Other hand rested on the gun at his side. Muscles bulged everywhere.

"Well now, what do we have here?"

We didn't move.

"Where are you headed?"

I felt the definite need to let Eddy do the talking, and he spoke right up. "Colorado, sir. My folks have a place there."

The officer studied him a bit, then looked me up and down, but didn't ask me anything.

"How about taking a ride with me to our police station, so we can have a little chat?" It wasn't really a question. He ushered us into the back seat of his vehicle.

At the station, he insisted we unroll our sleeping bags, besides taking off our coats, boots and hats. "Empty your pockets." He looked at all of it quite thoroughly.

I was so nervous. I chewed on my bottom lip. My heart jumped around a bit too, especially when he picked up my hat. Oh oh. I hoped he wasn't going to inspect it. Then I really needed to pee, but I tried to ignore my bladder. *Hush bladder.* Instead, I did my best to provide my 'proper girl' attitude, which included a demure smile. I intended to use Eddy's polite 'sir' responses if I personally got asked questions. Which did happen.

"Where are you from, missy?"

"I grew up in Downey, sir, but now I live in Isla Vista, sir."

"Where's that?" he asked without looking at me. The soles of my boots caught his interest.

I clasped my shaking hands behind my back. "Near Santa Barbara. You know, sir, by the coast."

"Uh huh. What do you do there?" He petted my fur hat.

"I work on campus, sir, for the photographer..........sir."

"Why is there a photographer on campus?"

I felt light headed. I grabbed Eddy's hand. "To take photos of the students, sir. If... if they want their photos taken... I mean, sir." I guessed that was the right answer because he didn't ask me anything else. But he still held onto my hat. Golly, I really hoped he would give it back to me.

"And you, buddy, got an ID?"

"Yes sir," Eddy quickly replied as he let go of my hand and whipped out his wallet. He seemed experienced with this question and answer routine.

Anyway, that was about it. The officer let us put our shoes and coats on. After we stuffed our extra clothes back inside our sleeping bags, we were allowed to roll them up.

The officer handed Eddy his cap. Then he escorted us to his car while still holding on to my hat. "We don't want no vagrants, nor Flower Children dirtying up our town. You hear me?"

"Yes sir, " Eddy and I chimed.

Again we had to get into the officer's car. He drove us to the far end of his town where he stopped and opened the back door. Eddy slid out pulling his sleeping bag behind him. I followed. As the officer closed the door behind us, without a word he handed me my hat. Then he drove away.

I really had to pee. I ran to the nearest bush and squatted down behind it. Just in time.

Another car came along, but passed right by. Two more cars. Finally a pickup with a load of hay stopped. The driver didn't say a word. Old guy. Smoking a cigar. Dropped us in front of a motel at the beginning of a little podunk town. A motel. Hurray. Eddy went into the office to rent a room. I was really glad because I had to pee again.

It was weird to all of a sudden have to pee so much. And for some reason it didn't feel good to relieve myself. There was a strong burning sensation. "Hey Eddy, have you ever heard of burning pee?"

"What do you mean?" he asked, blushing slightly.

"It burns when I pee. And I have to get to a toilet right away. It's a bummer."

"Maybe you need to see a doctor. Let's get something to eat and then find one."

And that's what we did. Even though the town was only two blocks long, it seemed to be well equipped. Besides our motel, it had a cozy little cafe, a market, movie theater, and an elementary school at the far end. There were some other places too, but the important one we found was the doctor's office.

We stepped into a waiting room. The lady behind the desk asked what we needed.

I was totally embarrassed. Undoubtedly my face glowed bright red as I whispered, "I have to pee all the time and it burns. Also, I can't hold it."

The lady smiled gently, "I'm sure that's something the doctor can help you with. Don't you worry. Sit down," she said as she patted my hand that rested on the desk. " I'll go tell him." She came right back. "Follow me."

The doctor turned out to be a young dude. He had a clipboard and pen, like he was ready to be serious. His hair was cut into a flat top like my brother. He shook Eddy's hand then turned to me. "I understand the symptoms that you told my receptionist. Don't worry. This is a common ailment for newly wed women."

He thinks Eddy and I are married.

"It's just a slight infection that will easily heal with an antibiotic, which I can give to you. Your body will adjust to this new intimacy. Just take a little extra time and precaution with cleanliness." Looking at Eddy he continued, "I don't mean to embarrass you, but do you understand that I'm saying to refrain for a few days?"

It became Eddy's turn to blush bright red, but he was able to nod.

The doc walked to a cabinet and took out a small bottle and handed it to me. "The directions are on the label. You'll be feeling better in 24 hours. There is no need to think that you have to please your husband right now. Give your body a little rest. You have a lifetime ahead of you to be a good wife."

Being the flippant person that my highschool English teacher declared me to be, I said, "Thanks for your help, Doc. And, by the way, we're not married."

Eddy did not hesitate to open the door for me. We took our exit without looking back. Outside he suggested, "Let's go back to the motel to take it easy for a bit. OK?"

"Sure thing," I cockily replied.

Back in the room I removed my peacoat and hat. From inside its hidden pouch I pulled out my stash of a dozen rolled joints. "Let's celebrate our journey to Colorado."

The look on my boyfriend's face was priceless when he realized I had that marijuana in my hat the whole time the cop was interrogating us and looking through our clothes. His mouth fell open, but he didn't say anything. I thought for sure he would be proud of me for being so clever. I handed him the lit joint.

He hesitated in accepting it. "Not right now, Kimmy. I think I'll take a shower."

The rest of the day was quiet. Eddy didn't talk much. I guessed he was just worn out from all the excitement of our run-in with the cop, as well as the embarrassing stuff with the doctor.

We did go back to the cafe for dinner. But once again in our motel room, he was standoffish. He read the Gideon Bible he found in the drawer of the bed stand. No cuddling happened either at bed time. Eddy went right to sleep. I figured that probably made it easier for him to follow the doc's instructions for no intimacy.

Early the next morning we easily caught a ride with a long haul trucker heading to Chicago. That ride took us past Las Vegas and all the way to Grand Junction, Colorado.

It wasn't far from there to the little town of Delta where Eddy would get his folks' jeep. Then we'd take the road to the homestead in the Uncompahgre National Forest.

Catching the next ride took longer because there wasn't as much traffic. The air got colder. The overstuffed clouds looked like they wanted to dump their load of snow. Eddy and I did jumping jacks to stay warm.

The driver who picked us up looked like he hadn't bathed in awhile. He smelled that way too. Also, he could barely sit still. He squirmed all over the place. Holding on tight to the steering wheel seemed to be what kept him in his seat. The music from the car radio blasted away. So we didn't do any talking. I was glad that Eddy sat in the front seat, while I was in the back with our sleeping bags. I hoped, if necessary, he could grab the steering wheel to save us from disaster.

Suddenly the car screeched to a stop when we entered the town limits. The glassy eyed driver grinned at Eddy with a mouth full of blacked teeth stubs. We scrambled out and he roared away.

"I don't care how cold it is, I'm glad that ride's over." I released a deep sigh and settled my hat a little lower to cover my ears. "What do we do now, Eddy?"

"We walk a ways." He held his sleeping bag in front of him like a shield. I didn't know if that was to keep him warm, or if he protected himself from something.

The sun lay low in the sky. Darkness approached. The cold increased.

As we walked, my handsome fella pointed out the highlights of this tiny country town. "There's the Frosty Freeze with two flavors of soft ice cream. Up the block is the movie theater. It shows the best B-grade films. You know, like 'Godzilla,' where you can see the zipper on the back of the costume." He grinned and chuckled.

We turned a corner to walk on a side street lined with

houses. Eddy's grin changed to a frown. He held his sleeping bag even tighter.

"You look worried, Eddy. Is there a problem?"

We stopped walking.

"No. Sort of. I mean I have to get the key for the jeep. It's stored in the Fetterman's garage. They're friends of my dad. They met at church. They know me, but..." He looked up and down the street like he was searching for an escape route.

"So?" I couldn't see a problem.

" I need you to wait here while I get the key."

"OK." I was always willing to do what he asked.

Eddy handed me his sleeping bag. I parked myself under a tree and watched him walk to a house a couple of doors down the street. A man answered Eddy's knock. They shook hands and Eddy went inside.

The sky faded from tired blue to yawning twilight. I did more jumping jacks.

Finally my boyfriend emerged from the house. He slid up its garage door and drove out an older model Willys Jeep. I got in and turned on the heater. Before we left town, Eddy bought a sack full of groceries from a little market.

A winding dirt road took us into the hills that only revealed themselves within the Jeep's headlights. We had entered Uncompahgre National Forest. It was a long ascent into the rugged landscape. Tomorrow, in brimming daylight, I intended to feast my eyes. The glow from the headlights onto the falling snow created an ambiance of long ago history. I imagined the pioneers carving out their homesteads and adjusting to an arduous lifestyle.

The homestead we came to did not have a log cabin. Instead it had a two story, white clapboard house. A more modern cabin with bare plywood exterior nestled a few yards away.In between the two buildings stood a generator. Eddy parked the jeep to shine the headlights on it. That would enable him to see well enough to get it running by charging it from the Jeep's battery.

While he attended to that, I took our sleeping bags and the sack of groceries inside the cabin. Before I remembered the electricity was off, I tried the light switch. But the dim light from the headlights let me see where the furniture was, so I didn't bump into anything.

Suddenly the inside lights came on and Eddy walked through the door carrying an armload of wood and a huge grin. Soon he had a fire blazing in the metal heat stove. Warmth allowed us to shed hats and coats. My dark haired, handsome boyfriend startled and delighted me with a hug. I hadn't known him to demonstrate affection, being the 'strong silent type.' I understood that this hug meant he felt really good about all he had accomplished.

I hugged him back and kissed him on his cheek. "We're here, Eddy. Safe and sound. All the way from Isla Vista to this cozy cabin. You did it. You got us here."

He stepped back and again displayed that huge grin, barely able to contain himself. After lighting the propane cook stove, he unloaded groceries and made us hot cocoa with marshmallows on top. He also pulled out peanut butter, jam and bread for our dinner.

Two games of checkers, and a shared doobie brought us to bedtime. With my assurance that my bladder no longer bothered me, there was no hesitation to warm the sheets with our love making. Twice, in fact.

The next day me and my fella walked around the property. Forty acres with a pond on the canyon ridge gave us a lot to explore. Ravens flew over the tree lined canyon. Snow capped peaks glistened in the distance. The pasture erupted with gopher mounds and a spring fed pond which provided the sweetest water I had ever tasted. Deer must have agreed with me, because their tracks in the snow marked all around the pond's edge. Towering cottonwood trees surrounded the white house. Crisp mountain air enriched my lungs as I breathed deeply. An industrious, distant woodpecker tapped his song of revelry. All of these sights and sounds joined together to enwrap me the thrill of being alive and free.

While helping me wash the dinner dishes, Eddy had a suggestion. "Tomorrow let's go to Denver. The Jeep has 4-wheel drive, so there'll be no problem on the mountain pass." Naturally I agreed to more adventure.

That evening, after my loving man fell asleep, I lay awake sorting through the events of the last three days. I realized that Eddy didn't talk about the doobies I had stashed in my hat. He didn't tell me that I was clever. Nor did he chew me out for the danger of the situation with the police officer. He also didn't tell me I shouldn't have told the doctor that we were not married. I assumed he was ok with that. But his coolness to me when we left the doctor's office, and that night, clued me to his disapproval. Why didn't he say anything?

My thinking went further. *When we went for the Jeep, he didn't want Mr. Fetterman to see me. Why? And why did I agree to wait under a tree, in the increasing cold, while he went into a warm house to get the key? Why didn't my discomfort bother me? Why didn't I speak up?* I fell into a restless sleep.

The next morning, right after breakfast, I cleaned up the cabin while Eddy turned off the generator and made sure the wood pile was covered. Then we were on the road again. The sun shone brightly on our three hundred mile drive over the Rocky Mountains. It was breathtakingly beautiful. Aspen and alders were swathed in the white paint of frozen snow. Dark green evergreens announced their majesty as they studded the stalwart slopes. The craggy mountains dared us to assault their heights. I was delirious with the beauty's rawness.

We didn't drive far into Denver. I think Eddy mostly wanted

the challenge of driving there in Winter conditions. He picked out a hotel for us that looked like it was left over from the Civil War. The guy behind the check-in counter didn't ask for any ID. He barely looked at us, even when he handed Eddy the key. We put our bags in our second floor room, then agreed to stroll around to find a place to eat. The little diner, a few doors down, seemed cozy, with good aromas and cowboy music coming from a jukebox. I felt special being there with my boyfriend. Last night's doubts and concerns faded away.

The snow was pouring down by the time we left the diner, so we went back to the hotel. We took a better look at our room. It was not spic and span. We carefully pulled back the bed covers. Nothing jumped out at us, so we ventured into the sheets. Stretching out released screeching from the bed springs. They definitely needed oiling.

"This bed must have seen a lot of action," I whispered. Then for some reason I started giggling.

Eddy placed his hand over my mouth and signaled 'shh' with a finger from his other hand to his lips. He pointed to the wall behind our heads.

I got quiet.

Neither of us moved. We could hear our neighbors. Oh my.

It sounded like two men were taking turns with one woman. Her voice was audible. "Wait 'til I get settled. We got all night.....Put out yer cigarette first. Use the ashtray, dammit. You ain't gonna start no fire in here."

Mostly grunts came from the men. There wasn't much of a pause between their encounters. Off with one. On with the other.

Eddy and I halted our cuddling. The neighbors' actions were definitely a downer. I grabbed my hat and searched for a joint. Maybe smoking would create a shift in consciousness to make it possible to ignore the goings on next door. We gave it a good try. But then we heard a knock on their door.

"It's the manager here. Can I come in for a minute?"

The lady's voice responded, "Well, ya. We don't much mind."

"I got this fellow here who was trying to get out of this weather by lying in the front doorway. All the rooms here are full up. I thought maybe he could sleep on your floor so he don't freeze to death outside. He smells like he's had a lot to drink. He's not talking. Likely he'll fall asleep real soon."

One of the men's voices said, "As long as he keeps to hisself, I guess it'll be alright."

Shuffling and banging sounds came through the wall.

"I brought this blanket for him."

Their door closed and the grunting noises began again.

Eddy and I leaned back on our pillow. We lay there quietly. I watched snowflakes beyond the window. He hummed a bit of classical music.

"What's that smell?" the lady next door blurted.

"Well I don't know. It ain't me," retorted one of the grunty bed voices.

"Oh shit," said the other grunty voice. "That guy just peed all over hisself.

The lady spoke up again, "Well, git off me and do somethin' about it."

"What kin I do?" whined Grunter Number One.

"I ain't touchin' him," declared Grunter Number Two.

Silence ensued.

Eddy's symphony continued a bit longer.

I fell asleep.

12

RETURNING

A big open nothingness greeted us on the lower east side of Nevada. The Mojave Desert was how I imagined the moon looked, or Earth before God sprinkled the trees and plants on it. Sure, there were plants, but they were prickly. Grass didn't hang out anywhere that I could see. Instead, the ground consisted of sand, sand, sand, and not the good kind like at the beach.

Eddy and I were hitchhiking back to Isla Vista from his parents' other home in Colorado. This driver was dropping us off in the middle of the cactus, snakes and sharp edged boulders.

"This is as far as I go, People. I gotta get to my minin' claim," announced our driver as he pulled to a stop by a dirt road that looked like it led to Nowhere. "There'll likely be a few more cars to pass through. Otherwise, there's train tracks over that way." He swung his arm out the window and waved his hand like he was swatting away flies.

The looks Eddy and I gave each other conveyed the message, *This is not cool. What do we do now?*

We eased ourselves out of the dust ridden rattletrap car. Our driver, who I now saw fancied himself as a genuine prospector, shifted into first gear and revved the exhausted, knocking engine into a high whine.

Before he abandoned us in this distraught absence of common beauty, I reached through the window and grabbed his arm. "Wait a minute. Are you sure about the train tracks? Where do they go?"

"See that silo over yonder?" the miner swatted more invisible flies. " That round, wood thing?"

With my hand shading my eyes from the sun glare, I peered in the direction he indicated.

"Well, that there is an old water tower for when there was steam engines. It stands right next to the tracks. And them tracks go east and west, just like you told me you wanted. So there you go, lickity split."

Still holding on to his arm, I basically pleaded, "Do you know when the trains run?"

"For Christ sake, Lady, are you kiddin' me? Let go of my arm," he shouted as he stomped the gas pedal.

Eddy grabbed and pulled me a safe distance from the spitting gravel and stones the spinning tires kicked out. A cloud of dust billowed behind the car.

Coughing, Eddy and I walked back to the highway and sat down on our sleeping bags to assess the situation. I still had three joints tucked inside my hat. I lit up one of them and we shared it. He produced a Red Delicious apple and a Milky Way candy bar from his coat pocket. We shared those. In a little bit we both felt calmer.

My handsome guy suggested, "Let's go to the other side of the road so we'll be in position to catch a ride headed west."

I whined, "Ride? What ride?" I slapped my hand over my mouth. "I'm sorry." I realized I shouldn't have said that. I didn't want to make the situation worse and cause Eddy to be disappointed with me.

He didn't seem to notice my slip. "I can see a car coming," he said as he pointed into the distance.

"Oh, hurray."

We picked up our bags, scrambled across the road and stuck out our thumbs in the traditional hitchhikers' request.

I could see it was a black sports car of some kind. It stopped. The driver leaned across the passenger seat and brought his face into view. He looked about my dad's age with slightly gray hair and a mustache. "Hey, there. I've only got room for one of you. I pick you, Girly. Your boyfriend can catch the next ride and you can meet up in Vegas. What do you say?"

My whole body stiffened. "Are you nuts?" Not only was I shocked with the offer, I was irate. I looked at Eddy. I wanted him to step up to the car window and punch the guy in his nose. But nothing like that happened. Eddy looked more like he was in a state of shock. So I reared up and yelled, "Get lost, Daddy O!" I picked up a handful of gravel and threw it at the shiny sports car. I looked around for more when I spotted bigger rocks that I liked better.

"Whoa, Girly. OK OK. My mistake, you little freak." The creep's eyes widened as he jerked himself back to the steering wheel. The tires screeched when the rejected driver sped down the road.

I let the rocks fly anyway.

Dust from the spinning tires settled.

Eddy had not moved. He stood like he was part of the dead landscape. Where was my knight in shining armor?

As gently as I could muster, I asked, "Hey Eddy, do you want to take a stroll to the railroad tracks to see if there's any water there?"

With a nervous stomach, I tried again to reach him. "What

just happened? What are we doing here? First that miner dropped us off in nowhere land. Then that dude in the black car tried to steal me. I'm scared and really thirsty. Do you want to walk to those railroad tracks and wooden tower to find out if there's water?"

Finally Eddy came out of his trance. He looked around, tightened his lips, took a deep breath, puffed his cheeks and blew out the air. He said, as though I hadn't spoken, "Let's go see if that water tower is still connected to a water source."

We picked up our bed rolls and walked in silence, which didn't bother me so much. I didn't want to be grumpy. Afterall I was with my boyfriend. He had taken me on an adventure all the way to Colorado. But I suddenly felt so alone.

We found a faucet by the water tower. Eddy turned it on and made me wait while it ran long enough to clear out any debris. We cupped our hands and drank. It had a metal taste, but what a relief it was.

A dilapidated platform with two rickety buildings stood nearby. Behind them I saw an empty corral and a barely visible dirt road. I couldn't figure out where it came from, but a dented and rusty pickup truck idled there. Two scruffy men climbed out of the back of it. They also had bed rolls. Maybe they knew something about trains passing through here.

The pickup drove away and the men walked towards us, aiming for me. They stopped a foot away, and looked me up and down. One of them walked completely around us.

He asked, "Are you them Flower Children that there's been talk about?"

Eddy shifted his sleeping bag to his chest. "Sort of." His breathing became shallow.

I piped up, "Do you know anything about trains coming through here?"

"We shore do, Little Missy. You aimin' to hop a ride?"

"Maybe," Eddy answered for me.

"Yes, " I said, feeling bolder now that my boyfriend appeared to be standing up for me. "We're heading back to Santa Barbara."

"Well, ain't no train here that will git you there. But this one'll git you across Nevaddy. Sure enuf. Right Joe?"

"Uh huh. Say, got any of that marijuana with you?" From under the brim of his Yankees baseball cap, the man looked right at Eddy without blinking.

I heard Eddy's breathing pause. But he didn't shift his gaze. He actually held steady. "No, sorry. I don't."

I kept my mouth shut.

"You ever tried any?"

Eddy's voice didn't waiver. "A little bit."

The talker elbowed his companion in the ribs. "See, I told ya. They are them Flower Children." He had a big toothless grin.

From the distance came the sound of an approaching train. All of us turned our heads in that direction.

Joe said, " This here train is going the way you want. It'll stop long enough to make it real easy to pick out a car and get settled."

I asked, "Are there any bulls here to chase us away?"

"Naw, ain't none here. You got nothin' to be worried about. You take good care of yourselves now."

They turned and walked away.

The train arrived.

Eddy picked out a boxcar with an open door. He boosted me up and followed.

It was a fairytale moment for me, riding the rails with the man I loved. The freedom and adventure of traveling across the vast unknown. Beneath the dome of brilliant cobalt blue sky I felt a deeper sense of my own being. The scenery that we now traversed took my breath away. The sand alternated sparkles of white and gold. Strangely twisted Joshua tree branches pointed here and there like disarrayed sign posts. Tumbleweeds tumbled like clowns at a circus. A red fox slunk between ominous rock formations. A pair of hawks graced the sky.

I was truly happy. Being with my boyfriend, exploring life as it came, not worrying if I fit in with my society, this was all I was looking for. This carefree moment made sense to me. I wanted more of them. I wanted to be with Eddy forever, sharing these grand experiences.

13

WITHOUT ANY NOTICE

After crossing Nevada in an open boxcar, it was easy enough for Eddy and me to hitchhike on the main roads of California. Once we were back to our homes in Isla Vista, we agreed we needed to visit our parents for the rest of Christmas break.

My folks weren't as thrilled to see me as I expected. As it turned out, my brother had been hit by a drunk driver when he was in a crosswalk. Most of my visit was spent in the hospital at his bedside. I couldn't talk with him because he was delirious. Of course my mom was really upset and her focus was on him. My tender hearted dad was silent with his worry.

I was sort of background scenery. At least there was no interest in knowing what I had been up to since they had last seen me. My shenanigans would not have been welcome information. Being kicked out of the dorms and then dropping out of college was their breaking point. It was kinder and smarter of me to not share the events of my life with them.

Our silence gave me the opportunity to think about the fragileness of my brother's life and what that all meant to me. I didn't want to lose him. I didn't want him to die or be seriously injured. Those thoughts led to thinking about how important Eddy was to me. I wanted to spend the rest of my life with him.

Back at my folks' apartment, I did some housework for my mom and played cribbage with my dad. He asked how my car was running, and if I still worked for the campus photographer. He also made his yearly batch of fudge. Yummy.

My brother stabilized, and my mother calmed down. She cooked my favorite pot roast dinner for me. She made no comment about the hiking boots I wore, although her eyebrows raised when she looked in the direction of my feet. Her old habit prevailed of pushing my long hair back from my face. So we stood on stable ground with each other.

Two days remained before I had to be back at work. Early the next morning I returned to Isla Vista, did my laundry and bought a few groceries. Then I drove over to Eddy's to find out if he was home. There was no sign of him. I put a note on his door letting him know that I was here.

Life on campus was jumping and work was busy. My roommates had also returned with their stories about what they did for Christmas break. They wanted to hear about my adventures, too. "Wow, Kimmy, you are so daring. Weren't you scared?"

"Nope. I was with Eddy. He kept me safe. By the way, have you seen him? When I go by his place, he's never there."

Finally, by the end of the week, I took the short walk from my home to Eddy's little cabin behind the front house. Again he was not there, but his roommate, Howard, was outside opening their mailbox. "Hey, Howard. How's it going? I can't seem to catch Eddy here. Have you seen him?"

Howard took off his glasses to clean them on his shirt. He was in no hurry to answer me. After settling his glasses back on his face, he looked me up and down then cleared his throat.

"Eddy moved. He came back from seeing his folks, packed his stuff and moved."

I was not expecting that reply. My spine stiffened to attention, and my smile slid from my face. "What? Did he go back home? Did something happen? Did he leave a message for me?" My breathing came in short, quick draws. Nervously I licked my lips.

Howard was slow to answer. I stared him down.

Dropping his eyes and shrugging his shoulders, in a faint voice he said, "He moved to Goleta. He got new roommates. Two girls from his music classes. That's all I know."

I didn't cry. Not then. I thanked Howard for the information. With my shoulders pulled back as far as they would go, I held my head high and walked back home in the sunshine. I didn't allow my thinking to go beyond the words Howard gave me. I had to see for myself if this move really happened.

Nearby Goleta was a really small town, just a few blocks. It was easy for me to find him. I spotted his clunky old station wagon parked in front of a little house with a garage on one side. Lilac bushes clustered around the cement path to the door. The lawn had been freshly mowed. The cut grass left its enticing green smell in the air.

Eddy's car was here. Why? I fought back tears. I would not act like a baby. *I'm a grown woman. I'm looking for my boyfriend. I have a right to be here.*

As I knocked on the front door, I could hear voices. A girl my age answered. She had a dish towel in her hand and a smile on her face.

"I'm looking for Eddy. I see his car out front."

She opened the door wide and invited me in. I followed her into the kitchen. It was all sunny and full of laughter. The girl I followed returned to wiping and putting away dishes. Eddy and another girl stood by the counter cutting up apples. Their hips touched.

He didn't look surprised to see me. "Hi, Kimmy."

I didn't respond as the three of them stared at me.

Eddy took the cue to fill in the silence. " This is Amy and this is Julie."

I nodded at each of them. My breathing began to increase with the beating of my heart. I froze a smile onto my face and looked as solidly as I could at this man whom I thought cared about me as much as I cared about him. "Howard told me you had moved."

Before Eddy had a chance to say anything, Amy, who still had her hip smashed against his, spoke up, "How do you two know each other? Are you a music major too? I haven't seen you in any of my classes."

"No," I responded, not taking my eyes off Eddy. "I'm not a student at UCSB. I find other more interesting ways to occupy myself..... I was just surprised that Eddy had moved without telling me, since we had spent a lot of time together recently."

I didn't have anything else to say, and Eddy was silent, as usual. He also didn't introduce me as his girlfriend. So I left. I walked right out of that happy little kitchen. Eddy, of course, didn't offer to stop me.

I cried for three whole days. Two of those days I didn't go to work. I knew that I needed to pay my supposed boyfriend an unannounced visit to find out if he was sleeping with either, or both, of his music cuties. He certainly seemed to be enjoying his new living arrangement.

It was just after sunrise on the fourth day of my torment when I let myself into Eddy's new dwelling. I walked past the kitchen and through the living room. I noticed a piano against one wall, with a cello leaning against it and Eddy's French horn on the piano bench. *How cozy!*

I found Eddy's room. I didn't knock. I opened the door and stood looking down at the sleeping pair. Amy snuggled in his bare arms. Their discarded clothes mingled in a pile on the floor. I left without disturbing them, while I felt my heart being ripped asunder. *How could he do this to me?"*

Instead of going back to Isla Vista, I drove to a hardware store in Santa Barbara. I bought two cans of spray paint. *How could he so easily betray me? Without saying a word to me? Without any explanation? Without hearing what I have to say? Apparently I have no value to him. He just tosses me aside. Well, I have a message for him!*

The handsome, black haired man, who had taken me on an intimate adventure to Colorado, discovered me an hour later, with one can of spray paint in my hand and the empty can tossed onto the lawn. I was very busy changing the color of his beat up station wagon from dull gray to obvious purple.

He didn't say a word, nor try to stop me. He just stood at a safe distance and watched.

14

VISITING MATT IN PRISON

Two months after Eddy switched his affiliation from me to Amy, he knocked on my door. "Hi, Kimmy. Amy and I are going to visit Matt this weekend. Would you like to come with us?"

Of course I agreed. Although I had decided I didn't care about Eddy anymore, nor did I want to see him ever again, I very much wanted to see Matt. Afterall, my friend was in prison because I had asked him to roll up a lid of my newly purchased weed into joints, ten of which he got to keep.

They picked me up in Amy's car. I shared the backseat with a food basket. Maybe we were going to have a picnic lunch with Matt at the prison.

Eddy talked with Amy almost the whole time. I didn't know he had so many words in him. Their theme was the university musical performance they were preparing for. Both of them played in the orchestra.

I didn't understand the jargon so I spent my time looking out the window. There wasn't much of interest to see. Hills, flat, huge open spaces with some trees here and there. Mountains hung in the distance. Maybe it bored me because I didn't look closely enough. I mean, there were houses, farms and orchards. People lived here. They must like it. Maybe it had interesting places, if you knew where to look.

Finally, after three hours of driving, we arrived at Tehachapi State Prison east of Los Angeles, in the Mojave Desert. The snow draped Tehachapi Mountains rose in the distance. If anyone escaped he'd have to know how to survive in this isolated and rugged landscape.

We parked, and walked to the visitors' entrance. Before we left Isla Vista, Eddy told me to bring I.D. He also said we might be searched for weapons. Pocket knives were not allowed. I assumed he also meant that it would not be a good idea to smuggle in a joint, or two.

We arrived by one o'clock. Other people were also waiting to visit. Mostly they looked like family members, including children. Wow, I couldn't imagine coming to visit my mom or dad in prison. All the guards and personnel looked so serious and sort of mean. No smiles anywhere. But I didn't see any guns, just billy clubs like the bulls carried at the railroad stations when Gil and I hopped the trains.

There wasn't much of an inspection. No pat down or strip search. We had to show our I.D., empty our pockets and sign our names in a ledger book. The picnic basket that Amy carried was thoroughly searched. The potato salad and ham sandwiches passed inspection. So did the cake, after it got prodded to make sure no weapon was being smuggled in. When Amy retrieved the basket, she was directed to leave her purse in a locker.

A dozen tables with attached benches filled the outdoor area next to the building we had been in. A chain link fence, topped with barbed wire, surrounded the enclosure. Eddy and Amy agreed on a table in the sun. I accepted that they were in charge of that decision. Besides, that's the spot I would have picked. The other visitors chose locations that gave them as much privacy as possible. Everyone sat down to wait for our relatives, or friends, to appear.

I tried to comprehend what it meant to be incarcerated here. Obviously you couldn't go anywhere. Guards watched everything you did. Everyone wore the same clothes and ate the same food (whether or not you liked it). Mostly you stayed in a tiny cell with no privacy. And what kind of people could be your friends? Part of me knew this about prison. That's why none of us wanted to be there. But this was real, not just a scary story our parents, or teachers, or Scout leaders told us. "Be a good citizen, or end up in prison." Yet, what made a good citizen, or a bad one? I knew Matt was a very good citizen. Kind, smart, a great cook, generous, and fond of dogs. So why was he here?

He was here because the law said we were bad if we smoked marijuana, which caused no harm to anyone. It made us feel good about ourselves and each other.

A door opened at the opposite end from where we came in. Men in matching blue jeans and button down blue shirts came through, looking expectantly for recognizable faces.

Matt was one of the last to appear. Even though I'd known him to be slim, all muscles, and sort of boney, he looked like he'd lost weight. He looked haggard. When he spotted us, he approached slowly. The look on his face was so sad. I wanted to hug him. But we weren't allowed to have physical contact. Can you imagine coming to see your husband, or son, or grandfather and not hugging? I guessed it was ok for the little kids to hug because I saw them get lifted and even held for brief moments.

"I'm really glad you came. I wasn't sure if you'd make it. After all, it's a long drive." Matt looked a mixture of relief and nervousness, as he rubbed his hands together and shifted his weight like he was trying to straighten his back.

Eddy spurted out a response, "Of course we came. It was an

easy drive. Amy made a swell lunch. The cake is especially good. We'll save that for last."

Amy set out the food and we served ourselves. Matt explained, "I just had lunch, hotdogs and macaroni. But this homemade potato salad looks really good. I do miss home cooking. Thanks Amy."

He and Eddy talked for a while.

Eddy said,"I don't really know what's going on in Isla Vista these days, since I moved into Goleta. I'm really focused on my classes, orchestra and up-coming track season. But I've seen Ray a bit. He drives that Porsche everywhere. He visited one night and played some new songs on his sitar for us."

'Us' meaning him and Amy, which I don't need to hear.

Matt glanced at me, as though he could hear my thoughts. I felt his compassion. He responded to Eddy. "We don't really get music here. Sometimes during lunch, church songs come from the overhead speakers."Pause."Have the Stones or Beatles put out any new tunes? What about Hendrix or Jefferson Airplane?"

Eddy and Amy filled him in as best they could. I just listened.

Finally I said, "Matt, I'm so sorry for....."

He held up his hand with his palm towards me to stop my words. "No, Kimmy. Don't say another word. You are not to blame. It was Dwayne who narked on Will and me." His hands tightened into fists. "He planned it for a long time. You did not cause this." His voice was firm as he looked deeply into my eyes.

So much I wanted to hug him! "Thank you, Matt. You are a true friend."

Eddy leaned forwardand quietly asked, "Have your folks come to see you?"

Matt sighed and turned his head away. I heard a slight cough before he looked back at Eddy. "No, not yet. But my mom writes and puts in what my dad tells her. I get weekly letters from her."

Amy looked at her watch and nudged Eddy. "We only have a

little bit more time. So let's eat some cake." She took it out of the basket along with four pretty little plates and forks. She gave me and Matt generous slices, while she gave herself and Eddy thin slices.

"This sure is good, Amy. Thank you," Matt said after wiping the crumbs off his lips.

Eddy explained, " You get to keep the rest, but don't eat it all at once. Maybe you've got a couple of friends here to share with and that would give you a better standing. Just know that this cake has special ingredients that need to be savored." He stared at Matt, until the hidden meaning took hold.

All of a sudden Matt got a huge grin on his face. "This is just what I've been needing, besides you all coming to see me."

"Well then, we should get going because Kimmy ate a really big slice, and you know how she gets."

When I heard my name, I put my fork down and looked at my former boyfriend. "What do you mean?"

Eddy replied, "I'll tell you later when we're on the road, safely headed back to Isla Vista."

I shrugged my shoulders and asked Amy, " Do you think I could have just a little bit more? Chocolate cake with chocolate frosting is my favorite."

Together she and Eddy replied, "No, Kimmy. We really need to get going now." Amy took the fork from me and pushed the cake towards Matt.

I didn't mind. It was all good being here with Matt and finally seeing him smile. I still wanted to give him a hug but Eddy must have read my mind. When I stood up he was right beside me. He took hold of my upper arm and aimed me towards the door. He lined me between himself and Amy. I leaned past him and blew Matt a goodbye kiss.

When we stopped to get Amy's purse I suddenly had something to say, "Do you know that octopuses have three hearts? "

"OK, Kimmy, let's get all the way out of the building before we hear more."

Well that was really funny to me and I started to giggle. We had just walked through the door that opened to the outside of the penitentiary. Eddy had let go of my arm.

"Eddy, why do I feel like I am stoned?"

"Because you are."

"What?"

"The cake, Kimmy. The cake."

" Amy, you baked a cake filled with marijuana? And we delivered it to an inmate of a state prison? I am totally impressed. Why didn't you tell me before we went in there?"

Eddy put a hand over his mouth to stop a laugh. Gently, and with a smile he said, "Because we all know that you don't know how to lie."

"Is that why you shoved me out the door?"

"No, that was a simple precaution. When you are stoned, you get silly and there's no telling what will come out of your mouth. Now what do you want to tell us about the octopus?"

15

ACAPULCO GOLD

Once again Bob wanted to score marijuana. This time he aimed for the best, which was Acapulco Gold. He learned, somehow, that the place to make a good connection was in Mazatlan, which was a thousand miles north of Acapulco and 1,400 miles from Isla Vista.

Summer vacation had begun at UCSB. Bob came to my home. It had been awhile since I had seen him, so I assumed it had to be important to hear what he had to say.

"Hi, Kimmy. How's it going?"

"Pretty good, Bob. I haven't seen you in a while."

"That's true."

He really didn't do anything. He just stood there on my front porch, leaning slightly against the railing. Yet, here it came. I don't know what to call it. I could almost actually see the molecules lift off him and swoop through the air to envelop me. It was like the transfer of a cosmic space suit that settled around me. It had to be a spell of some kind, even though I don't think he knew it was happening. That's just the effect he had on me.

"I'm thinking about going to Mexico for a little bit. I hear that Mazatlan is the place to score the Gold."

"Mexico again?" Not only did I stammer, I flinched. "You've got to be kidding. Our other two trips had been close to disasters."

"That was Tijuana, Kimmy." Bob paused while he enjoyed a slight chuckle. " This time we'll go south of there. It's beautiful in Mazatlan. Like a resort. We can take a bus, which is really cheap. So's the hotel and food. Zip down and zip back."

That enticing man came and stood next to me. I slowed my breathing to keep my heart from pounding its way through my chest. How could I be so affected, when going places with him always got me into trouble?

"We can drive your car to San Diego, park it there, and catch the bus."

Each word that he spoke resonated like the background music of Spartacus or Lawrence of Arabia. Every note shouted "Adventure" to every cell in my quaking body.

When I didn't respond right away he placed his hand on my shoulder and said,

"Maybe your girlfriend, Nancy, would like to go. I've asked Les. You know Les. The more, the merrier, as someone said. What do you think?"

I saw myself riding across the golden sands of Arabia, the wind streaming through my raven tresses. My true love galloped beside me on his charging white steed. The sun blazed across the endless sky. A hawk gave a shrill cry, as it began its mesmerizing dive back to its master's outstretched gloved hand.

I felt like a fly caught in his web. *What choice do I have?* I released a deep sigh andasked, "You want to do this when?"

"Soon. Like in a couple of days. I don't want to be away from Suzanne for long. She's planning our wedding and she likes to know what flavor cake I want, and stuff like that." His eyes sparkled and a blush rose to his ears.

"Well, OK. I'm a bit interested." I shoved my hands into the pockets of my Levis and leaned back against the door, as though I was in no hurry to commit myself. "I'll talk to Nancy when she gets home from work. Come back tomorrow when she's here and we can discuss this further."

Bob nodded his approval and left.

That evening, after sharing sloppy joes and salad with my roommate, I told her about Bob's offer.

Her eyebrows lifted and she folded her arms across her chest. "Hmmm. Really? Bob wants to go all the way to Mazatlan to find some Acapulco Gold? There must be more to this scheme than that."

"I have no idea what that could be. He did say he didn't want to be away from Suzanne for long. Maybe he just wants a last hurrah before settling down to marriage and fatherhood. But, Nancy," I bounced around a bit in my chair, "he invited both of us, and Les, to go to Mazatlan. This will be nothing like when we went to Tijuana to score pot. That place was weird and filthy. No wonder we had trouble there. This trip'll be different. Acapulco doesn't just have the Gold. It's also where the beautiful boys dive from high cliffs into the ocean. That's what I would like to see."

"Yes. That would be something to see," Nancy sighed. "Thanks for dinner, Kimmy. I'll see if I can get some time off from the diner. Now that UCSB is on summer vacation, there's not as many customers and I'm only part time anyway. I'll ask tomorrow if I can have a week off. Are you sure Les is coming too? He's a real sweet guy who could hopefully tone down some of Bob's crazy ideas." A smile began to form on her pretty face. "It would be amazing to go there. I'm beginning to like the idea."

The next day Nancy came home from work at the same time Bob showed up. I hadn't had a chance to find out if she got the time off. I really hoped she did because I didn't want to do this without her. She would be my safeguard from me succumbing to Bob's charms. He leaned against the porch railing again. My o my.

Nancy noticed my nervousness. "Kimmy, are you OK?"

Jerked out of my nonsensical day dream I answered, "Sure. Of course. I would just like to get out of Isla Vista for a while. A trip would be good for me."

Nancy must have thought I was thinking about Eddy, who didn't want to be my boyfriend anymore. She slipped her arm around my shoulders and gave me a little hug.

With a direct look at Bob, she said, "We both want to go. Kimmy explained the details to me about the bus and money. Is Les coming?"

Bob shifted his weight from leaning to standing straight. "Good. Great. Yes. He's coming. Can you be ready the day after tomorrow?"

"Yes," Nancy and I declared.

Bob pulled out a five dollar bill from his pocket, " Kimmy, here's money to fill your gas tank." He turned to walk away, then stopped. "Be sure you both bring I.D.s with you. We have to get visas at the border. OK?"

"OK."

Bob responded with one of his rare smiles. "Great. Les and I will be here at 7:00 a.m." He stepped lightly off the porch and sauntered away.

Two mornings later I was on the road again seeking adventure. As usual, Bob knew where to go. He directed us to the bus depot in San Diego. I found a place to park and locked my car. We picked out our seats on the bus, crossed the border, and stopped for our visas. No problems. It looked like this was going to be an easy, fun trip. Nancy brought her big suitcase, undoubtedly filled with every emergency precaution.

Although it was a thirty hour ride, the plump seats on the Greyhound bus were comfortable. I watched the desert scenery go by. We drove east along the border to Mexicali, then abruptly headed south. I knew we were in a different country when I saw pale green cactus with fat, prickly arms stretched to the clear azure sky. Smaller cactus with thick flat palms bunched against each other. Underneath them, and spread as far as I could see, scraggly leafless bushes nestled and soaked up the dry heat. Soft red, windworn rock formations jutted forth offering scant shade for sharp edged boulders. Here and there tumbleweeds scurried, shooing long eared jack rabbits out of their way. Now and then two or three large birds circled overhead. Small flocks of tiny birds flitted by, the brave ones perched among the spines of the stately cactus. And dull colored sand everywhere. Obviously no humans lived in that challenging environment. I wondered what I would do if I were suddenly abandoned there. Where would I find water?

Our bus stopped for breaks so everyone could get off to stretch. A snack, or meal, could be purchased from local vendors who perched alongside the highway under their makeshift sun shelters. The four of us bought sodas and bananas. Then we grouped together, away from the bus, to share a doobie that Bob had carefully hidden in one of his socks. The driver and other passengers did not seem to be offended by our actions, or the smoke. In fact two of the old guys who rode in the back of the bus shuffled up to us. So, naturally, we shared our joy. Bob chatted away with them. I think they told each other dirty jokes because the three of them laughed a lot and the old guys wouldn't look at Nancy and me.

Before getting back on the bus, I needed a restroom. But we were in rural Mexico where that didn't exist, so like the other passengers, I ducked behind my own scraggly bush. I guess my friends did the same. Although, during the night, when the driver had no intention of stopping, Bob was desperate and peed in his empty Coca Cola bottle.

After sunset, and since there were few passengers, Bob and Les made room for themselves in the overhead storage racks. They shoved our luggage around, climbed up, stretched out and went to sleep. Nancy and I stayed in our seats and played gin rummy using the flashlight that she dug out of her suitcase. When we tired of that, I gazed at the star studded sky. Eventually I fell asleep.

Mazatlan was bigger than I imagined it would be. It was a full sized city. We came to a broad street that curved along the lovely bay. The adjoining wide sidewalk, called a malecon, separated the water from the car traffic, the businesses and the multistoried hotels for the rich tourists. Side streets branched and wove out into the density of all Mazatlan had to offer, which looked clean and inviting. It was a mixture of grand old Mexican buildings with pastel colored brick and the encroachment of its modern northern neighbor that offered steel and glass structures for the comfort of rich tourists.

My friends and I were tourists, but we were not rich. We could, however, afford one of the nicer, though not fancy, hotels. The bathroom was down the hallway from our room, like in Tijuana, but here it was clean. Everything was clean. Nancy and I gave sighs of relief.

"No need for my disinfectant spray here," she announced.

Since we arrived close to dinner time, we put our bags in the room and went looking for a place to eat. The little cafe next door drew us in with enticing aromas. Bob helped us order with his fluent Spanish skills. The food soon arrived and we settled in to enjoy it. The long bus ride had made us all hungry.

There was a lot of chatter from the other diners. To me they sounded nervous, or excited. Bob listened intently.

I laid down my fork and leaned across the table towards him. "Bob, what's going on? What are they saying?"

He raised a hand with the palm facing me, as a signal to be quiet. He continued to eat the last two bites of his chicken enchilada. After wiping his mouth and resetting his fork, he quietly revealed what he had overheard. "Off shore from here is an island with a penal colony for hardened criminals. Last night two of the convicts escaped. They probably swam here. They could be anywhere in the area. They are murderers." He held up his palm again to stop the questions that we all had. "Let's go for a little walk," he said.

We crossed the street to the malecon, and walked until we got a clear view of the island with the penal colony. The buildings sat on top of the one large hill that swelled over the island. Thick foliage spread everywhere.

Les spoke up. "It looks like it's at least a mile away. Maybe more. But a strong swimmer would have no trouble getting here."

I nodded in agreement.

Nancy batted at a honey bee that circled her head. "Are there sharks?"

Bob responded, "Not likely. Let's get our swimsuits. This looks like a good place to hang out for a while. After all, isn't this what we came here for?"

Back at the hotel room, as each of us rifled through our bags for our swimwear, there was a knock on our door. Bob was nearest so he opened the door to reveal a tall man in a tan suit and a Panama hat.

"I apologize for this intrusion." He showed Bob his police badge. "May I come in?"

He had our attention.

"I am Señor Alvarez, chief of police." He spoke very good English.

"I do not want to alarm you, but two very bad men have escaped from our penal colony. We have every available policeman searching for them. They will be caught."

He paused, looked steadily at each one of us, then continued. "For your personal well-being I am requesting that you remain here in the hotel until they are apprehended. You will be informed when it is safe to enjoy our lovely city." He reached into his inner coat pocket. "This is my card with my phone number. If you have any kind of difficulty, please contact me." He handed the card to Bob, tipped his hat and excused himself.

"I guess this means we're not going swimming right now." I pouted and slumped down on a bed.

Les cleared his throat. "Señor Alvarez was pretty clear about us not going anywhere. He has enough to do without us getting in the way. In other words, he doesn't want us to do anything stupid that would cause an international incident."

Nancy and I exchanged looks and shifted our complete attention to our usually quiet friend. She asked him, "What are you saying, Les?"

He rubbed a hand across his forehead. "I'm saying, not only does Señor Alvarez have the responsibility, as chief of police, to recapture these escaped criminals, who are murderers and could murder again to keep their freedom. Now he also has four gringos from the USA to worry about." Les puffed his cheeks, blew out the air and continued. "If anything, anything at all happens to us, it could cause our government to bombard his country with major accusations of endangering our lives. Newspapers would bounce such an incident around the world. And of course that would lead to him losing his job, and who knows what else." Les shrugged his shoulders as if there was no more to be said.

I certainly didn't have anything to say, except, "Phooey.

What lousy timing. That ocean water is just calling me to jump in and splash around."

Nancy shook her head and flung her curls around like she was trying to unstick something that was lodged there. A bee flew out. She swatted at it until it flew towards the door and Bob let it out. "Well, at least we can do what he asked of us and stay put here until it's safe. Maybe just go to the cafe."

Les and I nodded in agreement.

Bob's reaction was different. "Yeah, that's a good idea. You guys stick close here."

Les snapped his head around to gape at Bob. "What do you mean by 'you guys'? What are you up to, Bob?"

Bob didn't look at us. Instead he studied his thumb nail and began to chew on it before he offered an explanation. "I speak Spanish. I can understand what anyone says. I'll know what's going on and where to stay clear of." He rolled his head to crack his neck.

Les stepped closer to Bob. "Just where do you have to go that's so important?"

Bob straightened his back. "I'm supposed to meet some people."

"When?" Les jammed his hands on his hips. He didn't back off.

"Soon." Bob's face smoothed from all expression. His voice was cool and calm. "You can stay here with the girls to make sure they're OK."

Silence. Nancy took out her deck of cards from her suitcase. She dealt out a hand of solitaire on the bed where she was sitting.

Bob started pacing back and forth from the window to the door.

I kept focused on Les.

Les looked at me and Nancy, then again faced Bob. "If you go,

I go. If something happens, hopefully one of us could make it back here to tell the girls. Leave the chief's card with them, to use, if necessary."

Bob stopped pacing. "OK. Good. We'll leave our visas and IDs too, so they can't be stolen from us. We'll go after dinner to make sure the girls have eaten."

No one said another word. Nancy played solitaire. Les sat at the table and watched. Bob counted, and recounted, his money. I stood by the window looking out at the beautiful ocean.

An hour later we went to dinner at the little cafe next door. Afterwards the guys walked Nancy and me back to our hotel room.

"Be sure to lock the door. And don't wait up for us." Those were Bob's parting words.

Nancy and I played several hands of gin rummy. Neither of us had a watch, so I don't know how much time ticked by. But when I struggled to stay awake, and the guys had not returned, I asked my girlfriend, "Why didn't you argue about them leaving?"

She put the cards away and pulled her pjs out of her suitcase. "How could we have stopped them, Kimmy? Tie them to the chairs with ripped up sheets? You know Bob does whatever he wants. I'm just glad that Les went with him. At least one of them has common sense."

We lay down on the bed farthest from the door and left the other bed empty for our delinquent friends.

16
THE SEARCH

I woke up groggy and needed the bathroom. When I returned, Nancy was sitting on the bed with her arms clasped around her knees. We had both fallen asleep with the ceiling light on. Bob and Les had not returned.

I stood still in the middle of the floor, not sure where to sit. "Where are they, Nancy?"

"How in hell should I know? This is crazy. And I'm hungry."

We tidied our appearances, took the room key and went to the cafe next door. With both of us using made up sign language and clucking like chickens, we received scrambled eggs, tortillas and salsa. Bob had thoughtfully left us some Mexican paper money. Nancy and I both felt energized, but didn't know what else to do, so we returned to our hotel room.

We went over again, and again the events of yesterday trying to understand what was happening.

I covered my eyes with my hand trying to recall the events. "Supposedly, Bob's main purpose for coming to Mazatlan was to score Acapulco Gold, because it's known to be the best marijuana in the Americas. He probably invited me because I had a car to drive us to San Diego to get the bus which brought us here." I paused to massage my forehead. "He suggested that I invite you."

I looked to see if she had any reaction. She didn't. Her head sagged on her knees.

So I kept talking. "As for him inviting Les, I didn't even know they were acquainted. Bob also told me he expected this to be a quick trip because he didn't want to be away from his girlfriend for very long."

I sat down next to Nancy with my hands locked between my knees.

She lifted her head and gave me a weak smile.

I offered a suggestion. "Maybe that's why he was nervous last night. Maybe he didn't want to be held up here and worry her with taking longer to get back home. Maybe that's why he would risk meeting whoever it was. Maybe...."

"That's a lot of 'maybes', Kimmy. I'm sure we could come up with more. But that's not bringing the guys back. And it must be lunchtime, because I'm hungry again."

Suddenly my mind lit up. "OK, I know what to do. We need to contact Señor Alvarez. He told us we could, for any reason. Remember? Where's the card he left us with his info? I mean, it's our only choice."

Nancy agreed at once. We took the card with us, as well as our visas and IDs. We stopped at the hotel desk and showed the card to the man who worked there. We showed him the chief's card. Nancy put her hand above her eyes, like she was shading them, and then swiveled her head left and right.

The man figured out that we were looking for the person whose name was on the card. He pointed and told us something. Our blank faces finally made him realize that we didn't under-stand Spanish. He seemed glad to help us so he led us to the door, pointed at the card and the direction for us to go.

Holding each other's hand for a sense of comfort and inner strength, we showed the card to other people as we walked in the hot sunshine. We shrugged our shoulders and the people pointed. We must have walked for an hour when we finally arrived at a two story, old adobe building that had bars on its windows. The sign above the door said "Policia.' Inside we again showed our card to a man in police uniform, who stood behind a counter. At first that man looked puzzled.

Nancy told him, "We don't speak Spanish." She pointed at the card.

He must have understood what we wanted, because he quickly turned and walked down a short hallway to a closed door. He knocked, opened it and talked to someone, showing the card.

Instantly Señor Alvarez appeared. "Señoritas, you are here?"

In relief Nancy and I squeezed each other's hand. Our sighs were quite audible.

The Chief of Police led us back into his office where we poured out our story, minus any mention of Acapulco Gold. He took off his hat with one hand and let it fall limply to his side. He pulled his other hand down his face like he wanted to wipe it away. "Please sit down here." He motioned to a well worn wooden bench. "I will make some phone calls." In a short time he hung up and handed us the paper he had been writing on. "Your friends have been arrested. They were discovered last night, during our enhanced efforts to locate the escaped criminals. They were in a cantina. They had no proof of their identities. They are in our jail. This is where you must go to bring their visas and IDs. I am sorry. For now I can do no more. I must go. The escaped ones have been spotted. Adios Señoritas. Buena suerte."

Señor Alvarez ushered us to the main door, turned abruptly

and joined several officers who ran outside and dashed away in two vehicles.

Once again Nancy and I were alone on the streets of Mazatlan. This time however, we didn't ask anyone for directions. We knew which way to go.

"It looks like we just keep putting one foot in front of the other," I said, sighing heavily. " This is one weird trip we're on." I realized I'd been doing a lot of sighing in the past twenty-four hours. "Nancy, I'm hungry and those miniature tacos that the vendor is selling sure look good to me. How about you?"

The little tacos were delicious and boosted my energy. But it was a hot walk in the noon sunshine. The warmer weather here made me extra thirsty. Soda pop did not help. I wanted water to drink. I had been filling myself from the bathroom tap in the hotel. Here on the streets of Mazatlan I found no drinking fountains. I hoped it wouldn't take long to get back to our room. I began to slow down. Nancy was several paces ahead of me with the space between widening.

No one told me not to drink the water in Mexico. No one told me about Montezuma's Revenge, the sickness that hit with lightning speed to strip my internal body. Suddenly I was dizzy. Then cramps hit me and vomit spewed out of me into the gutter. All I could do after that was collapse on the sidewalk.

Nancy ran back to me. "You can't lie down here. We have to get back to the hotel," she said as she grabbed my arm to help me to my feet. "Be your strong self, Kimmy."

Those were the words I held onto as I trusted her to find the way. My vision was swimming and the cramps were horrible. I knew I would need a toilet soon.

We made it to the hotel in time for me to find relief. Back in our room Nancy opened her suitcase and pulled out bottles of aspirin and pink Pepto-Bismol. I was grateful as I collapsed on the bed and closed my eyes. All I wanted was oblivion. She covered me up, stood watch for the rest of the day and played lots of solitaire.

I don't know how my girlfriend handled all of this. First we arrived in a city with murderers on the loose. Next Bob and Les got thrown into jail and we had to find the police chief to know where they were. Then I got raging sick and she brought us safely back to the hotel. All this happened in a foreign country where we didn't speak the language. Through all of this craziness Nancy kept her cool.

17

THE BUS TO JAIL

Fortunately, by morning I felt so much better. In fact, Nancy and I went looking for breakfast. Besides eggs and tortillas once again, I drank bottled soda. No more Mexican tap water for me.

After our meal, when we walked through the hotel front door, there was a different person behind the desk. He was a younger, cuter guy who beamed a smile at us.

"Ahh, young ladies from the U.S.A." Each syllable was precisely enunciated. "My name is Miguel. I speak very good English. I will talk with you. Si? Por favor?"

Nancy and I were thrilled with this announcement. We threw our names back at him. I wished I could throw my arms around his neck. English speaking Miguel could be our lifeline for finding and helping get Bob and Les out of jail.

"Miguel," Nancy began, "our friends were arrested two nights ago because they didn't have their visas or IDs with them. We found that out from the Chief of Police, Señor Alvarez. We met him when we arrived in Mazatlan because the murderers escaped and he didn't want us to get hurt. But Bob and Les left the hotel. They didn't come back. So Kimmy and I went to the police station, and the Señor made phone calls. That's how we found out." She paused to catch her breath.

I continued, " Nancy and I are supposed to take their visas and IDs to the jail to prove who they are, so they can be released. The chief said there is a bus to get there. Do you know where we can find it?"

"Si, si. Of Course." Our new acquaintance was not ruffled by our verbal onslaught. Instead he looked ready for action. With his shoulders pulled back and his chin held high, Miguel led us to the front door. He pointed to the corner where the bus stopped. He showed us how many pesos it cost to ride. He slipped Señor Alvarez's card from Nancy's hand to write on the back of it. Handing it to her he explained, "Show this address to the bus driver so he will know where you want to go."

Miguel's parting words to us, as we headed up the street, freaked me out. "Señoritas, be very careful. Do not go into the jail. Only enter the front door. No further. Bad men are in there. Very bad men. They might not let you out."

We caught the bus, showed the driver the card with our destination and found a seat. Nancy closed her eyes. I wrung my hands and took a couple of deep breaths to calm myself. "Wow, Nancy. What's happening? Can this trip get any worse? Did you hear what Miguel said?"

"Yes, Kimmy. I heard. So it's up to us to make sure that nothing else bad happens. We've got the visas and IDs for the guys. And we've got Señor Alvarez's card. They have to release Bob and Les."

"We just have to make sure we don't get pulled into that hell hole."

"Right. How do we do that?"

Silence from both of us. We felt the bus bump along on the cobbled streets in this shoddy part of the city. I looked around at the other passengers. It was a full load. All kinds of people. None of them fancy looking. I mean, I saw two little boys chewing on sugarcane. A mama took the cap off a soda bottle with her teeth. A grandpa held a cage full of squawking chickens. Some guy in a sombrero strummed a guitar. And lots of people chatted with everyone. It was noisy, but they all looked happy.

I said, "Maybe we won't go all the way in the front door. Maybe we'll just hold it open and shout."

Nancy nodded, like that might be a good idea. "And we can hold on to each other too. It'll be harder to grab us that way."

"The card!" I cried out. " We have the Chief of Police's card. We tell everyone that he is our friend and he sent us here. He knows where we are." That was it. That was our plan to rescue our dumb ass friends.

The bus driver stopped to let us off across the street from the jail. He said something to us which we didn't understand. "¿Habla usted español?" Blank looks hung on our faces, so it was his turn to make up sign language. He jabbed his finger at his window, patted his chest and flapped both of his hands over his shoulders. Nancy and I understood that he was telling us he would return to pick us up in front of the jail. We all gave each other big grins, and my girlfriend and I stepped out into the unknown.

We held each other's hand as we crossed the street.

The jail was a big, two story building, made out of some kind of old bricks. The only window was barred. We had to walk up steps to get to the front door, which was all glass. It looked dark inside. I definitely did not want to go in there.

I checked my purse to make sure the guys' visas and IDs were safely there. Of course I double checked for my visa and ID. All I could think to do to keep from screaming was to turn into 'Proper Girl." That worked for Nancy and me when we got stopped at the border crossing in Tecate and we had that marijuana hidden in the spare tire of my car. *Just stay calm, Kimmy. Put on your nice girl smile. Remember to say yes sir and no sir. You can do this....You have to do this to get Bob and Les out of jail.*

We opened the door and peeked in. It was so noisy! I don't even know what the noise was. Maybe it was all in my head, because no one was there. Not even behind the counter. Nancy and I looked at each other. We looked around.

Nancy said, "Hello?"

Silence.

She tried again, "HELLO?"

Still no response.

Suddenly a big, surly looking man emerged out of that darkness.

Nancy and I clung to the door and held tightly to each other's hand.

The surly man approached us. Was that a smile on his mustached face? He wore a khaki colored uniform and black leather boots. He stopped in front of us and glared. No words, just glared.

Nancy jerked, letting go of my hand and the door. She rifled through her purse and pulled out Señor Alvarez's card. Her action caused me to dive into my purse. I pulled out Bob and Les' papers. The really big man took what we offered.

¿Habla usted español?"

Nancy and I answered in unison, "No sir, no Spanish."

Jumbo sized man continued to glare. Then he turned his head and barked out something to someone. He stepped backwards and motioned us to follow.

What? Go inside the hell hole?

The giant stopped moving. He stood beside a counter. Next to that was another door. An overhead light barely lit up the area. He pointed at something. I could see it was a wooden bench, like at the police station. He still held our guys' info and the Police

Chief's card. My hands no longer gripped Nancy, nor the door. My consciousness had no grip on anything. *Are we going to be thrown into jail, too?* My heart felt like it was going to pound a hole through my chest.

Monstro continued to point at the bench.

The ingrained "Proper Girl" took over. My legs unglued from the floor and walked me to the bench. Nancy was right behind me. We sat down.

Our supposed guide shook his head, chuckled lightly.

Another man came through that other door. He wore jeans, a white t-shirt and Mexican sandals. He was fair skinned and very thin, but all muscles. His dishwater blond hair was pulled back in a low ponytail. The two men talked and blondie was shown the papers. They looked at us, and talked some more.

Blondie walked over to us. "Hello. I am Doctor Feliciano."

English. He spoke English.

"Your, ah friends, are here. I have kept them safe. They will be most glad to see you. They are being sent for now. It will be a few moments. Worry no more." He turned and walked back through that other door.

Nancy and I didn't talk. I think we both held our breaths. We waited. My mouth was dry. I tried to swallow. I heard her stomach growl.

With a loud thud the door burst open again. Out bolted Bob and Les like bulls from their shute.

Les spotted us immediately and charged. First he embraced Nancy and then smashed me to his breast. "Thank you, thank you," he panted .

Bob talked with the Doctor. They shook hands. Then he ambled over to us. "Thanks ladies. I knew we could count on you."

That totally flattered me, but I wasn't sure why.

Bob and Les rode the local bus with Nancy and me back to

our hotel. The guys changed their clothes and Bob treated us to dinner. Afterwards, back in our room, he and Les told us some hair-raising accounts of their short stay in the hoosegow.

It turned out that Doctor Feliciano was an inmate who was serving a life term. He could have been sent to the penal colony on the island from where the two murderers escaped. But he agreed instead to use his medical skills in exchange for better accommodations at the local jail.

Bob explained, "The doc found his wife in bed with another man. He killed them both with a big kitchen knife. The judge ruled it a passion murder. Since the doc was a well respected citizen, the judge tried to find a lenient sentence. This was the best outcome. He has a lot of freedom within the jail, and he gets the choicest foods."

Les spoke up. "He also gets his choice of the women inmates."

"What do you mean?" I gasped.

"There's another side to the jail. For the women. Most of them don't have any family who will pay their bail or for their food."

"Pay for their food?"

"Yes. That's how it goes in Mexico. So once a week the women are brought to the men's side to prostitute themselves to get enough money to pay for food for the next week."

Bob smugly added, "Don't look so shocked, ladies. Probably every one of the women are in jail for prostitution. It's nothing new to them." He paused to take out a pack of Chiclets from his shirt pocket and popped two of them into his smirking mouth. "Let me tell you what Les and I had to do to keep from being locked up in there forever."

He made it sound like he had a better story to tell. I was curious. "What could be worse than that?"

"Well, the policia were on overtime looking for those escaped murderers, right? When they found us, we were in a cantina, just having made a score. They worked through the room checking everyone's IDs. Since we left ours safely with you, they decided to arrest us. In the squad car the two dudes talked about performing a strip search when we reached the police station. They were laughing so hard that they didn't see when I motioned to Les to do what I did, which was to shove the baggie up my ass.

With hands on her hips, Nancy countered that disclosure. "OK boys, let me get this straight. You had something other than kilos, or even ounces, of Acapulco Gold. You're implying that you possibly scored heroin. Or maybe you're saying your asses are big enough to hold a brick of weed. Now, how could that be, I wonder?"

Bob choked on the gum he just swallowed.

Les didn't say a word.

I had no clue about what Nancy said. But I definitely understood that Bob did.

"You are just so proud of yourselves, aren't you?" Her eyes smoldered at them as she shook her hands in the air. "Neither of you has bothered to ask how we found you. Or what we had to go through to get your visas and IDs to the jail. You two are out of there because of us!" She turned her back on them and sat down at the table with her deck of cards.

I was shocked. I mean, I was flattered when Bob told us he "...could count on us" to get them out of jail. Recognition for my efforts given to me by any man was important to me. That was how I was raised. It was assumed that whatever men went through was what really mattered. But Nancy saw it differently. And she said so. *What am I missing?*

I looked at Les, who sat on one of the beds with his head hung low and his hands clenched between his knees. He raised his head and his woebegone face spoke the truth of his words, "

You're absolutely right, Nancy. I'm so sorry to have put you and Kimmy through this."

Bob stood by the door fidgeting with the knob. "I'm going out for a while." He left, and quietly closed the door.

That was the end of our very full day. Nancy told Les to step outside so we could change into our pjs. She and I shared a bed. Les turned out the light and slid into the other bed. I lay awake for a while trying to understand where Nancy got the courage to say all of that. My mom didn't talk to my dad that way. I never before heard any woman talk to a man that way. And Les said she was right.

Sometime during the night Bob returned.

18

DUMB LUCK

The next morning I slept in. The onslaught of Montezuma's Revenge had weakened me. The extra bedrest felt good.

My friends were all up, dressed and ready to go.

"We're just waiting for you, Kimmy, to go to breakfast," Bob said as he stuffed a package into his backpack. A similar package lay on the table.

The Gold! Bob had scored two bricks of Acapulco Gold last night. Today he was beaming. "Shall we try some before we go to breakfast?" There were half a dozen joints also on the table.

"Yes," I said. I was eager to try it. "Let me get dressed." I grabbed my clothes and toothbrush and headed to the bathroom down the outside hallway. When I returned the room was filled with wonderful smelling smoke. My friends had started without me, but I didn't care. I entered the circle as a joint got passed around.

After letting the euphoria settle somewhat, we happy four went to breakfast. Once again Bob treated us. Perhaps he was trying to make up for the recent havoc he had caused. Whatever.

I took full advantage of his gesture and practically gorged myself with yummy fish tacos. But no tap water to drink. Oh no. I treated myself to a bottle of Dos Equis beer.

As we pushed ourselves away from the table and walked into the sunshine, Bob announced that he had another treat for us. "I met a fisherman last night who agreed to take us to one of the offshore islands for the day. We have to meet him soon. So let's go grab our swimsuits and some food for lunch. Nancy, you've probably got a bottle, or two, of sunscreen in that suitcase of yours. Be sure to bring it."

Nancy blushed, and we all laughed.

A sinewy, gray haired fisherman waited for us at the shoreline across from our hotel. He wore cut off pants, a faded t-shirt and a scruffy Dodgers baseball cap. He stood next to what looked like a big canoe. Other similar boats lined the shore. He bundled up a large net from its floor and put it into another nearby boat.

Bob explained, "Mazatlan is a fishing town. Rather than poles, nets are used to catch the fish. The old man probably doesn't want to take any chances on a bunch of clumsy gringos getting their feet stuck in the precious net and ripping it apart. This is how he makes a living and feeds his family."

Nancy and I bestowed big smiles on our captain and thanked him for this opportunity. "Gracias Señor."

Bob and Les followed our lead, "Si Señor, muchas gracias."

The old fisherman seemed happy for the opportunity to make some extra money by rowing us across the bay to one of the three offshore islands. The one he took us to was called Isla de Venados, Island of the Deer. Its single hill claimed dominance over the land. Yet it looked enchanting with its strip of creamy colored sand and the backdrop of thick, dark green vegetation. It was such a beautiful day. Gentle waves rocked our canoe. Clear azure seawater sparkled from the sunlight. Soft, warm air whispered across my bare arms. We smoked another joint and shared it with our guide.

Landing on the sandy beach, Les helped pull the boat out of the water. Nancy and I carried the bags of lunch supplies to a shady spot under a tree. Bob stuck the beer and soda bottles into a depression he hollowed out in the sand, at the water's edge, to keep them cool.

I watched the old man walk away from us and disappear into the density of the hillside. *Where could he possibly be going? What am I missing?*

My attention returned to the warm soothing sand beneath my feet and the glimmer of sunlight on the lapping waves. I was eager to get into the watery wonderland and experience its magic. I liked diving in and shutting out the sights and sounds of the upside world. I could move without walking or running. Somersaults, dives, bubble blowing, frogging my legs within the shimmering liquid delighted me to no end. Multicolored fish wove in and around me. They explored my wiggling fingers. My undulating hair mimicked their movements. Coming to the surface for gulps of air, caresses of sunlight and the cries of sea-gulls propelled me into another realm of wonder. So many colors, smells and temperatures to consider. I laughed at the realization that I moved through my usual world from a vertical viewpoint, while beneath, and on the surface of the ocean, I was horizontal. The contrast of these two worlds made me aware of the gift of life that I had. I wanted to explore so much more of it.

After swimming for a while and looking for perfect seashells, I spread out my hotel towel next to Nancy. She had been working on her suntan. I watched Bob and Les for a while. They seemed to enjoy shoving and dunking each other in the briny deep. There were many hoots and hollers. Guys were so strange.

Nancy rolled over onto her side. "Kimmy, are you awake?"

I shaded my eyes with my hand to look at my girlfriend. "Sure."

My dear friend sat up. She took a deep breath, released it and said, "I'm not doing this anymore. This crazy stuff. I can't. I've got my sister and mom to think about." She paused. The edge of her towel was squeezed in her fist. I could see she was trying to keep herself calm.

"Kimmy, look what's happened to us on these trips with Bob. This time Bob and Les were thrown into a Mexican jail. If we hadn't gotten them out of there, they would probably have rotted away, with their parents never seeing them again. And what about us? We're two white girls in a foreign country. We don't speak the language. We have hardly any money." Another pause and deep breath. She fought back tears. "Apparently the only thing we have going for us is luck. Just like when we crossed the border in Tecate. Dumb luck, Kimmy. We've got dumb luck."

She reached for her bottle of suntan lotion and rubbed a bit on her arms. "I don't know how you see all of this, but this is my last adventure. Going places with Bob is dangerous. He takes no responsibility for what distress he causes. Instead, he entices us with a charming adventure, which is really a coverup for his drug smuggling. And when the trip goes awry, he eases himself out of the picture. He lets the mess fall on his friends to clean up. And we are his friends." Nancy could no longer stop the tears.

I didn't know what to do or say. I had been jolted from my reverie. My lovely world of fun, excitement and friendship shrank before my eyes.

With a quivering voice Nancy whispered, "Bob never tells us what he's really doing. He just slips in and out. And when we pull the mess together for him, he offers a nonchalant 'thank you,' or 'I knew I could count on you.' Like here. Like it was no big deal that he and Les were thrown into jail, or what we had to do to get them out. No recognition, no apology. Nothing!"

Nancy was breathing harder and her voice sounded stran-gled. "And Tecate! Kimmy, do you understand that he had us smuggle the weed across an international border for him? If it had been discovered, we would have been the ones to be arrested and jailed! Not him or Eddy. Oh no, they had the task of crossing a mile or so of desert with an American highway waiting for them at its edge. They could have hitchhiked out of there and back to Isla Vista if we didn't show up. And when we did show up, they acted like we had breezed through the inspection station and that they had accomplished a dangerous feat."

She stopped talking. Tears streamed down her face.

My mind was reeling. Nancy had jarred something loose within me. I knew she had spoken the truth and I had been a fool.

Nancy lifted her chin and made the effort to calm herself. She stood and straightened her shoulders. Gathering her suntan lotion, and the book she'd been reading, she rolled them into her towel. Then she looked out over the water to where we had come from this morning. " I'm going back to Isla Vista with a different attitude. I'm going to concentrate on my studies and get a degree from UCSB that I can use to create a future for me. I'm not going to jeopardize the scholarship that I worked so hard for." She paused to wipe away the last of the tears. "I'm not mad at you, Kimmy. I don't blame you for anything. I'll never forget what we've experienced." She bent down and hugged me. "I really hope you figure out what you want for your life, and come up with a plan." Then she walked away and left me to face my actions and their intentions.

19
CHANGE

After our return from Mazatlan, change came for me and my friends. I don't know how it was determined, or what caused it, but it felt appointed and precise.

Last night after our arrival, when I dropped Bob off at his place, he took his pack with the Acapulco Gold out of my car's trunk. Hefting it onto his back, he walked to the driver's window. There he stooped to my eye level and said, "Thanks, Kimmy, for getting us there and back. You have a way of keeping afloat when our trips take unexpected turns. You must have been born under a lucky star." He stood, turned and strolled up to his front door. Two weeks later I read in the Santa Barbara newspaper about his marriage to Suzanne.

Nancy awoke the next morning knowing exactly what she needed to do to graduate from UCSB. She told me she clearly saw the steps to earn a degree that would land her a great paying job. She would be able to reasonably take care of herself, as well as her mother and sister. I overheard part of her phone call to them.

"Mom, I'm coming home this weekend to visit for a few days. I went to Mexico with my friends. Yes, I did. It was beautiful there and the change of scenery helped me see what I want to do with my life.”

Next, my determined roommate called the diner where she had been working. Even though she had been absent longer than requested, the boss told her to come to work that afternoon. I listened to Nancy shuffling around in her bedroom. “Kimmy,” she shouted, “I’m on my way to the laundromat, then to work this afternoon.” I heard the joy and excitement in her voice. From the living room window I watched my dear friend ride away on her bike, with a laundry bundle slung over her shoulder.

I returned to the warm comfort of my bed.

Les’s change shocked me to my core. He’d been arrested. The narcs raided his apartment while he was in Mexico and found a small stash of marijuana. We never learned who tipped them off, but his roommate was coerced into informing them of his return. There was no hope for leniency. A two year prison sentence was the outcome, and his roommate was not charged with possession. Another one of my sweet friends would be ruined and his life completely altered.

As for me, my change was slower. Nancy’s words from the island beach by Mazatlan swirled in my head. “Kimmy, I hope you find out what you want to do with your life, and then make a plan.” She had made it very clear that adventures with Bob were dangerous, and he only cared about himself.

As I lay on my bed, I reviewed my other escapes from danger. Riding the rails with Gil thrilled me because it was daring and not something that girls did. I felt honored that he had asked me to go with him. But the danger of almost being crushed by train wheels truly scared me. Gil must have known about the risks. Why hadn’t he told me?

On the other hand, I supplied my friend, Matt, with the pot that got him arrested and thrown into prison for two years. But he didn’t rat me out to the narcs. Thanks to his generosity of protecting me, I could freely continue to experience the wonders of life. I felt somewhat ashamed, as well as very grateful for my freedom. Why him and not me? Was I spared because I was a girl, or was I overlooked, because I was a girl?

And what about hitchhiking to Colorado with Eddy, while wearing my stash lined hat? That certainly gave me mixed feelings. I was thrilled to be on an adventure with the man I cared about. I wanted to impress him with my daring attitude. Yet, how could I have presumed that antic was ok? We could have gotten into serious trouble. No wonder he slipped away from me, into Amy's arms, and then moved back to his parents' home in Southern California.

Finally I reflected on the three trips to Mexico with Bob to score pot. Those events were definitely exciting, but they resulted with me (and my friends) escaping incarceration by 'the skin of our teeth.' Three times I did that! And it took Nancy telling me how crazy that was, for the realization to break through.

What had I been doing? Did I think I was invincible to being harmed by my risky behavior? Did I assume my friends would always look out for me? The truth was that I hadn't even considered my behavior, and apparently I took our friendships for granted. However, this knowledge just skimmed the surface of my conscious thinking. Maybe being stoned so much fogged my awareness, which was dominated by the need to explore the totally cool time in which I lived. There was a lot going on. Change was busting the seams of society's mores and confinement. Unconsciously I responded to its vibrational force field. Impulses drove my actions. I wondered what would happen if I moved out of Isla Vista, and the land of psychedelics.

A week later I settled into a little house in Goleta, smack dab next to the railroad tracks. At 3:17 every afternoon the passing train shook my home as it rumbled by. The returning train rocked me in my sleep sometime during the night.

In the next few years that completed the Sixties, there were other dwellings where I haphazardly resided while I galloped, or squeezed, through the distorted events that beckoned my participation. I did not sit still.

Mixed in among these locations, my search for purpose and understanding of my need for adventure expanded. My soul had been captivated by a myriad of sights and sounds. Temptations of mind altering drugs, free love and shifting landscapes continued to woo me. Within these fragments of reality, nothing was crystal clear. Often I felt like I was in a clothes dryer, being spun, tossed, scorched or smothered. Yet, I wasn't alone in my confusion and desire for change.

The culture of the society that raised me was in turmoil. An illegal war in Vietnam slaughtered thousands of innocent people, for some unknown purpose, and ruined the lives of so many young men that were forced to partake in the atrocities. A nuclear war with Russia was barely averted during the Cuban Crisis. Our president and his loyal brother were assassinated in broad daylight in two major cities. Flags were burned. Women rose up, marched in the streets to demand equality with men. They burned their bras in protest. Rosa Parks, Martin Luther King Jr, Cassius Clay, Malcolm X and the Black Panthers were courageous with outspoken words and actions to bring attention to human rights. Black children became pawns for school integration. All this went on while our government focused on the exploration of outer space.

The balance, sanity and joy came through music that broke open boundaries and burst through taboos. Politicians were discredited for their lies and greed. Those musical geniuses were the vanguard of honesty, brotherly love, and solutions of peace.

It was a messy time. New voices, viewpoints and consciousness emerged.

Where did that put me?

I rode the undercurrents of the tumultuous force that hit our nation, and the rest of the world, during this particular decade. Although I was not always aware of those dynamics of change, the vibrations electrified my spirit.

20

THOUGHTFUL PLANNING

The little house in the avocado orchard, I shared with Ruth, a gentle and introspective person. After reading several library books, she taught herself to make wine. She concocted and bottled a dozen gallons of smooth, rich nectar from apricots, prunes and other fruit. Not the typical grape drink. She set them to ripen in the cupboard by the backdoor. Two months later we tasted them. Even though I didn't like wine, I declared the prune drink to be excellent.

One dark and rainy evening, when Ruth returned from work, her car slid off the road. The front end was smashed and her neck and back were jolted. That slowed her down a lot, but she didn't complain. Instead, she walked daily down and up our hillside road to realign and strengthen her spine.

Ruth's younger sister, Pat, just out of high school, moved in with us. Her boyfriend, named Chris, soon appeared on a frequent basis, making it a full house.

One day Ruth told me, "Pat wants to hitchhike to Pingree, Idaho to visit a friend. She wants to experience the open road.

But I'm just not ready yet for that." She still wore a back brace. "I trust you, Kimmy. Will you fill in for me?"

Even though I was an experienced hitchhiker, I was only a few years older than Pat. It would be my responsibility to keep her safe and to get us where we were going. So I gave this request a bit of thought. I told Pat, "You'll need a bedroll with a change of clothes and a few dollars in your pocket for food. We will not have any marijuana on us. That's too risky. (I had learned that lesson from hitchhiking with Eddy.) We can leave in the morning, if you want." Ruth gave me her smile of approval, and I was quite proud of myself for thinking about possible needs and pitfalls.

Thoughtful planning turned out to be a good move. The first day on the road, a cop pulled up beside us, where our ride had dropped us off outside a little podunk town in the middle of California. The sturdy looking, and well equipped, officer insisted that we get into the back of his squad car. He was a big burly guy with aviator glasses, a billy club and revolver. Without hesitation we obeyed. He drove us to his police station. Once inside he asked, "Where are you ladies coming from? Where are you heading?" He motioned for us to put our bedrolls on the counter.

Before we had a chance to answer, he turned to the woman sitting at a desk, behind a typewriter. "Martha." he snarled, "escort these ladies to the restroom and do a thorough search."

Five feet tall and five feet wide Martha was not the chatty type. Getting up from her desk and setting down her romance novel, she approached Pat and me by pointing down the hallway. She followed directly behind us into the restroom. "Strip," she barked.

We obliged. What else could we do? Speechlessly we disrobed, rubbed our goosebumps, and turned full circle for Martha's viewing pleasure. Pat was no cry baby. Me neither.

"OK. OK. Get dressed."

She ushered us back to the officer. He looked at her. "Well? Anything?"

"Nope."

"OK ladies. Let's go. You earned a free ride to the other edge of our fair city. Grab your bags."

Obviously the cop had rifled through our bedrolls while our personal boundaries were being violated in the restroom. Young Pat and I were vulnerable victims. A man in a uniform that represented protection, morality and justice had ordered a woman to view our nakedness. She became his eyes. I felt shame, fear and confusion.

Since there was also nothing to be found in our bedrolls but a change of clothing, we apparently passed inspection on both counts. What had he been looking for? What did he expect to find?

The far edge of that town treated us more hospitably. We quickly caught a ride with a grandma in a silver Volkswagen van decked out with lots of travel stickers. She was sweet, with a soft voice, and a big smile. "My name's Bessie. What are you girls doing out here in the middle of nowhere?"

I slid into the front seat while Pat arranged herself among the four tail wagging assortment of dogs that hogged the bed that filled out the back. I let her do the talking, since this was really her trip. "Thank you for picking us up. We're going to visit my friend in Idaho."

Grandma Bessie shifted into gear and we were on the road again. "Well now, it's not really safe for you pretty little things to be hitchhiking like this."

"We haven't had any trouble except for the policeman who took us to jail. He was not nice. He told the lady who worked there to take us into the restroom and make us take off all our clothes so she could take a good look at us. She even looked at our bottoms." Pat burst into sobs.

"Oh, Honey, are you all right?" Bessie looked at Pat in the rearview mirror, then glanced at me.

"Yes, ma'm," Pat whispered.

"Hah, that's not OK! And it sounds like something Homer would do. Was he a big man with a real thin mustache?"

"Yes."

"He thinks it makes him look like a movie star. He fancies himself as a ladies' man. You were lucky he had Martha do the strip search."

Pat looked at me with tears pouring from her eyes. I wanted to give her a hug. I think the possibility of sexual violation just hit her.

"I'm driving up to Mt Shasta. You'll be able to get a ride from there into Oregon, and then go east to Idaho. You're welcome to take a nap, or stretch out there in the back. The bed's real cozy. Just shove the dogs aside."

Grandma Bessie and I listened to a country music station. That would not have been my choice, but we were her guests. I learned that cowboys sure were a sad bunch of singers. It seemed that none of them knew how to keep a girlfriend.

It was nighttime when we got to the cozy little town of Mt. Shasta. The mountain was huge! It had such a powerful feeling to it. I bet the Indians who lived around it worshipped there. I would have.

"It's just too late for you girls to continue hitchhiking. I'm visiting my friend here. You come in and say howdy to him. Then you can use the bathroom and sleep in the van tonight. What do you say to that?"

Grandma Bessie and her friend, Peter, fed us macaroni and cheese with tiny sausages from a can. Cucumbers on the side. The dogs in the van kept us warm during the night. We got an early start the next morning after being served pancakes and orange juice. *You just never know when nice people are gonna appear.*

Although we still had about five hundred miles to go, we caught rides easily enough. Oregon wasn't all green like I thought it would be. Half of it was high desert with black cattle spread here and there. I didn't even know there was such a thing as black cows. I'd only ever seen black and white milk cows, or the reddish ones called Herefords.

The sky spread far and wide. Such a deep, clear blue. Birds seemed to love it as they rode invisible air currents or chased each other around. I liked what I saw of Northern California and Southeast Oregon. Idaho pulled me in too. It wasn't much different. Lots of space to roam around in.

Pat's friend and her family were nice. They had a farm. The mom canned corn from her garden, and fed us three yummy meals a day. We bunked in the basement rumpus room.

The girlfriend, and two other friends, showed us what they did for fun, which was mainly floating down the irrigation ditches on inner tubes. The clear and slow moving water irrigated acres of wheat and potatoes. There was a lot of laughter, and knock knock jokes kept them occupied for long stretches of time. For instance: Knock knock. Who's there? Luke. Luke who? Luke through the window and find out.

Oh well. They were nice friends.

Two days later Pat wanted to go home. She missed her boyfriend. So she called Ruth for a bus ticket home. The mail took three days for delivery. In the meantime we roamed the surrounding fields and hills. I really liked that. Wild flowers and butterflies abounded. It all smelled good too. Fresh and real.

The morning she left, I walked Pat the half a mile to the Greyhound station. She chattered about her boyfriend, Chris, the whole way. That made me wish I had a boyfriend to go home to.

As I watched her bus leave, I wondered what came next for

me? I didn't have the money for a bus ticket, and I didn't feel like going back to the little house yet. Also, it wouldn't be right to stay with the friend's family in Pingree. They were nice to me because I came with Pat. So I decided to keep on moving. I would hitchhike to Eddy's folks' homestead in southwestern Colorado, where they lived during the summer. I thought I'd give Eddy another chance at wanting me.

21

LONG HAUL TRUCKERS

I snuggled my sleeping bag under my arm and walked the half mile to the highway. This was my first hitchhike alone. The rural landscape spread wide open before me, with gray mountains in the distance and a cobalt sky overhead. I breathed deeply, letting my lungs swell with goodness. Sunshine washed over my upturned face. I felt lighthearted with the freedom to wander and explore, to follow my own lead and promptings. Being surrounded by natural beauty, clean air, and new sights brought me deep peace.

My first few rides were from local farmers going to the hardware store, or picking up groceries. They dropped me off along the highway where semi trucks passed in abundance. Those long haul truckers were the lifeline for filling the country stores with hammers, chicken feed, milk and cereal.

Tucking my hair up into the straw cowboy hat that one of Pat's friends had bestowed upon me, I pulled it low over my eyes to block the sun. Wearing Levis and tennis shoes, I hoped to look like a teenage boy, so I wouldn't be harassed. The semis zipped right by my upheld thumb, but I caught rides from more locals going short distances. Once inside their vehicles I thanked them for picking me up. I think they weren't really sure if I were a boy. Sideways glances kept coming to me. Maybe my bright pink ski jacket confused them.

Finally I caught a longer ride from a rancher towing a trailer full of bawling cows. He dropped me off by a dirt road that trailed into the distance beneath a setting sun. That's when a big rig finally pulled over for me. I had to grab onto the outside handle bar to hoist myself up to its seat. The cab was high off the ground. Larger than what I expected, I noticed there was a broad space behind the front seat, but it was too dark to see what it was used for. Maybe another bench seat could fit there.

This driver looked the way I imagined a big rig truck driver to look, with a crew cut and in need of a shave. He wore a short sleeved plaid shirt with a pack of Lucky Strike cigarettes in the front pocket. I was relieved that he didn't bother me with a bunch of questions, just the basics. "Where are you headed?"

"Southwest Colorado, just past Grand Junction."

"Aren't you a little young to be out here on your own?"

"Maybe." I shrugged my shoulders. "I know what I'm doing. Anyway I need to get where I'm going." I turned my attention to the view outside my window, hoping that would stop the questions. Night was closing in. I couldn't see much beyond the headlights shining on the highway. I liked the sensation of the gentle bouncing as we sped along. It was like being in a moving fortress.

About an hour later the driver pulled into a big parking lot next to a roadside diner. Other rigs neatly filled the area with a few cars here and there. "Are you hungry? You got any money for dinner?" When I didn't respond, he tried again. "C'mon. I'll buy you a burger."

Definitely I was hungry. Surely he could hear my stomach growling. I hesitated, because for some reason I didn't want him to see me in the bright light of the diner. I wasn't sure if he'd figure out that I was a girl. I did not feel totally safe with this guy.

"C'mon. C'mon. Let's go. I need to use the john."

I hesitated to leave my sleeping bag in the truck, but it would look strange to take it with me. Following him into the well lit, noisy diner, he pointed to a booth. I slid onto the seat while he headed to the restroom. A waitress placed two menus on the table along with two glasses of water. She left.

When the driver returned he picked up the menu and asked if I wanted my burger well done or raw, I didn't answer, because I was working at keeping my head ducked low under my cowboy hat. The waitress took his order for both of us, and left. Leaning back in the booth, I could feel his eyes boring into me. He didn't say anything, but after the waitress delivered our food, he leaned forward and took a closer look at me. That's when he knew. That's when I got worried. I wouldn't look up at him. Instead, I focused on stuffing as much food as I could into my mouth because I didn't know when I'd have a chance to eat again. But my stomach was turning into a big knot of dread.

I went back to the truck with the driver because I needed my bedroll and I didn't want to be stuck here in the middle of nowhere. I knew he was on a deadline and would have to concentrate on his driving. Hopefully that would keep his attention on that, and not on me.

A few miles down the highway he suddenly reached over and jerked off my hat. My hair tumbled onto my shoulders.

"Well now. What do we have here, Little Missy?" He licked his lips then, took a deep breath, and pulled the back of his hand across his mouth to wipe it clean. "My buddy, Jim's been sleeping back there." The driver nodded toward the bunk behind us. "It's about time for him to wake up and take over driving. He's going to want more than this extra hamburger I bought for him."

Suddenly I realized that the extra space in the cab was a bed, and another man had been there all along. I grabbed my hat and jammed it on my head while keeping my eyes straight ahead. I didn't know there was a buddy who had been sleeping. He sure had been quiet.

We drove maybe five more minutes. Nobody moved, nor said a word. The headlights revealeda desert area. Sand, sparse, low cactus, sage brush and not much else appeared, except for the brilliance of the star studded sky. We passed a speed limit sign. There was little traffic.

"Now that you've got a full belly, and you're closer to your destination, thanks to me picking you up, how about hopping in back and spending some time with my partner? You can be the tomato on top of his pickle." He released a snigger as he squeezed both hands tightly to the steering wheel.

"Oh, no thank you." I steadied my breathing and kept my voice low and calm. I focused on looking out the front window. In the distance, at the edge of the headlights, I saw a road sign.

"Well, I think you and Jim would get along real fine. Go on. Fair is fair. Dinner and a free ride in exchange for a good time."

My bag had been on the floor, under my feet. I reached down, picked it up and pressed it against my chest. " Yes sir. You're right. I certainly can't argue with that. Fair is fair. But you see, that's my turn off right up there. That's where I'm going. Yes sir, I know right where I am. Right there. That's where you can let me off."

"Oh come on now, girly. Cut the crap. You can't be hitchhiking, and acting all innocent like you don't have to pay the price. You've been trying to pass for a boy. What goddamn boy wears a pink jacket?"

From the bunk, Jim spoke up. "Let her go, Carl. It's not worth it. She doesn't want it. Drop her off here in the middle of nowhere. It serves her right. The rattlers and scorpions can deal with her."

Carl braked hard. The truck tires screeched as the huge truck jerked to a stop just past the road sign. I got out fast. The big rig cranked back into gear and merged into the deep black night. The smell of burned brakes hung in the air. It was so quiet and very, very dark.

With my sleeping bag clasped tightly to my chest I stood by the side of the road, alone. The black sky, full of distant stars, was all I could see. I rocked myself back and forth to steady my nerves. The quiet was so complete that it frightened me. Anything could come out of it, from any direction. Then within a couple of minutes my eyes adjusted, so that I could separate the pavement from the pale land. Completely encircled by the vast stillness, I cleared my throat and sang a song from my childhood. "O, give me a home where the buffalo roam. Where the deer and the antelope play. Where seldom is heard, a discouraging word. And the skies are not cloudy all day."

Right then the passing clouds moved away from the half shell of the moon. Still clutching my bag, I turned from the highway and gingerly stepped onto the sandy landscape. I walked until I tripped. I figured that was where I was supposed to lie down. I unrolled my bag, bundled my spare clothes into a pillow, climbed inside and fell asleep, entering into a dreamless void. When I awoke in the coolness of the morning, and saw where I was, I thought to myself, *Look where I am and what I've done! All by myself. I hitchhiked on my own. I talked my way out of being fucked by some creepy old truck driver. And I slept out in the middle of a desert....just me under the stars. Besides all that, no rattlers, or scorpions stung me, and no coyotes tried to eat me.* I felt very good about myself.

Returning to the highway, I crossed it and stepped onto the sideroad that headed East. Again I would take my chances on catching rides from the locals with their short trips to markets and hardware stores. No more long haul drivers for me. I hoped a ride would happen soon because I was hungry and thirsty.

22

EDDY

An hour later my luck changed. Several rides from nice people took me all the way into Colorado to Delta, where the road to Eddy's homestead began. Some of those people shared food and sodas with me. Two of them each gave me a dollar.

From a small market I bought a package of bologna, two candy bars, an apple and a Dr Pepper. That left me with a dollar. I saved one candy bar for later. Fueled enough to begin walking on that dusty, uphill road into the Uncompahgre National Forest, I felt like I was coming home.

Sweet memories surfaced of my time there with Eddy. The winter snow had covered everything with its stillness and serenity. Now Summer was nearing its end, which made it seem like I was in a different place.

I really liked the smells from the pine trees that poured in through the open truck window of the banged up Ford pickup. An old guy named Ralph was the driver, who greeted me with a warm smile that was missing a tooth. Hay bales filled the bed of his truck. An alert border collie leaned against his side to make room for me on the seat. A rifle rested in the gun rack on the back window.

My pink jacket was wrapped up in my bag and my hair hung loose beneath my hat. He didn't seem at all bothered that I was a girl hitchhiking on this road that he frequently traveled for most of his life.

"So what brings you out here, young lady?"

I gave him a big smile and offered him my last Milky Way candy bar. "I know the people who own the old White homestead. I'm going to visit them."

We shared a few stories about our different lives in the mountains of Southern Colorado to the shore of the Pacific Ocean. Then Ralph dropped me off at the top of the driveway of my destination.

The sun had lowered itself onto the crest of the hill across the canyon. There it rested, offering its softened light to guide me to the man I loved. My hope for sharing love with Eddy still lingered deeply within me. *What will his first words be to me?*

Eddy and his folks were home. It was dinnertime. His dad answered my knock on the front door with a scowl and a grunt. "Oh, it's you."

His mom rushed out of the kitchen to see for whom she needed to set another plate. She was careful efficiency wrapped in politeness. "Kimmy, how unexpected of you. Come join us for dinner."

Eddy hung back in the archway between the living room and dining room. He leaned against the wall. His face displayed a look of shock. "How did you get here?"

Those were his first words to me. *Why weren't they, Kimmy, I've missed you so much. I owe you a huge apology. I can't believe you're here. How wonderful. I'm such a lucky man.*

"I hitchhiked."

Three faces gaped at me. His dad's scowl got bigger. His mom blinked and cleared her throat. Eddy's face readjusted from surprise to.....to what? I couldn't tell. It just sort of became a guarded false front.

I ate with them. Eddy's mom did the talking. She enthusiastically explained that she was fixing up the wide open second floor for the hunters who would be coming in the Fall. She had made privacy partitions by hanging curtains around each bed. Proudly she announced that Dad and Eddy were building up the stockpile of firewood for the big wood burning stove. "You're welcome to sleep in the cabin while you are here."

Eddy and his motorcycle slept in one of the two downstairs bedrooms. I didn't learn why the motorcycle was in the house. But I did learn that he was not interested in joining me in the cabin.

The next day, the man I loved allowed me to walk with him while he manipulated the irrigation gates in the tiny ditches that crisscrossed the pasture. Alone with him, away from his parents, I thought surely he'd say what I had been waiting to hear. Instead he spoke to me about the irrigation process and that the pasture was the summer home for their two horses. One of the horsesEddy had brought with him to Isla Vista. Sometimes he rode her on the beach. But here, on the rustic hillside by the canyon, the finicky mare was not about to let him near her.

"I can't get within ten feet of her. I guess she likes her freedom."

We returned to the house where Eddy tended to his wood chopping chore. I felt lame just standing there watching him. I looked around for something to do and picked up two apples from beneath the old tree that leaned next to the house. Slipping through the pasture gate I sauntered into the field. Not walking in a straight line towards the grazing horses, I meandered, so as not to spook them. Every now and then I stooped to admire a wildflower. When I was a few yards from them, I stopped and pretended to eat one of the apples. The ears of the dark horse perked up. Her nostrils flared. She walked to me. I held out the apple on the palm of my hand. She stretched her powerful neck until her velvety lips encircled the apple. Her gleaming white teeth cracked open the juicy treat. All of this was carefully observed by Eddy's buckskin mare. She moved closer to me and rubbed against the other mare. I showed her the second apple. Her rear end bumped the dark horse away from her. I stood still. With my left hand I held the apple close to my chest. She sniffed and then stretched for it. Slowly I raised my right hand to feel along her neck. She didn't bolt. Gently she nuzzled my shoulder. I released the apple to her. She nickered and accepted. Then she let me move to her flank and hoist myself onto her back. The dark horse followed us towards the pasture gate.

I could see Eddy outside, chopping wood. I hollered to him. "Eddy, look who I have with me. Open the gate."

He looked up at me, but continued chopping.

I thought he saw me. Maybe not. So I hollered again, sure that he would be delighted that I had achieved what he hadn't been able to do. Certainly he would realize what an asset I was. "Eddy, come open the gate."

By the time the horses and I arrived at the gate, Eddy was slowly walking towards us. He wasn't smiling. His face was blank. But he had gone to the barn for their halters and lead lines. That must have been why he hadn't rushed to open the gate for me and congratulate me on my clever conquest.

In a barely audible voice, the man I cherished mumbled, " Thank you, Kimmy." He strapped halters on the horses and led them to the barn. Then he went back to chopping wood again.

I stood there watching him, not knowing what to do. I felt invisible and non-existent. The joy of my achievement evaporated as I was obviously being shunned.

Suddenly a car arrived in a swirl of dust, and out stepped two of our friends, Gerry and Brigitta, from far away Isla Vista. Eddy greeted them with handshakes and a big smile. His face lit up as he asked them questions and listened to their plans.

" We're on a cross country trip to New York. We're gonna catch a ship to Sweden to meet Brigitta's parents, get married and live there."

Eddy's parents also gave the couple a rousing welcome. "You can sleep in the cabin. Surely Kimmy won't mind sharing."

I shifted from the bed to the couch. My night's sleep was restless. Gerry and Brigitta were in love, and although they tried to be quiet, their passion was evident. That made me miss Eddy even more, but I knew I needed to face the reality of his rejection of me. All the signs and reactions that I had received while here at the homestead were painfully clear. That's why I decided to ask Gerry and Brigitta for a ride to New York.

Brigitta shoved aside some of her belongings to make room for me in the backseat of their Studebaker. The plan of travel consisted of a nonstop drive to New York City, with potty breaks. Gerry intended to drive straight through the night. We would eat enroute from the picnic basket that Brigitta supplied. They hadn't counted on sharing with another passenger, so I was careful to take tiny portions.

That was basically the only interaction we had. Otherwise I was ignored. That gave me the opportunity to ponder the situation I had thrown myself into.

A silent turmoil roiled inside my self-imposed cage of blindness, confusion, stupidity, and arrogance. I didn't know what to call the mess I had created. Maybe I could squeeze between the bars of this cage. Freedom lay just out of reach, beckoning to me. Then where would I go? It was a big world. Or was it?

My viewpoint from the compact area of the backseat was quite limited. Gerry and Brigitta made the decisions of where to go and when to stop. It was a safe, free ride without any responsibility. I was simply a passenger on my way to the big city. It appeared that I didn't have to do anything, just enjoy the ride. But joy was far from my reach.

I tried to understand why Eddy didn't love me anymore. What had I done that turned him against me? He didn't tell me, and I didn't ask. We never talked about what we did, or why we did it. We hadn't shared our feelings, needs, or desires. This situation felt like the home I was raised in, where I had no voice of my own. Sitting in the backseat of the Studebaker, surrounded by someone else's personal belongings, I didn't know how to question what I was doing, or what was being expected of me. Again I realized that my culture emphasized that girls and women were meant to follow the instructions of men, and that we were inferior to them. We were expected to obey and to be 'proper girls.'

So, there I was, on my way to New York City with only a dollar in my pocket and no place to stay. No one was telling me what to do, or where to go. I was free floating without any idea of where I would land.

I held onto the thought that before I hitchhiked to Idaho with Pat, I had visited Lori, her husband, and their little boy. We used to be roommates in Isla Vista before I attached myself to Eddy. She told me how she had spent some of her summers with her Aunt Joan in New York City. She liked the hustle and bustle of that huge city. In fact she intended to go there in a week, although her husband needed to stay behind because he couldn't get time off from his job. She said she had made arrangements with her Aunt. For some reason she told me her aunt's address.

The day after that, I bumped into Michael, whom I vaguely knew, at the laundromat. He was also getting ready to return to New York for the summer. He grew up there. We talked about

Lori going to visit her aunt. He compared his address with hers and declared they were practically in the same neighborhood.

"Hey, Kimmy. Maybe you ought to come to the Big Apple for the summer. If ya do, I'll show you the Guggenheim and take you to some great places to eat. What do ya say? I mean, now you got my address, so you might as well come."

I was putting those coincidences together when I heard Gerry say, "So where are we dropping you off?"

Next thing I knew, I was standing on a sidewalk in the middle of New York City. Once again I clutched my bedroll to my chest. I watched the Studebaker slip back into traffic. Then I turned and walked up the steps to the address I had given for Lori's aunt.

23

NEW YORK CITY

The address for Lori's aunt put me in front of a multi-storied apartment building that was wedged between two other apartment buildings. Eight steps were required to get up to the front door, which was locked. The aunt's name was included with other names on a plaque beside the door. I didn't know how to go any further. Then two people, who I guessed lived in the building, arrived and unlocked the door. The woman paused before entering and told me, "You press the button next to the name and wait for the tenant to speak to you or buzz you in."

I pushed the button and waited. I felt so exposed, waiting for a voice from a box on the doorstep of a building, in a place I'd never been before. It felt like being in a stall in a public restroom and any second someone would shove open the door while I was sitting there with my pants down.

"Hello."

I was jolted back into the moment and blurted out, "I'm a friend of Lori's. She gave me your address so I could find her when I got here."

"Lori's here in New York?" Buzzzzzz. "Come up. I'm on the third floor.

The front door magically opened. I walked through and went up the stairs to the aunt's apartment, and knocked on her door.

The woman who opened the door was an average looking, aunty type person, my height, with shortish brown hair. She wore tan slacks and a soft green blouse. She welcomed me into her home. She was so nice to me. I was so relieved.

"I didn't know Lori was here. I haven't heard from her in two years. Why did she give you my address? How will you find her? What will you do?"

Those were all great questions. No answers came to my mind. And I did not really want to think about them because the void they created was really scary to me. If I looked too closely I would see the pit of nothingness that loomed up at me. This was not a happy reality. So I gave the vaguest responses that I could and hoped I would sound like a proper girl, and not some deranged nut who showed up unannounced on her doorstep. Finally I murmured, "I guess I'll figure out what to do tomorrow. For sure I'll try to find my other friend, MIchael, who lives some-where near here."

Aunt Joan continued to ask me questions about myself and life in Isla Vista. She also fed me, showed me how to work the shower, and let me sleep in her spare bedroom. I crashed into a deep, dreamless sleep.

The next morning I got up early, before Joan. Quietly I dressed and left the apartment. I had to find Michael. He was my only hope. I knew his address so I asked strangers on the street for directions. Annoyed expressions and curt answers were the general comeback. People were in a hurry to get places and didn't want to be bothered.

Everywhere looked the same. Apartments or stores were jammed together. Honking cars and trucks jostled each other on over-crowded streets. There were so many people on the side-walks that they reminded me of a herd of cattle. Finally I asked a traffic cop who was helpful.

After what seemed like hours, I found Michael's home. It looked more like a house than an apartment. There was not a little box with names on it beside the door for me to buzz and talk into. I knocked loudly. Then, lo and behold, the door swung open and boisterous, fast talking Michael stood before me! I threw my arms around his neck.

"Hey, Kimmy, let go of me." He dragged my arms off him. "How did you get here?"

My relief in finding Michael burst forth in a whirlwind of words. "I caught a ride with Gerry and Brigitta. They showed up at Eddy's place in Colorado. They're on their way to Sweden to get married. Lori's not at her aunt's. She didn't even know Lori was here. Where is she? Did she come to New York? I have nowhere to go. I have to find her." I steadied myself from the shaking inside that wanted to break loose. I knew I had to be tough and not show my feelings.

My blast of information did not phase my New York City bred friend. Michael stepped out onto landing and closed the door behind him. "I was just going to get something to eat. C'mon, I'll take you to the best deli in town. It's kosher, of course. They have these great turkey necks."

"OK. But is Lori here? Do you know where she is?"

"Sure. Sure. Don't worry. I'll show you where she is." He grabbed my elbow to turn me around and charged ahead. Two blocks later he asked me, "What do you think of the big city? I bet you ain't seen nothing like this before."

"You're right. There are so many people here. The traffic is screamingly noisy. But it's just like the Moon Dog album I have, where he blends all the city sounds in with his saxophone. This is so cool!" I was relieved to have found a friend in this giant cauldron of bursting activity. Now it didn't seem as rude and threatening. I didn't feel as lost.

We ate turkey necks and coleslaw at a boisterous Jewish diner. Everyone yelled at everyone else. From a booth in the far corner I heard, "Hey, Reuven, where ya been? Hurry up with my latkes, will ya, I gotta get to a very important meetin' in ten minutes."

A man at a table in the middle of the room declared, "You call this gefilte? It's more like boiled bird turd."

A man at the counter, with a big brimmed hat and baggy overcoat, shouted, "Hey Shlomo, I saw your sister with the rabbi yesterday."

"What's that supposed to mean?"

"Nothing, nothing, I'm just saying."

There was hearty laughter everywhere. It seemed to be understood that insults were well meant. I guessed that all those people were old friends.

Michael was included in the banter.

"Hey, Mikey, I heard you went to college in California. What was it like hanging out with them goyim flower children? Did you get high or find any pretty shiksas?"

"Michael," I whispered, "what's a shiksa?"

My friend turned to me. "It's an alluring gentile girl. Stand up, will ya, and take a bow."

I didn't know what was going on, but I knew enough to honor Michael's request. I stood. Seeing all the expectant faces turned towards me, I gave my best proper girl smile and curtsied. The whole diner burst into cheers! Michael beamed.

After that event, my friend took me to Lori's third floor apartment. It was in a different part of the city, several long blocks away. Michael led us at a brisk pace.

It was a cold water flat. That meant it had no hot water or heat. It also meant that the bathtub was in the kitchen, next to the front door. When not in use it had a metal cover that substituted as a countertop. Water was heated on the stove and poured into the tub. Next to the stove there was a small refrigerator. The toilet was in a closet off the bedroom. Two windows brought sunlight into the living room, which kept the cockroaches in hiding during the day.

Michael announced my presence with, "Look what the cat dragged in."

"Kimmy, Kimmy, Kimmy!" Lori's little son, Aaron, ran to me, wrapped his arms around my legs and beamed up the best smile to me.

Lori greeted me with, "You found us. I am not surprised. You're capable of anything. Are you going to stay awhile? The couch is available."

Then Chris stepped out of the bedroom. Michael hadn't told me about him being here. When Pat and I left for our hitchhiking trip to Idaho, Chris was very much her boyfriend. He was the reason she wanted to get back to our little home on the hill as soon as possible. But here he was, with my married friend, Lori. Were they sharing a bed? Did her husband, Brian, know about this? No wonder Lori hadn't told her aunt that she was here. *What world have I stepped into?*

Lori wrote a message for me to give to her aunt and I needed to get my bedroll. Michael walked me back to Joan's apartment building. He pointed to the street signs and some landmarks along the way so I could recognize where I was. It was late afternoon when we got there. I said goodbye to my friend and rang the buzzer to announce myself. Aunt Joan again let me in, but this time she chewed me out.

"Where have you been? What made you think you could come here and expect me to take you in? Which I did, because you claimed to be my niece's friend. Then you just disappeared! I was worried about you." She spoke calmly but she was angry, as she made it clear that my thoughtlessness was unacceptable.

I apologized, gave her the note from Lori and grabbed my stuff. With my head hanging low, I left as fast as I could and returned to the cold water flat.

My time at Lori's consisted of adjusting to the Lori-Chris duo. He had a genuine interest in Aaron and the three of them went for walks to a nearby park. I also met some of the other tenants. Most of them were creepy to me. Dirty, dull-witted, or drugged out. I wandered around the neighborhood but the buildings crowded out the sky and the traffic noise never stopped. There wasn't anything interesting to see or do.

Michael came by a week later and took me to the Guggenheim Museum, which was actually an art gallery. It was awesome! This giant-sized, multistoried, round building, with its breathtaking open space, housed the artwork of the world's greatest painters. Picasso, Warhal, Lichtenstein and many others were honored here. I filled my eyes with the possibilities of expressing our human experience. I gave my friend a hug.

"Whoa, whoa, Kimmy. Let's not go overboard here," he said, laughing, as he unwound himself from my exuberance.

That was a good day for me, however, everything else about this enormous city confused me. It acted like a hive of ants devouring a corpse. I saw no beneficial purpose to the erratic driven behavior of its inhabitants. To protect myself, and blend in with the masses, I cut my hair short. I hoped the removal of my prettiest asset would enable me to go unnoticed.

When Chris offered to introduce me to meth, I accepted, hoping the novelty of shooting up this drug would relieve some of my anxiety and loneliness. He took his time, and was careful to find a good vein in the crook of my arm. The effect of the drug caused me to be quiet. I had no need to go anywhere. Instead, I drew. When I had a pencil, I drew people or objects. When I had a pen, I drew intricate fantasy. I went into the depth of my imagination. On the other hand, I only shot up the meth five times. I didn't like the self-absorbed isolation it produced.

I wanted human interactions, which didn't come easily here. I liked being with my friends in Isla Vista, who, in comparison, behaved normally. We gathered together to smoke pot, but it was more than that. We shared food, music, stories and laughter. We cared about what happened in each other's lives. It felt good to be with them. Here I was always on guard, not knowing whom to trust.

For instance, one night I went to a party on the top floor of our apartment building. The space was a sprawling loft. Maybe the people there were happy. Lots of talking and drinking occurred. I wandered around the room, saying hello to anyone who noticed me. One man seemed interested. He was a bit older, fast talking and approached me with an attachment of onlookers.

"Hi, my name's Oliver. My friends and I are wondering if you are a boy, or a girl. We can't really tell." The attachment of faces leaned forward and gawked at me. "I mean, you're dressed like a boy and your hair is short, except it's fluffy. And your face is a girl's. So we don't know. Tell us. Please, please tell us." He bounced back and forth from one foot to the other. The eyes of the adjoining faces bulged, their mouths grimaced, while they tittered and snickered.

"Even better," this weirdo continued, "You can live with me. You don't have to pay for anything. You just have to be there for everyone to come and see." He and his cohorts burst out laughing and moved in a cluster to the other side of the room. I stood there stunned as I realized those people considered me to be a freak.

Before I had a chance to gather my wits and leave, two other men came up to me. Their vibe was closer to normal. One of them looked about my age. He wore a gray sweatshirt, khaki pants and tennis shoes. In other words, he looked like a regular guy.

The man with him appeared several years older. He wore black pants and a matching sweatshirt. "Don't worry about those assholes." He paused to give me time to settle back into myself. "My name is Darrell and this is my friend, Robin. We're on the first floor, so we've seen you come and go a few times. Where are you from?"

We talked for a while. The drumming in my chest eased. I learned that Darrell had been in the Navy, and Robin was from the Midwest. I told them that I came from California and I was staying with Lori. We hit it off and spent more time together in the upcoming days. It was Robin who was interested in me. He came to my rescue a few days later.

I had gone for a walk and ended up in the garment district. That's where long racks of clothing were being shoved out of buildings and into large vans to go to different cities worldwide. To me it seemed like tedious, uninspiring work. By the time I returned to my apartment building I was thirsty and tired. I didn't want to stick myself back into Lori's cockroach domain. Instead I approached another man's door. He lived on the second floor and was rather decent. He was definitely attractive. Most of his days were spent looking for acting jobs. I knocked anyway, hoping he was home. When he didn't answer I tried the doorknob. Hurray, his door was unlocked. I went inside because I just needed some place to be that wasn't the city, or Lori's.

I walked through his tiny space, and even looked in the refrigerator. Orange juice! Just what I needed. There wasn't much left. I finished it, and sat down to read one of his magazines.

About twenty minutes later I laid down the magazine and noticed that the apartment was shifting. It wouldn't hold still.

Not like an earthquake. Instead like the walls moved in and out in breathing mode. The sunlight coming through the windows jiggled and produced flying creatures. My hands melted and reformed. *Oh my god, I'm having an LSD flashback!*

I didn't like what was happening and the disturbances increased. My vision became more distorted. I tried to reason out where I was and how I got there. Panic formed in me. I had to get out of there. Somehow I found a door and stepped through it into a dingy hallway. Having no idea where I was, I pressed myself against the wall. The walls billowed and shrank. I threw my arms over my head to protect myself from what appeared to be a collapsing ceiling. Someone passed by me, stared at me with bulging eyes and a purple face that tried to drip off his skull. I stumbled down the stairs, heading for the sunlight that pierced through a doorway window. Outside I felt completely disoriented. The movement from people walking by caused brilliant colors to flash and swirl around me. My breathing increased. My tongue stuck to the roof of my mouth. I stood there, not knowing where to go, or who I was.

That's when Robin and Darrell appeared. They had been to a deli for lunch. When they found me, it was obvious to them that I was distressed. "Hey, Kimmy. Are you ok? It's me, Robin."

When I didn't respond, he gently took hold of my arm and led me into their nearby apartment where I sat on their couch with my arms wrapped around my knees.

The owner of the orange juice soon knocked on their door. He had come home and discovered he no longer had a full jar. He had thought for sure that it was a safe hiding place until he was ready for it. He went throughout the building, knocking on doors, to ask every tenant if they knew who drank his orange juice. When he saw me huddled on Darrell and Robin's couch, they all realized that I was the culprit. A few hours later I came out of my LSD episode. I was exhausted. I was also very grateful for the protection that had been given to me.

The next day I stayed in Lori's apartment and mostly played with little Aaron. He was such a sweet child. We colored lots of pictures and sang nursery songs. He fell asleep in my lap at naptime. I felt safe again.

Then I began to visit Robin and Darrell more often. We played checkers and Darrell made popcorn in a pan on the stove. Two days later they told me about their plan. They weren't happy being in New York City. Darrell was a sailor at heart and needed the open sea. Robin was raised in the cornfields of Iowa. He too missed the sky, fresh air and big spaces.

Robin said, "Me and Darrell are going to Buffalo. It's next to Lake Erie. Come with us. We can take a bus there."

24

BUFFALO NY, ETC

The cold, dreary place that we landed in, was smack dab next to enormous Lake Erie. Darrell found us a tiny two bedroom apartment right away. He had a pension from his time in the Navy because he was injured from malfunctioning machinery. I don't know what the injury was. He walked and talked ok. Like a benevolent big brother to Robin and me, he provided our room and board.

There wasn't much interesting to see or do in Buffalo. Robin and I walked around, and the huge gray lake was impressive for its size, but that was all. Mostly we stayed indoors improving our sex lives. Then the weather turned cold, and I needed warm clothes. Somewhere I had lost my pink jacket.

It didn't seem right for me to ask Darrell for money. So I went looking for free clothes. In Isla Vista I could go behind the small market and rummage in the box where anyone could drop off, or pick up, used clothing. Nobody I asked on the streets in Buffalo knew of such a thing. But someone did direct me to a welfare agency.

The dingy, dank building was crowded with people waiting

for help. When my turn came, I sat down at a desk, across from a man who looked like he just crawled out of bed after a long night of partying. His rumpled clothes did not distract my eyes from the hair around his bald spot that stuck out in oily clumps.

"I need warm clothes."

Setting aside the liverwurst and limburger cheese sandwich he had been gnawing on, the guy looked me up and down. Without verbally acknowledging my presence, he reached for the phone on his desk and dialed. While staring at me, he talked in German to the person on the other end. Obviously he didn't want me to know what he was saying. The smug look on his face told me that he was quite proud of himself for being so clever. *"Ich weiss nicht wenn es ein Knabe oder eine Mädchen ist."* (I don't know if this is a boy or a girl.) Laugh. Laugh. Snicker. Snicker.

Two years of German in high school fully enabled me to understand the insult he shared with the person on the phone, and the contempt he felt towards me. I stood up and said, *"Ich bin eine Mädchen."*

The creep choked on his food.

"Oh well," I added, *"Solch ist Leben."* (Such is life.)

He hung up the phone, pushed his sandwich aside, ripped off a piece of paper from a pad, wrote on it and stamped it with some official stamp. "Here, take this to the Salvation Army. They'll give you some clothes." That was it. The bald, greasy haired guy was done with me. He had his amusement for the day.

I found the Salvation Army thrift store two blocks over. I didn't get to pick out the clothes I needed. The woman who assisted me made the choices. Ugly. Just plain ugly. I ended up looking like a refuge from the old country. Big, bulky, beige wool coat with brown buttons the size of door knobs. A wool scarf to fold in half like a triangle and tie under my chin. I could have called it a kerchief and felt right at home jabbering away in

German. The sweater wasn't too bad. Of course it was dull beige wool, with a skirt to match. The excitement of the skirt was the pockets, which were just large enough to stick in a folded hanky. The lady offered me three of those. What could I say? " No, I don't want any of these horribly ugly clothes." Knowing I would be warmer, I thanked her for her help. I wore the coat out of there, pulling up its collar against the bitter wind that raced across the lake. Back at the apartment, I modeled my new wardrobe for my roommates. They pitied me too, after they stopped laughing.

Darrell read a lot and sometimes went out at night. Probably he was lonely. I mean he was older, and Robin and I always hung out together. Maybe he went to bars. What else was there for him to do, except go bowling at the alley on the corner of our block.

One morning, however, he told me that lately he had made really poor choices. He said that he got stinking drunk and shacked up with a woman who turned out to be dirty. That shocked me because Darrell always kept himself clean. He had a good, aftershave smell. However, he paid a big price for his stupidity. Almost immediately he broke out with two huge canker sores, one on his lower lip and one on his penis. I know because he showed me.

What could I say? Did he want sympathy? Or advice? "Golly, Darrell, have you been to a doctor?" Were these trophies? I couldn't tell if he was proud of them. He didn't show them to Robin.

After taking a shower, he went to the hospital and got antibiotic medicine. Apparently the syphilis sores would go away on their own, but the medicine protected the body from worse outcomes. A few days later he was feeling much better and came out of his self-imposed isolation.

We regrouped for a conference. Unanimously, the three of us

agreed that a month in Buffalo was long enough. It was just too depressing. A few days later Darrell came up with a plan for getting us out of there. He'd connected with an agency that transported cars and needed drivers. If we went back to New York City, we could drive a private car from there all the way to New Orleans, to its owner who had left it in the city when he flew south.

"Yes. Absolutely. Let's do it!" was Robin's response.

"How soon can we go?" was my question.

"I have to iron out the details and get us bus tickets. But as far as I'm concerned, the sooner the better," Darrell said as he grinned.

Being the designated driver, he normally would have received payment for that task. But since he wanted to bring his "relatives" as passengers, there was no payment. Our free ride was the payment. We eagerly waited for the announcement that a delivery was available. Darrell had been calling the agency twice a day.

When the confirmation came, all we had to do was get ourselves to the city in time. We grabbed our meager belongings and hurried to the bus depot. Darrell had bought the tickets a week ago. Lucky us, we made it there with half an hour to spare. We used that time to grab food and drink for the journey.

I was not happy, even for a few moments, to be back in New York City. The overwhelming noise of the traffic, the herd of people jammed together like in a stockyard, and the confounded blockage of the sky by the scrapers slammed a cage door shut on my well-being. Gloom spread around my heart as I witnessed the drowning of normal, worthy human existence. Between clenched teeth I growled at Darrell, "How much longer do we have to be here?"

"Not much longer, Kimmy. Let's grab a taxi to go to the agency."

On that drive, I slumped in the back seat, with my face buried in Robin's shoulder. I didn't feel like me at all. I kept my mouth shut to keep from complaining.

The transaction at the agency went smoothly. Darrell signed paperwork and showed ID. The man behind the desk looked me up and down. That seemed to be all that I was worth these days. I mean, the guy at the welfare agency, the creep and his cronies at the loft party, and the people who stared, or bumped against me, when I was freaked out on LSD, all treated me as if I were nothing more than a piece of furniture. Is that what city living does to humans?

Then the keys were handed to another man who had been quietly standing near the door. He was going with us as the driver for the first part of the trip. He would take us to Richmond, Virginia, leave, and Darrell would take over. We rode in a Lincoln Continental with all the luxury extras: power windows, brakes, steering, air conditioning and AM radio, plus plump leather seats and a walnut dash. It was so cool! We practically floated down the road.

The journey south along the coast interested me because we passed Civil War sites. Little stone walls everywhere bordered farms and graveyards. Lots of those farms, homes, and families got destroyed by fighting about slavery. It was very sad and unimaginable to me. There were way too many graveyards.

The Atlantic Ocean struck me as different from the Pacific. Darrell said the Atlantic was generally warmer, and waves were milder. Seeing it and smelling the ocean air made me miss Isla Vista. Majestic condors and migrating monarch butterflies floated through my inner vision. I wished I were there with my friends.

Since we were ahead of schedule, Darrell suggested that we take a side trip to check out a bit of Florida. The beaches were lovely with long stretches of white sand. Southern California had that too, which made me homesick. The citrus orchards that covered the northern part of Florida had been moved to the southern area to be safe from winter freezes. When my family moved to Southern Cal, after WWII, there were orchards everywhere. As the population increased, houses replaced those orchards.

Our sightseeing took us into Florida for about a hundred miles. Then Darrell headed us west across the Florida Panhandle. He was really tired from all that driving without any sleep. By seven o'clock he couldn't go any farther. We ate at a diner and stayed in the motel next to it. At dawn we completed the trip to New Orleans.

25

SHINY NICKEL

New Orleans looked like it might be a town with possibilities for sanity and joy. After dropping off the Lincoln Continental, Darrell asked the lady behind the desk if she could recommend a neighborhood with decent housing. Thank goodness she did. The three of us were sick of living in ghettos. We got a furnished two bedroom apartment on a street where neighbors said hello to us, and the children wore clean clothes and smiling faces.

I think we were on the edge of the French Quarter. That was the old, hip area of town, where parties happened all night long. Streets named Bourbon, Rampart and Canal carried the main flow of traffic, while the Mississippi River snuggled up to the shore. People were not in a hurry. The corner pay telephones only cost a nickel. Sometimes a Negro man in a black suit came out of one of the clubs, stood on the sidewalk and blew his horn. It was pure New Orleans jazz. And that was so cool.

I tried to be happy. Really I did. But I wasn't.

Robin was boring. All he was interested in was sex, which

included me admiring his erection. He was thrilled when I agreed to draw a picture of it. Otherwise, all he talked about was his single mom who only fed him tomato soup and toasted cheese sandwiches. He didn't read and wasn't interested in music. Besides, Robin mostly listened to baseball games on the radio that Darrell had bought him. There was no need for him to work, as long as Darrell paid for everything.

I never understood that arrangement. I cooked the food that he bought, washed dishes, swept the floor and took out the garbage. In my free time I wandered around town on my own, wondering what kind of job I could get. I needed my own money. I especially needed, and very much wanted, my own place and my own life.

Wandering through the French Quarter, the older architecture delighted me. It looked like it belonged in a cowboy, or pirate, movie. Double glass doors opened onto second story balconies that wrapped around the buildings. The wrought iron railings wove into lacy patterns. I imagined pretty ladies with flowing, colorful gowns and dainty parasols strolling there, enticing the passing men in the streets below to visit them.

The main boulevard was split down the middle with trolley car tracks. Tourists eagerly clambered aboard to enjoy the novel transportation. When they discovered the street artists painting out in the open, they acted like giddy little kids at the ice cream store crowding around oohing and aahing. All of these sights entertained me, better than going to Disneyland, which was built near where I grew up. Life was so different here from New York City or Buffalo. Even with lots of people and vehicles, there wasn't the crowdedness, constant noise, or dirty air. I heard laughter.

Two weeks after arriving, I came upon a musician performing outside his club. A group had gathered to listen. It was awesome to hear the sweet sounds that man would play. All of us were thrilled and applauded loudly. He played several mind boggling songs. For an hour the crowd swelled.We stood shoulder to shoulder in harmony. Someone lit up a joint. The smoke rose among us. I was reminded of the camaraderie of my friends in Isla Vista. I noticed some of the audience bent down to put money in a hat that rested on the ground nearby him, to thank him.

Finally the saxophone's magic ceased. The gifted musician picked up his hat, tucked the horn under his arm and returned to the darkness of the club. Members of the crowd again became individuals intent on their own destinations.

Too soon I was standing alone. I walked to where the man had stood, hoping to still feel the rhythms his fingers produced. To breathe in the melody's air and fill my spirit with its joy. Gone, all gone. I shrugged, feeling the weight of my sadness upon my shoulders. Above me the sky offered a few wispy clouds. Seagulls called out to each other. My loneliness escaped in a sigh. Tears began to blur my vision. Quickly I pulled the back of my hand across my eyes before anyone could see my distress.

Then a tiny flash of light caught my attention. On the ground, directly in front of me, where the musician's hat had been, a sunbeam reflected off a small, metal object. There, within arm's reach, lay a bright, shiny nickel. I picked it up. Rubbed it. Felt the warmth from the sun. Then, filling with hope, I knew that with that nickel I could make a phone call.

It had been four months since Pat, and I hitchhiked to Idaho, and my world turned upside down. Pat had called her sister, Ruth, for a bus ticket home because she missed her boyfriend. I missed Eddy and I hoped he still loved me. I hitchhiked to Colorado, to his parents' cabin, to find him. Instead I found heartbreak, rejection and confusion which twisted and grew, until I reached this moment.

Ruth had been in recovery from an auto accident. She was probably healed and back at work by now. It was likely she'd be home at seven in the evening. That would make it ten o'clock in New Orleans. Forming a plan, I had to come up with an excuse to leave our apartment, alone, to make that call from one of the pay phones (not that Robin would want to get off his lazy butt and come with me).

That night after dinner I approached Darrell. "Hey Darrell, I really don't like to ask you, and I'll certainly pay you back when I get a job....I've been asking around about maid work."

He glanced up from the paperback he was reading. It had a spaceship on the front of it. "What do you need, Kimmy?"

I couldn't look him in the eye because I was flat out lying to him, and I was terrible at that. Staring at the floor and clasping my hands behind my back, I squeezed them hard to steady my nervousness. "Well, I need to make a quick trip to the market. It's....ah,.... um,..... it's women stuff. You know what I mean." That part wasn't a lie, but I never talked to guys about my menstrual periods. I could feel my face and ears on fire.

"Oh." Darrell blushed too.

Robin wasn't even in this conversation. He sat across the room taking his shoes off.

"I don't want to hear this." He grabbed his one shoe and hobbled into the bedroom with the other one half off. He closed the door.

Darrell had left the room, too. Both of these men did not want to hear that I had this particular need. Maybe I needed to come up with a different reason to leave the apartment.

Then Darrell returned. He stood stiffly before me and handed me a five dollar bill. "This is more than enough, but you might need other stuff. So you don't have to ask again. You get a job and you can pay me back. OK? Go do your thing now." He sat down in his chair again and returned to his book.

"Thank you, Darrell." My feet stuck to the floor until he flapped his hand at me in dismissal.

There was a phone right outside the market. *Please, please be home. Please answer the phone Please help me.*

"Hello?"

"Ruth is that you? This is Kimmy. I am so glad to hear your voice."

"Kimmy, I've been thinking about you for two whole days now. Pat and I were just talking about you. Where are you?"

"I'm in New Orleans at a phone booth, so this call will hang up real soon. I need help, Ruth. I want to come home. Can you send me a bus ticket? I'll pay you back. I promise."

"New Orleans? What on earth are you doing there? Yes, Kimmy, I can do that. I'm working again. Where do I send it?"

"General Delivery, New Orleans. Thank you Ruth. Thank ...." There was a long silence. The phone went dead. My time ran out. But Ruth said she would do that for me.

As I stood on a street corner that was across the country from where I knew I belonged, tears streamed down my face. I bought what I needed and there was money left over so I would be able to get some food for my trip. Because I was going to leave. I had to. I didn't belong here living with two guys who did nothing. Or being someone's sex object, did not fulfill my yearning to explore life. I had to get home to my friends in Isla Vista, and the Pacific Ocean, and people who cared about me. And now I didn't have to hitchhike.

Three days later I started going to the post office every afternoon. Four days after that, Ruth's letter arrived. General delivery mail was asked for at the counter. The mail man behind it would not give me my letter because I didn't have any way to prove my identity. I had left my driver's license with Ruth for safe keeping.

"Who else would it be for? " I shouted. "Who else would know it's coming? Nobody else has my name. Please give me my letter." I was fighting back tears. "Please." I wanted to reach across the narrow divide of the counter and snatch my letter out of this pimply faced moron's hands.

The four people standing in line behind me heard all this and talked among themselves. They were just regular people, tall, short, white skin, dark skin. But together, they spoke up for me. "Give the girl her mail."

The mail man shook his head, "I can't do that. There's regulations." Then he turned and looked at another man who had just come through a side door with a "Postmaster" plaque on it.

That second man heard the ruckus and came to see what was going on. He walked over to me, saw the tears welling in my eyes, took the letter out of the mailman's hand and gave it to me. Gently he said, "I'm sorry about the delay. You have a good day, child." He nodded to the people behind me and returned to his office.

I wiped my eyes with the sleeve of my shirt and hurried away. I did feel like a child. A helpless, abandoned child. Showing my weakness like that made me feel ashamed. What a mess I was in. But as soon as I was outside, I ripped open the letter and found my ticket home, with a sweet note from Ruth telling me that I was missed. More tears tried to embarrass me. I stomped my feet to jar myself back into the reality of the moment. With the ticket clenched tightly in my hand, I headed to the bus depot to find out the time of departure. A bus left for the west coast everyday. I could go home tomorrow.

That night I couldn't bear to have Robin touch me. Fortunately my period saved me from that intrusion. But he was a whiner. "Darrell told me that oral sex was more enjoyable than regular sex. Come on, Kimmy, you'll like it."

"Oh, right, Robin. I've got my period, which includes cramps, and you want me to suck.......No Robin, that's not going to happen." I rolled onto my side and flattened myself against the wall.

"Please, Kimmy. I'm all ready, so it won't take long. Please."

I threw back the blankets, grabbed one of them and crawled to the bottom of the bed, and then out the door to the living room. Making my escape, I slept on the couch. Darrell was still up, reading one of his books. I gave him a look that I hoped would keep him from saying anything. Sleep. I just wanted to sleep.

When morning came, voices woke me up. They came from Darrell's room. "Don't worry Robin, I'll talk to her."

Imagining what that was about, I got my clothes from the bedroom and locked myself in the bathroom. *This is my day. They are not going to ruin it for me.* The shower felt so good. I scrubbed every part of me to be rid of this crap life. I had my ticket out of here. From the kitchen I got a paper grocery sack and stuffed it with my few belongings. A change of clothes, toothbrush, hairbrush, my sketch book and the package of tampons.

Robin and Darrell stood together watching me. Darrell placed his hand on Robin's shoulder.

Before they had a chance to say anything, I pulled back my shoulders. Now I could look Darrell in the eye. "Thank you Darrell for getting me out of New York City and out of Buffalo. New Orleans seems to be a nice town, but it's not for me." Then turning to whimpering, pasty faced Robin, I clearly said, "Don't worry, Robin. Darrell will find you another girlfriend and make sure you get enough to eat."

"Don't go, Kimmy." Robin's bottom lip trembled and tears welled.

Darrell's arm was now slung around the younger man's shoulders. "Let her go, Robin. She doesn't want to be here. If she stayed, she'd make us both miserable."

I closed the apartment door quietly and headed towards the Greyhound depot, looking back to make sure I wasn't followed. My bus didn't leave for another two hours. That was ok with me. I walked around filling my eyes with the rhythms of this grand old town. With the money I had left over from what Darrell had given me, I hopefully bought enough food to last for the long ride. Then the bus, my bus, arrived and I boarded.

I loved the smell of the bus, and the sounds of its door opening and closing. For me they were the smells and sounds of freedom. I watched the other passengers jostle for just the right seat and put their small belongings in the overhead racks. Larger baggage was stowed in a compartment that opened on the outside. I held onto my paper sack. I wanted to sit by a window, so I could see what I left, and where I was headed. There were enough empty seats for me to get my choice.

As soon as the driver turned on the engine, and I felt the vibrations, my spine tingled with anticipation. The slight jerking of gears being shifted reminded me of riding the rails with Gil. The memory of that freedom to explore and to take risks again stirred my inner being. I settled into this journey and put my sack on the empty seat next to me. No one sat there to tell me what I could, or could not do.

The bus ride took four days and nights. I didn't mind, even though it would have been easier to have a pillow for sleeping. I was determined to stop feeling sorry for myself. Instead, I wanted to understand how I got into the mess of the last four months. It was difficult for me to admit, but I had been frightened and miserable. How could I have thought that it was ok to be dropped off in the middle of New York City with one dollar and only two addresses of people who may, or may not, be glad to see me? And shooting up meth? That was totally stupid. And taking off to another city with two men whom I barely knew, who assumed that my sole purpose was to clean house and gratify a sexual need ? Well I got what I deserved, didn't I? Maybe. But not any more. I was in charge of my life now.

Nancy's words of advice echoed in my mind, "Kimmy, you need a plan."

26

HOMECOMING

After the long bus ride from New Orleans to Santa Barbara, I called Ruth from the station. She and Pat picked me up in my Borgward. Their hugs felt so good. As the sun was setting on a bright Spring day, relief flooded me. A weight that I didn't know I had been carrying lifted from my shoulders. The car ride to our little house relaxed me even more. Familiar surroundings assured me that I was safe and my life would make sense to me once again. My hellish time in the cities taught me that not all people were kind, nor cared about me. Some of them were downright rude, belittling, or mean. I didn't want any more of that malignant lifestyle that seemed to fester in big cities. Trees, sunshine, ocean air and true friends were all that I wanted.

A delicious spaghetti and fresh salad dinner awaited me.

"I still have a little bit of my wine left," Ruth said as she offered me a small glass of her 'Apricot Special.'

We toasted with cheers of, 'For she's a jolly good fellow', 'home sweet home', and 'absence makes the heart grow fonder.'

"You returned just in time," Ruth smiled as she leaned forward. "Pat and I want to move into Isla Vista."

Pat wiggled in her seat. "I'm signed up for two classes at UCSB this Summer, and if we live in I.V. I can walk to them. Ruth won't have to go out of her way to get me there on her way to work."

"Speaking of the car, Kimmy, I really appreciated being able to use your Borgward. My car wasn't fixable after the car crash. The axle was busted and a hole got knocked in the engine. So your car got daily use." She reached across the table and laid her hand atop mine. "Thank you. She was a dream to drive. If you'd be interested in selling, I'd really like to buy her."

"I'm glad my car got put to good use. I knew you would take care of it." A yawn escaped from me as my eyes fought to stay open. "I'll do the dishes, then I'll crash on the couch. Wake me up tomorrow in time to drive you to work."

What a good night's sleep I had. I woke to the aroma of coffee. I had never acquired a taste for it, but I loved how it smelled. Plus, I liked coffee flavored ice cream. *Oh, wow, I could go to the Baskin Robbins 31 Flavors store today.*

I drove Ruth to work in Santa Barbara. She was an accountant with a quiet, detailed job which suited her nicely. Pat rode along. After we dropped off her sister, we headed to Isla Vista.

Pat cleared her throat and asked, " What was it like being in New York City?"

I took a deep breath to remain calm, because I wanted memories of the last several months to fade away. I tried to sum up my experience and leave it there. "It was huge, always noisy and extremely crowded with people in a hurry. I really didn't like it there."

With her mood deflated, and from a tiny voice, Pat asked what I had hoped she wouldn't. "Chris wasn't here when I got back from Idaho. I heard that he went to New York with Lori. Is that true? Did you see him there?" She looked directly at me as her voice quivered with sadness.

I didn't know how to dodge her question. I was a lousy liar. "Who did you hear that from?"

"Brian, Lori's husband. He came to the house looking for Chris." Her hands twisted together in her lap.

So, Brian knew. How awful. How could Lori, and Chris do that to him? I pulled the car over after I turned off for Goleta, the road that led to UCSB and Isla Vista. Shutting off the engine, I again took a deep breath and massaged my forehead, hoping to work loose the best answer.

"Yes, Pat... Chris and Lori, with little Aaron, were living together in a yukky apartment in a crummy part of New York City. I stayed with them for a short time. At least, that's where they were when I left a couple of months ago.... I'm really sorry."

"Did Chris ask about me?"

"No... It really wasn't my business to bring up your name. I mean, they gave me a roof over my head. I had nowhere else to go." I knew I sounded pathetic.

Pat cried softly with her hands covering her face. I restarted the car and turned in the direction of the auto repair shop where my friend, Don, worked. I parked by the curb to give Pat privacy. Then I walked to the open door of the garage.

There he was, with his back to me, bent under a car hood, as he leaned over an engine, the friend I married in Las Vegas to save him from the draft. I walked up to him with a grin spread all the way across my face. "Hi, Don. How's my favorite husband?"

Bang! He jerked and whacked his head against the hood. That didn't seem to phase him. He spun around, put down his tool, and bear hugged me with his still awesome biceps. "Ex-husband, Jennifer Rose. I annulled us. You are once again Kimmy." He released me and glanced towards my car. "Who's with you?"

"That's Ruth's kid sister, Pat," I said. " You remember her?"

Don gave a nod to Pat, and she returned a small wave.

I tapped him on his shoulder. "So why were you in such a hurry to get rid of me?"

With a rag he wiped grease from his hands, slid one of them into his pocket, pulled out a ring and stuck it on the finger of his left hand. "Because this is the real thing. You kept me out of the draft long enough for me to convince Bonnie to be my wife. I guess going to Las Vegas with you let her know that I might not wait forever for her."

"I'm glad I could help, Don, with all of that. Congratulations."

Inching back towards the car he'd been working on, he said. "We're living up the road from you, at Painted Cave. Bought a house. Come visit sometime."

"Absolutely. That's so cool. But before I let you get back to work, I'm wondering if you know of a good car that's for sale. I'm thinking of selling mine to Pat's sister, Ruth."

Don didn't hesitate with his response. "Yeah, sure, as a matter of fact. I've been working on a sweet little Triumph that I picked up from some guy passing through who didn't want it any more. At least the gussied up girlfriend, who was hanging on his arm and bitchin' a mile a minute at him, did not want it. He practically gave it to me before he jumped into her BMW. Anyway... It's not like the one I have. This one's a TR 2. Take a look."

We walked to the back part of the spic and span shop. There was a little silvery blue sports car, all right. I liked it immediately. "Is it running? How much do you want for it?"

"Yup. I just put in new spark plugs and wires and adjusted the timing. It purrs.... Four hundred."

"I have to get a job. But if I sell the Borgward for the down money, could I make payments?"

"Of course. Why not? Seein' as how you're my ex-wife, I think we could arrange a deal."

I gave Don a kiss on his cheek, then Pat and I headed into Isla Vista. I hoped to find some of my friends.

Driving by the sorority and fraternity houses, then past the Bank of America and a few other businesses, didn't turn up any familiar faces. I drove on the streets that were lined with the older beach houses and by the college's gated apartments. None of my friends were anywhere in sight. I don't know what I was thinking. Of course they'd be in classes or working, if they were still here. Afterall, I had left, maybe they had too.

"Hey Pat, what do you say we go get us ice cream cones? My treat." That brightened her face. I had found twenty dollars that I had stashed in my clothes drawer before we hitchhiked to Idaho.

Standing in front of the ice cream bins at the Baskin Robbins store on the edge of Santa Barbara, trying to make a choice, really released the memories of me and my friends smoking pot, getting stoned. "How about triple deckers, Pat?"

"Triple deckers! Seriously?"

"Yup. Why not? I'm going for peach, chocolate chip mint, and coffee. What looks good to you?

Pat produced the first smile I had seen on her since we talked about Chris. "Well I do have a hankering for rocky road, straw-berry, and blackberry swirl."

We walked back outside with our cones and stood in the sunshine. I got a 'brain freeze' from eating too fast. I had to slow down and just lick my way to the waffle cone. Yum. Pat was only down to her second level.

"Hey, Pat. We're sitting outside Baskin Robbins, basking in the sun like little birds. Do you get it?" I laughed at my own joke. Goodness, it felt great to be home again.

After returning to the house on the hill, I went through my clothes and stuff. I didn't have much except for a few books and my art portfolio. After I straightened that out, I walked up the road a ways to a spot where I could see the distant ocean. That gave me the time and space to think about going to see Brian. I knew I needed to tell him about Lori and little Aaron. I did not look forward to that, so I decided first to cook dinner for my roommates. We had the makings for burritos. I quick-soaked pinto beans and got them cooking. With flour, salt, Crisco shortening and a dab of water I rolled out big tortillas. All that was needed was an avocado from one of the two trees in the front yard. I found a ripe one on the ground and turned it into guacamole.

While I did that, Pat drove into Santa Barbara to pick up Ruth. At the dinner table we shared the events of our day. Of course Pat already told her sister about me wanting to sell her my Borgward.

"What do you think about that, Ruth? I figure two hundred dollars plus the cost of the bus ticket you sent me would be a fair price."

"Yes, Kimmy. Absolutely." Ruth flashed a big smile and we shook hands on the deal.

Then I excused myself and drove to Isla Vista to see Brian, which made me really nervous. He had the right to know about his wife and son, but I didn't want to be the one to tell him.

The startled look on Brian's face, when he answered my knock on the door, quickly changed to concern. His brow furrowed, his jaw tightened. "Kimmy, come in."

I got right to the point and spoke without pausing. "It's been over two months since I lived with them, Brian. Aaron always seemed happy. He drew lots of pictures and liked me reading to him. Lori and I kept him clean. She and Chris took him to a nearby park. They taught him to pull open the refrigerator door so he could get food for himself whenever he was hungry." I hesitated as I remembered little Aaron, still in diapers, tugging at the thick door and reaching for the chopped hotdogs and vegetables on the bottom of the refrigerator.

"Don't stop now. I need to know."

I took a deep breath to steady my voice. "It was a cold water flat with cockroaches. But the worst part is that Chris and Lori shot up meth daily."

"What the fuck!" Brian shouted. He took in large gulps of air, then turned and hit the wall next to where I stood. Realizing how close I was, Brian backed up and sat down on the couch, clenching and unclenching his fists.

I didn't move.

Brian's nostrils flared and his chest heaved. "I'm sorry, Kimmy. I mean you no harm. I can see this was hard for you to tell me. Thank you." He rubbed his hands back and forth across his knees. "Lori said she wanted to visit her aunt. But I didn't believe her. Chris had come by here after Pat left with you hitch-hiking to Idaho. I could see that he was hot for my wife."

Brian stood up and paced around the room. "I told my parents that Lori left and took Aaron with her. They sent me money for plane fare to New York, and for a divorce lawyer. I'm going to get my son and move us down to Texas to be with them. What you've told me gives me no other choice." My broken hearted friend stopped pacing. "I might need you to tell this to the lawyer."

I nodded my agreement.

"Thank you. You're helping to keep my son safe."

I quietly slipped out the door. Driving back home, I understood that sometimes doing the right thing did not feel good.

27

BEING RESPONSIBLE

The next morning I dug out one of my two dresses. It was sleeveless and loose fitting, so I borrowed a cardigan sweater from Pat to give me a more professional appearance. I intended to secure employment. Ruth gave me a ride to Don's garage to pick up the Triumph. We had stopped at her bank on the way there for her to withdraw two hundred dollars to buy the Borgward from me.

I approached Don with the money in my hand.

"Well you look fancy. What's the occasion?"

I told him that I would be looking for work in Santa Barbara. I gave him the money that we had agreed on. He handed me the key to the Triumph. He also gave me back a few dollars, reminding me to go to the DMV to put the car in my name and to fill the gas tank. I drove proudly away in my classy sports car, with high hopes of continued success.

By lunchtime I was hired at Ingalls department store in Santa Barbara. I would work in the men's department, based on my high school experience during Christmas break of my senior year.

The rest of that first day at Ingalls consisted of me being introduced to the sales women in the other departments. They were all lots older than me and not very friendly. I was shown where the storage and restrooms were, and that the drawers beneath the clothing counters held extra socks, etc. But that was done mostly by pointing. No one seemed to want to talk with me.

The one male customer that I had that first day was a middle aged nervous dude. When I offered to help him find his pant size he stammered, "Uh, no thanks, I don't need any help." He turned his back to me, fingered through the selection of khaki slacks and slunk to the dressing room to try on his choice. However, my suggestion for socks was appreciated. "Uh, thanks."

After two very slow, boring weeks of trying to look busy for the one, or two customers who wandered through my section, a familiar looking man walked straight towards me. He wore Bermuda shorts, a black t-shirt with the Rolling Stones on the front, a baseball cap and sunglasses. Despite the odd choice of clothing, I recognized him right away. The nonchalance clued me in.

"Hi, Kimmy. I never thought I'd find you in a place like this. How did you manage to land such a normal job?"

"Hush the fancy talk, Bob. Pretend you are interested in the pants."

"I'm not. But I do want to buy something for Suzanne. Some baby stuff."

"You're going to be a father?"

"Sure." He cocked his head to the side. " Why are you surprised?"

I took him to the baby section. The sales woman there popped up. "May I help you, sir?"

Bob slid his sunglasses down to look at her. "No. I want her to help me." I stood right next to him, so there was no mistaking whom he referred to.

"But this isn't her section."

"Well, maybe it should be."

Vivian, that was her name, backed away. She actually snorted and stuck her chin in the air.

I helped Bob pick out some teeny, tiny clothes, which I knew absolutely nothing about. He said Suzanne had explained that since they didn't know if a boy, or a girl was coming to them, the first clothing needed to be gender neutral colors like green, yellow, or white. He decided on a couple of items.

Heading to the counter to pay for his purchase, he told me that he and Suzanne were living in a big house, sort of like a hacienda, near Montecito. Other people lived there too. "Come visit. The people are mostly interesting and Suzanne would be happy to see you. She doesn't get out much now."

After work I drove to the address Bob gave me. It was a different area for me to explore. The road continued on to Depression Drive, which the Civil Conservation Corp had built during the Thirties. Its dirt road curved along the spine of the Santa Ynez hills. I thought that it would be fun to drive the Triumph there.

I never really noticed pregnant ladies before. Suzanne was my first. Her belly was so big. We sat on her couch, with pillows propped all around her. Bob sat nearby in a stuffed chair with his feet resting on a foot stool.

"Being pregnant is really intense, Kimmy. Just wait until it happens to you." Suzanne spoke softly and smiled sweetly at me, then showed me the baby blanket she was knitting with yellow and green yarns. She thanked me for helping Bob pick out the baby clothes. "I'm really glad you stopped by. I wish I could visit longer, but I get so tired now that our baby is almost here. I'm sure Bob would like to show you around the property."

I followed him outside where he told me that he and Suzanne had the whole bottom floor to themselves. It was the biggest living area in the hacienda. Its flagstone floor kept bare feet cool in the hot summer. The rooms were spacious. The upper floor held one big living room with combined kitchen space. Four bedrooms and one bathroom spread out from there along an open corridor. I thought that was a unique arrangement, except everyone would know when you needed to pee.

A driveway stretched in from the road and circled around in front. Beyond that I could see a garden area with a few fruit trees. A picnic table sat in a nearby grassy space with a fire pit and surrounding wooden chairs. We sat there for a spell, catching up.

Bob's typically laid-back attitude shifted to concerned friend. "Why did you hop into a car in Colorado, with no money, and let yourself be dropped off in the middle of a city? And not just any city. You picked New York! What were you thinking?" He had shifted his position from casually reclined to leaning into my face. "Your luck sure took care of you big time. I'm glad you're safe, Kimmy. But it sounds like the guys you were with in New York were real losers. I hope by now you've figured out better choices in men."

I shrugged my shoulders. "Well, for some unknown reason, I'm sitting here with you."

Bob hooted with laughter and shook his head. "Damn it, Kimmy. I've always gotten you safely home." He passed me the lit joint he had just rolled. "Come back Friday evening. We're having a little party. You need to hang out with cool people."

The next day at work, Mr Ingalls, the store manager took me aside and handed me an envelope that contained my paycheck. With that gesture he explained there would be no need for me to return. Apparently the sales lady in the baby section complained about me, and my rude friend, who had ousted her from her section and deprived her of the sale. Since she was an older, long time employee, and personal friend of the owner, I was fired.

What a relief not to have to work there any longer and be bored out of my mind. Besides, I had earned enough to fill the gas tank of my cool little car, and give Ruth some money for rent and food. Being responsible suited me for short periods of time. My life was looking good again.

It looked even better to me two nights later as I sat around a campfire at Bob's place, smoking some very fine weed with mellow, like-minded humans.

That's how I met Bill.

28

BEING DIFFERENT

I knew that Bill was different from my other friends. He was an artist. One of his instructors recommended his painting to hang in the Santa Barbara Art Museum. The painting was modern and daring in its composition.

I met him when he was living at the hacienda during Summer break. We had been sitting outside by the fire pit. I suggested we go for a ride on Depression Drive which wove along the nearby mountain ridge. I followed him to his room to get his gray tweed newsboy cap that he so often wore.

It was a warm day. He had left his door ajar to bring in fresh air. His drawing table was lined with different pens and charcoal sticks. Sitting on the high stool and using the various pens, sat a five year old girl with long blond curls, intently scribbling her creations. Several sheets of paper had already fluttered to the floor.

Bill abruptly halted, and carefully approached her. She was hitting one of the pens on the desktop. "Hi Mirabelle. What are you doing?"

"I can't get this pen open," she said without looking up. She had a sweet voice.

The tension in Bill's body was evident. I expected him to scold her for coming into his room without his permission. The pens looked top quality and expensive. Banging one like that was not a good idea. Instead he said, "Let me open that for you." Gently he took the pen from her hand, opened it, returned it to her, then stood back.

I thought that was strange behavior.

Almost immediately a voice called out, "Mirabelle, it's time for lunch."

That little girl with blond curls, a red polka dot sundress and bare feet set down the pen and studied her latest drawing. "I think this is my best one. Mommy will like it." She hopped off the stool and out Bill's door, with her drawing, to join her mom in the kitchen.

Bill straightened up his area, looking carefully at each uncapped pen and matching its lid to it. Then he picked up the child's drawings that were scattered about and stacked them on the chair outside the door. He put on his hat and said, "Let's go for a drive." He shut the door and locked it. The key went into his pocket.

Our leisurely drive in the nearby hills let the air blow away any disturbances. The convertible top of my Triumph was tucked neatly away. I gave the gears a good workout as we navigated the corners of that rarely traveled mountain road.

Bill spoke up. "I like where I've been living for the past two summer months. The people are nice and I do a bit of yard work in exchange for my room. In the Fall I need to be closer to campus, because I don't have my own transportation."

"Where did you live last year?"

"I lived in Santa Barbara with the family who sponsored me. Sort of like a scholarship. I rode the bus back and forth. This year

I'm on a work/study program, so I'll have income. I'm wondering if you know of anyone with a spare bedroom, like in Isla Vista?"

I really liked Bill. We seemed to have a lot in common, meaning friends, art, pot and free love. Ruth and Pat had recently found a place in Isla Vista and were in the process of moving out. So I suggested, "You can move in with me."

And that's how it went. Smoothly, too.

Towards the end of Summer, we each decided to visit our parents. It had been awhile since either of us had been home. My parents lived just south of Los Angeles, and Bill's mother lived east of there in Riverside. The plan was to drop me off and he could take my car to his mom's. He would return for me the following day.

When we arrived at my parents' home, I invited him in to see the building my dad had designed. The living space rested above the four offices below. His well established insurance business was in the largest office.

It was mid afternoon when we arrived and my mom sat in her favorite chair in the living room, reading from a Ladies' Home Journal magazine. That was her time of the day to find quiet pleasure, after she had straightened up her home and taken her bath. I hadn't told her I was coming.

I came through the front door, with Bill right behind me. "Hi Mom."

She looked up from her magazine. "Hello Kimmy." She wasn't startled, nor surprised, nor pleased to see me. She sat calmly, holding her magazine with her finger capturing the last word she had read.

"I came for a short visit. Just thought I'd surprise you." I stood in the doorway with my boyfriend beside me. "This is Bill. His mom lives in Riverside."

Bill removed his hat and nodded to my mother. "Hello Ma'am. I'm pleased to meet you."

Without acknowledging my boyfriend, my mother looked directly at me and said, "Kimmy, offer your friend a glass of water."

Before I had a chance to respond, my dad had come up the stairs and into our home. Probably he had heard my car drive up and came to investigate. Bill and I quickly moved farther into the living room to make room for him.

I was glad to see my dad. My smile was big. "Hi Dad, I'd like you to meet Bill."

My boyfriend stepped forward and extended his hand for a shake. "How do you do, sir?"

My father shook it lightly then glanced at my mother. No one said anything.

Bill twisted his cap in his hands, lowered his head, fidgeted and quietly said, "It was nice to meet you. You have a lovely home. But I need to be on my way. My mother's waiting for me." He backed up towards the door, paused and stammered, "Kimmy, I'll pick you up tomorrow at noon. Bye, bye." He squeezed past my dad and almost flew down the steps. He drove away.

My dad, a tall man, dressed in his business suit, didn't tell me he was glad to see me. Instead he said, "Your friend seemed nice and well-mannered, but I can't have him seen here. That would be bad for my business." He turned abruptly and went back down the stairs.

I stood there, stunned. I didn't know how to respond. I never questioned or argued with my dad.

When I brought Eddy home. My dad wasn't rude to him. My mom was eager to know him. She asked him all kinds of questions. Yet she had no comment about this boyfriend. Instead she said, "I'm making meatloaf for dinner, with mashed potatoes, gravy and green beans. We have ice cream for dessert."

I stumbled to the couch and sat down. "That sounds yummy, Mom. What are you reading?"

Ignoring my question, my mother responded, "Lash is going to barber school. I know he'll do very well."

"Uh huh."

She didn't ask what I had been doing, and I didn't offer to tell her. Instead,she continued reading where she had left off. Later when my dad came home, we all ate dinner together. No one talked. Then the TV in the living room was turned on for him and me to watch, while my mother washed the dishes.

That night, as I lay in bed in the room that had been mine while I was in high school, I tried to understand why Bill got so agitated. How could my father mean what he said about Bill being bad for his business? Of course I knew that Bill was Negro. That didn't mean anything to me except I really liked the color of his skin. I wished my skin were that color. Getting a suntan always made me feel better.

But the color of his skin is not what attracted me to Bill. He was an artist, and I really liked being pulled into bed with him. Besides that, he knew interesting people, and he had friends in San Francisco. We drove up there several times to catch music events and hang out in the city. There was always something new for me to experience when I was with him.

The town I grew up in was all white. There were no Negroes, and only a handful of Mexican kids in my high school, who lived on the other side of the railroad tracks. I never wondered about that. I unconsciously accepted how that was. Not anymore. I understood why Bill got nervous and ran out of my parents' home. *So that's why he didn't bawl out little blond haired Mirabelle for entering his room and using his expensive pens. She had parents that he couldn't risk upsetting. My parents were no different.*

29

SUMMER, 1967

It was 1967, "The Summer of Love" in San Francisco. Golden Gate Park was jam packed with people, music, marijuana and various psychedelics. The vibes were all about sharing, mind expansion, brotherly love and free love. In fact, as we strolled through the park, Bill and I were drawn to a gathering on the edge of the grass near a parking area. Music filled the air. The people, predominantly young men, were intently watching what was happening on the ground, in the midst of their circle.

A naked older man (maybe thirty) was sexually engaging with a younger woman (maybe eighteen), who appeared to be willing. The man explained his techniques and maneuvers to the surrounding, enraptured young men. Supposedly the writhing woman was in ecstasy from his expertise. She moaned, "Don't stop. Please don't ever stop."

I wondered how she felt to be on display like that. Did she feel special and important to have been chosen for that public performance? Did that man love her? Did she love him? Or were they both just showing off with an overwhelming need for attention?

Bill pulled me away and we walked towards the music and free food. There we ran into Louie and Brent, friends from the city.

Louie shouted out to us, "Hey, dudes, what's happening?" He wasn't a hugger, but Brent wrapped his arms around me and then knuckle bumped Bill on his arm.

Before I met Bill, some of the people from the hacienda would travel back and forth to San Francisco, until most of them decided to remain in the big city. That's how he met everybody in that big mixing pot. Louie wanted to be a DJ. He'd practice on us with different voices. Brent played several instruments. Classical, jazz, Beatles' songs. Anything. He played a guitar, or harmonica on street corners and the people who stopped to listen gave him money. He always earned enough for at least rent and food, and he ate a lot.

We filled paper plates with delicious free food and sat together on the grass in the warm sunshine. Between mouthfuls we talked about places we'd like to visit, and all agreed that we wanted to go somewhere we'd never been.

Louie told us, "I want to see Niagara Falls. I've heard that two little brothers went over it in a barrel."

Brent knuckled him on the arm. "A barrel? A wooden barrel? How old were they?"

Louie shrugged. "They were little, like seven and ten."

"Were they in the barrel together?"

"Yeah... they fit in it together."

"What happened to them?"

"What do you think happened to them?"

"Well that was really stupid."

"Yeah, but I'd still like to see the Falls."

Bill was laughing hard, but he chimed in. "Me, too. But I want to see the tallest building in the world, the Empire State Building."

Louie slapped his knee. "That'd be so cool. We could climb all those stairs to the top and look down on the Big Apple."

Brent slapped both of his knees. "The Statue of Liberty would be awesome to see. I heard you can climb up her too. inside her crown and look out. Do you dudes know that she was made in France and shipped here in pieces, and then put back together. How righteous is that! She's a symbol of brotherhood, or maybe sisterhood, between our two countries."

I flung my arms around Bill's neck. "Let's do it! Let's go see our country. From sea to shining sea."

We all cheered and decided that a road trip would be outstanding. Plans were made. Louie said he knew some guys in Vermont where we could stay. Brent said he had some money saved up. Bill had a bit of money too.

I spoke up. "I've got a different car now. It's bigger and it gets really good mileage."

We formed a plan. Louie and Brent would come back to Santa Barbara with us. Louie wanted to map the route to take. We'd bring sleeping bags so we could camp out. The car had a small trunk. We couldn't bring much else. Maybe two changes of clothes and a frying pan. We'd shop at markets along the way.

I was so excited to be going on the road again! And this time it would be with a boyfriend whom I could never even imagine tossing me aside, like Eddy did.

Brent brought his harmonica. Louie produced a well used frying pan and the map. Bill added a box of matches along with his drawing pad. I wasn't about to go anywhere without toilet paper. Toothbrushes were remembered.

Each of us smuggled a few joints in with our extra clothes. If one of us got busted for possession of this illegal substance, we all got busted. We knew we had to be careful.

We agreed that wherever we stopped for the night, if there were other campers nearby, we wouldn't get stoned.

By the time we were sleeping under the vastness of the Arizona desert sky I felt joyously alive. And deeply peaceful all the way down to my toes. For some reason I knew I was safe whenever I was in the midst of trees, rivers, wild flowers, and soaring birds. I felt the most like me. I felt free and safe. Soft kisses on my cheeks, from the cool evening air, soothed away any worries of whether or not I belonged in this world.

From out of nowhere bats swooped and darted back at our intrusion into their territory. I snuggled closer to Bill in our zipped together sleeping bags. In the distance coyotes sang to each other. Smoke wisped from the dying embers of our campfire. Stars in the black expanse of night sky sparkled with mystery. Was it truly the home of gods and ancestors? Perhaps remnants of our earlier laughter, and music from Brent's harmonica, reached them as our offering of thanksgiving for their guidance and protection.

I fell asleep remembering words my mother had given me, when she tucked me into bed every night with a pat on my forehead, "God's in His heaven and all's right with the world."

The next day we arrived at the Grand Canyon. It was superb! Better than any of us four mortals imagined. I viewed the immensity of the river's persistent eroding that had created themotley colored, stone walled depths. Ravens rode the updrafts that those deep corridors produced. I wondered if condors would like it here. Their wings would snap with the thrill of soaring and exploring this great untamed vastness.

Around our campfire that night, I told the guys about the time when I was four years old. I came here with my family, on the way from Iowa to our new life in Southern

California. My dad towed our little travel trailer where we slept and my mom prepared our meals. He had suggested to my seven year old brother that this place had special powers. "You can throw a rock a mile." In fact, they walked together to the rim's edge and each threw a rock. I watched with them to see where the rocks landed, a mile down to the Colorado River below.

The guys swore that they, too, would do that tomorrow. And they would throw them even farther.

Brent thumped his chest with his fist. "I'll throw a rock up really high, and then let it fall."

Louie thumped his chest with both fists. "I'll throw my rock out far, far over the canyon, almost to the other side. Then it can fall to the depths below."

Oh, my mighty warrior friends were so dear to me. The three of us looked at Bill, waiting for him to claim his manhood.

" OK, I can do that too. But I'll do it the hard way. I'll turn my back to the canyon, close my eyes and throw a rock over my head, daring it to find its way to the bottom."

We all burst out laughing.

Catching my breath, I announced that it was time for dessert. S'mores were on the menu. Earlier we had each found a thin, green branch from one of the various shrubs that grew near the campground. One end poked a marshmallow which was then held over smoldering coals to turn golden brown. With that accomplished, the hot, gooey, chewy succulent topped a square, or more, of Hershey's chocolate, sandwiched together between two Graham crackers. Yum. Yum. Yum.

Our road trip meals consisted of a standard dinner of hamburgers on buns, with the usual condiments, canned beans, and Fritos. Breakfasts and lunches sort of ran together. We ate peanut butter and jam sandwiches, various fruits, and candy bars, while we drove. We had a long way to go and not much money.

We also smoked our pot while driving, with the windows rolled up to hold in the goodness. I did not take a turn at the wheel because twenty-five miles per hour was all I could manage when stoned. I don't know how the guys did it, but we cruised along at the speed limit of fifty-five miles per hour.

Louie did most of the driving, and talked in one, or more of his DJ voices. "Here we are, lady and gentlemen, grooving to the vast panorama of the American West. Can you dig it?"

After throwing our rocks into the Canyon the next morning, we continued on through the Indian reservation. That, too, was huge and filled with displays of towering, oddly shaped rocks and arches in varying shades of gray, orange and brown. Mesas rose up, and sand covered the ground. The very straight highway offered little variety and no sign of houses or people. Except for the man who walked on the edge of the pavement.

From the back seat, I spotted him and stuck my arm, with a pointing finger, into Louie's view. "Look. Look." We all leaned forward to see that amazing sight. A man walking in the middle of nowhere.

When we were near the man, I could see that he was an Indian.

Louie rolled down his window. Crisp morning air streamed in. The sun was not yet high enough to offer any warmth. The man wore a short sleeved shirt, and no jacket. Where on Earth had he come from, out here in the middle of the desert?

Louie slowed the car and inched along beside him. "Hey, buddy. It looks like a long walk to anywhere. Want a ride?"

The Indian stood still, looking at a very small car filled with mostly white faces looking back at him. "OK."

I scooched closer to Brent to make room in the back seat for our guest. It was a tight fit because he had really broad shoulders.

"Are you cold?" I asked our passenger. "We can turn on the heater.

He shook his head. No. No.

"Are you hungry? We've got peanut butter and strawberry jam sandwiches." I held one out to him.

Again he shook his head. He looked worried. Well, maybe he wasn't used to white people. Or maybe he'd never seen a Negro. Or maybe he'd never been this close to a strange woman. Or maybe the radio music was too loud for him. Also, pot smoke still billowed out of Louie's window.

The Indian guy kept his eyes looking straight ahead, or out his window. He clasped his hands between his legs and hunched his shoulders. I think he was really relieved when we came to a gas station for a fill up. He opened the door before we came to a full stop. "Thank you."

Louie shook his hand. "Sure, buddy. Have a cool day. Peace."

Brent flashed him the peace sign with his raised hand.

We watched the broad shouldered man disappear behind the station while Bill paid the attendant for a tank of gas. As we drove away from the station, I could see the Indian, walking into the distance, across the desert, with his back to the highway. I wondered what his life was all about.

Niagara Falls, our next destination, was the opposite of the Grand Canyon. It was noisy, wet and blue. The Falls was not a narrow cataract that ended in a quiet pool which beckoned me to swim in its sparkling waters. No. Three falls actually combined to produce the sixteen stories high of roaring splendor. It spread across a mile of curved embankment. At the bottom, its water pooled into the bluest of blues caused by the reflection of its limestone bed. Rainbows appeared when the sun shined on the mist that sprang from the cascading water.

The magic that resided here exploded in my face. It told me, "You can't ignore me. I dare you." Over the years, a few people took the dare. A century and a half earlier a man walked over it on a stretched tight rope. Four decades later, in 1901. A sixty-three year old lady school teacher was the first to go over it in a barrel. She lived. I thought she must have been crazy to do that.

The guys and I were all impressed by our visit, but we were not enticed to stay any longer. Two hours convinced us that Nature deserved to be respected for her unending variety and power. We loaded ourselves into my car and continued our journey to Vermont.

30

JUNKYARD WONDERLAND

Louie navigated our way through the twists and turns of back country roads in the "Green Mountain State' of Vermont. We came to a dilapidated split rail fence, mostly hidden in tall grass and purple bushy flowers. A rickety sign with faded letters drooped from a post at the opening in the fence line. The sign read Victor's Vehicles. We had arrived at our destination.

With a deep sigh Louie, brought my car to a halt. "This is it." He had no official map to bring us to this last leg of finding his friends. We had driven from Niagara Falls to the little town they told him to find. Then the directions were, "Ask the locals how to get here."

We patted him on his shoulder, or knuckled his arm. "Well done, Louie. Way to go."

Turning onto the dirt driveway at the end of the road, I saw a small wooden house surrounded by colorful flowering trees. Louie's friends sat on the porch in old wooden rocking chairs. They bounded off the porch to greet us. "You made it here. Far out!"

The car was parked, we tumbled out, shook hands and shared introductions. Red haired Alex was tall and lean. Stocky Jason was all muscles and crew cut. Both were barefoot with cut off jeans and tee shirts. And they both had great smiles. My kind of people.

As they led us to a nearby patch of grass beneath a large maple tree, Jason told us, " From here we're within sight of the office, in case a customer drives up. Or we can hear the phone ring from the outside buzzer. Yet we are far enough away so our smoke doesn't drift there. Have a seat." He relaxed onto one of the two bucket seats from sports cars, and motioned to us to join him. I took the other seat, and my guys stretched out on the cool grass. Alex produced a fat joint that he lit and passed among us. The four of us travelers released all tension from our drive.

Jason and Alex told us that the previous year they spent their Summer vacation roaming the Haight/Ashbury district to find out if it was anything like the rumors they'd heard.

"Well, was it?" we all chimed.

"Oh, it definitely was," Alex spluttered between massive tokes from the fat hand-rolled joint. "It was totally outstanding. Pretty girls everywhere with loose flowing skirts and see-through blouses." He looked at me and winked. "And most of them offered us places to stay. 'Free love' really meant it was free. Meals included. No questions asked. No IDs needed."

Jason chuckled. "One chick got such a crush on Alex, that she wanted to come back to Vermont with him, in spite of herself already having a boyfriend."

Alex beamed. "She said she was enchanted with my adorable red curls and long eyelashes. Jeez, I felt like a doll, or something. But she was awesome in bed."

"Did she follow you here?" I asked.

"No. Her boyfriend convinced her otherwise. He reminded her that she was three months pregnant with his baby." Alex grinned. "Since then she's sent me two care packages of weed and photos of her baby. Apparently her boyfriend stuck with her even though she insisted on naming their little girl Alexa."

His story impressed me. *There was a girl who knew what she wanted and didn't settle for what her boyfriend expected of her.* I wanted to be more like that.

I looked at Alex, who definitely had sex appeal. His self assured attitude mingled with a cool manner that was enticing. He acted like anything he wanted would easily come to him.

On the other hand, Jason had his own appeal. Shorter, broad shoulders, and rock hard calf muscles, were sure signs of an athlete. His blond crew cut and lake blue eyes gave him a wholesomeness that suggested he could be trusted with secrets.

Louie stretched and shook out his legs. "How did you get this cool job?"

Jason squared his shoulders, leaned back and filled us in, while Alex rolled another joint and licked it closed. "A fraternity brother passed the gig to us when he graduated."

Bill's eyes lit up. "You belong to a fraternity? Do the other guys know you smoke weed?"

Jason flashed his lopsided grin. "The frat brothers were curious about what we experienced in San Francisco. They asked us what it was like to smoke 'dope.' We assured them that we didn't try it. Instead Alex and me told them about the cool dudes we met there who smoked it." He grinned at Alex, slapped his leg, threw back his head and laughed. "It was so hard to keep a straight face, but they believed us. And they assured us that they didn't want to ever try it, because everyone knew that 'dope' was bad stuff. It rotted your brain, et cetera. They admonished us to absolutely stay away from it."

Alex smirked as he explained, "Drunken orgies rule their fraternity lives while they conform to the age-old protocol of the educational system that prepares them to be lawyers and politicians."

Brent nodded in agreement and asked, "I dig you. Do you get paid for being here?"

"We do get paid," Jason responded after cracking the knuckles of his hands. "We receive enough to cover our bus fare here and back to the university in the Fall, plus cash for food and beer. That's in exchange for us to be available to customers and to be honest with the money transactions, so Victor, the owner, can have family time with his wife and kids."

Bill glanced around at the broken and smashed cars and trucks. "What exactly do you do here?"

Alex stood up, looked at his surroundings and said, " Well there's not much that needs to be done. I mean, we don't wash and shine the cars." He laughed at his own joke. "I guess we're the 'Junkyard Dogs.' We stand guard." He and Jason gave each other a thumbs up. "Come on, let's get a snack and then gather up stuff for dinner. Smoking pot always gives me the munchies."

We trooped back to the office and entered the back door to Alex and Jason's living quarters. All they had, that I could see, was a tiny kitchen and bathroom. Maybe the front porch, or that spot under the tree, served as their living room and bedroom. *Where do they sleep?*

We snacked on apples and oatmeal raisin cookies while Jason and Alex cooked up homemade macaroni and cheese, with giant sized sausages and a crispy green salad. Our plates heaped full in one hand, and glasses of iced tea in the other, we followed our hosts outside. The dirt road that we drove in on appeared to wind throughout the junkyard. We walked it a short distance to a clearing. Surrounded by heaps of discarded and mangled vehicles, old truck bench seats formed a circle around a fire pit, on the bare earth. Jason quickly built a roaring fire from nearby stacks of kindling and chopped wood. It seemed obvious to me that this was a favorite spot for them.

The sun was setting behind the maple trees and stars began to appear. I enjoyed my dinner, even the large Kielbasa sausage that I ate for the first time. I soon tuned out the voices of the guys as they bantered about chicks, soccer and Vietnam. The dark night sky and twinkling starlight caught and held my attention. The painter, Vincent van Gogh, and his famous painting, 'Starry Night', popped into my head. I bet he saw the same sky that I saw, except his didn't hold still. It swirled and shouted. It was my favorite painting, and I often wondered how his imagination took him there. Then I realized that whenever I used peyote, or LSD, my mind altered into giving me wild and vivid visions, just like that painting. But, supposedly, Van Gogh's mind naturally did that to him all the time. Wow!

Brent pulled out his harmonica from his pant's pocket, and played Bob Dylan's song, "Blowin' in the Wind." Sitting by a campfire in the middle of the green countryside, was the perfect setting for those sweet notes to lift above the fire's crackling flames and drift over the surreal landscape of a peaceful junkyard.

Alex folded his arms across his chest, smiled broadly and said, "Me and Jason met Brent and Louie on a street corner in the Haight. Brent was blowing tunes and Louie thumped bongo drums. The people who passed by, or stopped to listen, gave them money. They were good, especially Brent...No offense, Louie, but he's the one we stopped to hear. He was, I mean, you are really good Brent." He rubbed his palms together and his face beamed. " I think you will appreciate our musical endeavors. C'mon. We'll show you."

Jason lifted a hand, with its palmed turned out. "Slow down, Alex. Not now. It's too dark. Let's give them the show tomorrow.

They had a long drive getting here. Sleep first, then the performance. OK?"

Alex nodded his agreement.

"Speaking of driving here," Louie said as he stretched his arms high and yawned, "crossing three thousand miles was fairly smooth going, until we entered beautiful, green Vermont with its many winding country roads. The drivers here are crazy, or maybe drunk out of their minds. They passed us on curves that blocked the view of on-coming traffic. They passed us even when the road was straight but had an approaching car, or truck, going at least double the speed limit. There was no time to pass us. They did it anyway. I had to swerve half a dozen times...at least. Those crazy ass drivers scared the shit out of me!"

Alex and Jason nodded in recognition. "Seriously," Jason said, "Vermont has the highest suicide rate in the nation. On the road and off. Drinking and driving is a favorite pastime. A lot of smashed up vehicles end up in this junk yard."

"Why?" I asked. "I mean, why so many suicides? It's so beautiful here."

"I don't know. Probably because the unemployment and depression rates here are so high. Not having work can really get a guy down. Anyway, sleep cozy. You can roll out your bags under the maple tree that's near the office. The grass is soft and it's a clear night. No rain is expected. We'll call out when breakfast is ready. Kimmy, feel free to use the bathroom inside."

Bill had zipped our sleeping bags together by the time I returned from the well scrubbed bathroom. Jason and Alex were neat housekeepers. I snuggled close to my boyfriend and quickly fell asleep with a full tummy and a very full day of adventure.

Our hosts were good breakfast cooks, too. Blackberry pancakes and maple syrup were in ample supply. The aroma of coffee and bacon wafted through the air. We again loaded our plates and headed to the campfire sitting area.

Between mouthfuls, my curiosity overflowed, " The kitchen and bathroom were all I saw of your house. Where do you guys sleep?"

Alex raised his eyebrows as he turned his gaze to me. "Did you see the ladder attached to the wall, next to the bathroom door, and the hole in the ceiling that it led to?"

"Yes, I did."

"Well, up that ladder, and through that hole is our sleeping loft. Perhaps you would like to take a closer look?" His eyes locked onto mine.

I had trouble swallowing my bite of pancake. My cheeks blushed.

Bill tensed, stood up and carried his plate back towards the house..

Oh my. What have I done?

"Oh, no, no thank you." I stuttered. "I was just curious." I put my fork on my plate. "The breakfast was delicious. Thank you."

I hurriedly followed Bill to the kitchen. "I'm sorry, Bill. Really, I am. I was just curious. I didn't mean anything." I filled the sink with hot, soapy water and began washing dishes.

Bill didn't say a word. He stood back and quietly watched.

Brent entered the room and brought his plate to the sink. He came close to me and whispered in my ear, "Don't worry, Kimmy. Alex was just being an asshole, giving you a hard time." He patted my shoulder and rapped Bill on the arm, the way dudes do.

The rest of the guys brought in their dishes. I washed them. Bill dried and stacked them on the open shelf. The pans lay drying on the counter top.

Back outdoors, in the sunshine, Jason bowed and with a flourish of his arm bid us, "This way, lady and gentlemen."

He and Alex led us towards the farside of the property, through a canyon of more rusted, dilapidated cars and trucks piled higher than our heads. Brent spotted a Model A Ford that had to be at least forty years old. Ivy and morning glories snaked through its missing windows. The open rumble seat was devoid of padding. Instead, brilliant red geraniums filled the space.

We stopped in front of a disaster zone of discarded junk. Cut off tail pipes of various lengths hung from the limb of a maple tree. Hub caps swung on another branch. I spotted what looked like a xylophone made out of more tail pipes with some kind of wooden slats for the keys. Cut up rubber inner tubes stretched over an old barrel keg, two dented pails and several large pork and beans cans. They looked like bongo drums. A multitude of beer bottles, filled with different levels of water stood on the dropped tailgate of a Dodge. Another bucket yielded an assortment of sturdy sticks with rubber stuffed knobs on the ends.

I stood still, my mouth dropped open, and my head cocked to the side. *What is going on here?*

Jason pulled a battered top hat, a pink feather boa and two sets of drumsticks from the front seat of the Dodge. He handed a set, and the boa, to Alex, who draped it around his neck. Both of them bowed and together they announced, "Welcome to Maple Mountain Musical Mayhem. Please join us."

Brent grinned, immediately responded, and moved straight to the xylophone. Louie and Bill looked at each other, grinned, and sat down with the bongo drums. Finally I figured out what was about to happen, and I chose the water bottles to blow on.

Alex and Jason twirled from fenders to hanging hubcaps, while they rat-a-tapped with their drumsticks. They pulled out bigger, padded sticks to bang on car hoods and roofs. Brent left the xylophone and joined me on the whistling bottles. Bill tried out the big sticks on a dilapidated Jeep. Jason and Alex joined together in a bongo duet.

It was indeed a musical mayhem, and I loved it. Putting down the bottles, I beat on a couple of cars with a stick in each hand and whooped "yahoo." Throwing up my arms, I danced. My bare feet stomped the ground as I gyrated backwards and forwards. My hair billowed around me. My joy soared.

Bill embraced me and we attempted to polka.

More whoops and hollers burst out of the guys. Louie performed some kind of hilarious rooster dance. Brent burst forth with "'gobble, gobble, gobble." The rest of us joined in with pounding our feet, clapping our hands, and laughing until tears streamed down our faces. Eventually we collapsed on the tattered car seats. Alex lit up a joint. It passed around the circle, and Time stood still here in Wonderland.

31
THE QUARRY

After a lull in our musical mayhem Alex looked at Jason. "I wonder what Lucille brought us today." He turned to me and my guys. "Every Sunday on their way to church, Victor stops here so his wife, Lucille, can give us desserts she has made to last us until the next Sunday."

"This food talk makes me hungry," Jason informed us as he rubbed his rock hard stomach. " I need to feed these muscles for the upcoming soccer season."

The walk back to the office filled up with soccer talk, which Brent seemed to know a lot about. I tuned it out. My sweet tooth busily fantasized dessert possibilities.

Wow, besides a chocolate cake with chocolate frosting, there were peanut butter cookies, gingerbread and two pies arrayed on the kitchen table.

Jason poked one of the pies, which was still warm. "Hot damn! Peach. My absolute favorite. And there's two of 'em. That means I get one all to myself. You guys can have everything else." He glowed like he'd just found the pot of gold at the end of the rainbow.

Alex had already started making lunch. "I heard you've been eating burgers and beans for your camp outs. I'll stay away from that. How about tuna sandwiches with fresh garden veggies on the side?"

Bill and I washed, scraped and cut up cucumbers, carrots and tomatoes that came fresh from their garden with dirt still clinging. "You have to show me your garden." I insisted. " I want to know all about it.....You guys are full of the best surprises."

Alex grinned and declared, "You bet we are. But first of all, Kimmy, it's soil, not dirt."

"Huh? What?"

"Dirt is dead stuff. Soil is the live earth, full of nutrients, that the plants grow in and are nourished. That's why our veggies taste so damn good." And OK, after lunch a quick tour of our garden patch. Then we're off to the quarry, but no questions asked about that. You just have to experience it. Let's eat."

It's amazing how much food guys can eat. I think none of them breathed while they devoured every morsel on their plates. They didn't talk. They just fully concentrated on the task before them, which appeared to me, to eat more than anyone else in the shortest time possible. Then came the burps. The loudest, the longest, the extra sound effects, and if possible, a culminating, super sonic fart. I left the table and went outside. Their boisterous laughter reached my ears.

After that sumptuous and entertaining meal, Louie, Brent and Jason cleaned up. Alex gave Bill and me the garden tour. Cucumber vines sprawled everywhere. Tomatoes grew out of old tires used as pots. There was a strawberry patch, green bean bushes and something I didn't recognize, which looked like giant green onions and turned out to be leeks. Alex talked about which veggies were happier next to which other veggies, and the benefits of rabbit and chicken manure, which he traded veggies for with a nearby farmer.

Before we left for the quarry, Jason told us to wear shorts or cutoffs. Brent and I were prepared, and our hosts loaned what they had to Louie and Bill. Two towels were grabbed from the clothesline that led from the back of the house to a nearby tree. I was getting curiouser and curiouser. "Come on Jason, Alex, what's up? Where are you taking us?"

They remained mum, while we marched through the music zone and kept on going into a wooded area. Maple trees shared the grove with oak and birch. I didn't recognize the bushes, but several of them had berries. Alex halted, turned towards us and pointed to a ferny looking bush with red pointed pompoms. "Don't get near that. It's sumac which will give you a terrible, itchy rash."

"Like poison oak that grows in California?" I asked.

"Yes. Beware."

We continued walking and I was in no hurry to get to our destination. I loved being in the woods. It felt like home to me. I mean, it felt like that's where I belonged. All the colors, smells and sounds I just wanted to soak up somehow. I imagined myself sleeping there in a hammock, or on a pile of leaves with squirrels, foxes, even skunks sharing their secrets with me.

"Keep walking, Kimmy. We're almost there."

I shook the dream out of my head and jogged to catch up to the guys who stood in the sunshine of a clearing. Alex and Jason brought us to a quarry, which was the local swimming hole. It greeted us with the bluest of blue water.

Jason walked away while Alex explained, "This used to be an open pit for mining granite. Other quarries in Vermont mined limestone or marble. When the stone ran out, ground and rain water filled the hole. It's cold, and absolutely fun." He dropped the towels to run and jump in.

On the far shore, Jason was swinging out over the water from a thick rope tied to a tree branch. "Bonzai," he hollered when he let go and pummeled down to create a big splash.

My friends were hesitant to get into the water. This was a new experience for those of us who were raised in cities or suburbs. Cautiously I stuck my toes into the water's edge.

"How cold is it, Kimmy?" Bill asked as he stood beside me.

Without answering, I stood up and dove in. After coming up for air, I went for a deeper dive, with my eyes wide open. Another world revealed itself to me. The coldness made me swim and swim to warm up. Breaststroke, backstroke, and the crawl all loosened my muscles and transformed me into an aquatic marvel, or so I imagined.

I never did answer Bill about the cold water. He'd have to find out for himself. Besides, I was too busy trying to be everywhere at once. I scrambled ashore and headed for the rope swing. Jason showed me where to grab it and how to get a running start. "The important part is knowing when to let go at the apex of the arch."

The first time I tried, I didn't let go. I ended up back on shore in the trees. No one made fun of me.

With a big brother attitude, Jason said, "Don't worry, Little Sister. That's how it is for everyone the first time. We need to feel when the projection stops and the energy falls back."

My next attempt had me ready. I let go of the rope at just the right spot and flew, spreading my arms wide and flapping to keep myself vertical instead of ending up in a belly flop. Surfacing, I shouted, "That was totally groovy. I want to do it again!"

Then my friends lined up to try, with varying degrees of success which depended on how much they wanted to show off. Brent tried to somersault in midair. Bill and Louie grabbed their noses before they hit the water. Each of them claimed to have made the biggest splash.

"Boo. No way," Jason hollered while beating his chest with his fists. "I am King of the Vine."

When the sun lowered to the treetops, that was the signal to gather towels and go back to the house. It was wisest to travel the woods with enough light to keep from bumping into the sumac.

By the time the sun had set, we had returned and put on dry clothes. Again grouped around a campfire, we stuck hotdogs on sticks for roasting, ate the potato salad that we all helped to make, and crunched on more cucumbers from the garden.

I stretched out next to Bill. "I could live here forever."

Brent's voice cut through the silence, "Enjoy it while you can, Kimmy, 'cause you never really know what tomorrow will bring."

With that thought, we headed back to the kitchen for thick slices of Lucille's chocolate cake. With full tummies and satisfied taste buds, we compared sunburns and again argued about who launched the biggest splash from the rope swing. Jason still won unanimously.

Once more I filled my role of being 'one of the boys,' hanging out, and being accepted by them. That was so natural for me, because they did what I wanted to do, went where I wanted to go, fulfilled their curiosity and sense of adventure. I didn't expect anything of them, although I hoped they would care about me and keep me safe. That's how it usually went, if they were my friends. My boyfriend was the frosting on the cake.

Sometimes I wondered if we would marry. I had even asked him what he would name his children. He'd thought about that. He had names in mind.

The fire's flames mesmerized me. Dancing colors and shapes jolted my memory to Nancy's words from our time together in Mazatlan. My mind rang clearly with her words, "Kimmy, I hope you figure out what you want for yourself, and come up with a plan."

Well I didn't have a plan yet, but I finally knew what I wanted. I wanted a boyfriend who loved me, a close circle of friends who wouldn't disappear, and to live in and explore the wondrous outdoors. And I wanted a garden. I didn't know how to make that all happen, but I knew, without a doubt, that's what I wanted.

32
VIEW FROM THE TOP

After two more days of swimming, music, laughter and delicious food, my guys wanted to continue our trip to New York City and beyond. Being at the junkyard, with Alex and Jason, had been pure joy for me. I could have stayed in Vermont forever. But I was outnumbered. Reluctantly I agreed. I turned over the keys of my Volkswagen Bug to Louie, who seemed to have a map in his head. I do not know how he navigated with unfailing accuracy in foreign territory.

A full day's drive from the refreshing green of Vermont to the clamoring gray of the city happened smoothly. Louie, Brent and Jason had spent part of the previous day going over my VW Bug to give it a tune up. Nothing much was needed except an oil change, filters, air in the tires and whatever else they did. Bill and I cleaned the inside spic and span for the next part of our road trip.

Our arrival in the gigantic city unnerved me. The guys oohed and aahed about all the skyscrapers and pretty chicks everywhere, while I feared that something bad would happen. Memories of my time there flooded me. I kept my head ducked and sat on my hands as we drove through the towering structures and the masses of people in a hurry to get somewhere, anywhere. I felt like I was being thrown into a deep, dark pit with no end in sight.

Bill sat next to me in the backseat and saw my discomfort. "Hey, Kimmy, what's wrong? Look where we are!" He nudged my arm with his elbow.

I didn't look up. Thin words eased from my lips. "Yeah, I know. It's just that it was a total bummer when I was here before. People were so weird. I was scared a lot."

My boyfriend leaned closer to put his arm around me. "Don't worry. You've got three bodyguards and Louie can get us in and out of anywhere. Right, Louie?"

"Absolutely. No worries." Louie glanced at me in the rear view mirror and beamed me a smile.

Brent twisted around in the passenger seat and patted my knees. "You're safe with us, little sister."

Amazingly, Louie found a parking spot in this mega city. We locked the car and walked in the flow of the bustling, jammed together crowd. The guys' eyes were practically popping out of their heads as they looked everywhere at once. Their energies radiated off their bodies like a force field around us. Instantly caught up in the rhythm of the jostling throng of people, they no longer resembled laid back guys from the junkyard in the boonies of Vermont. The three of them seemed to dig the vibe of the cement and skyscrapers. I held onto Bill's arm.

The first thing they wanted to do was taste New York hot dogs from a street vendor. Brent zeroed in on a cart's bright umbrella from half a block away and over the heads of the scurrying crowd. His enthusiasm pulled all of us to his goal. Without taking a breath, he ate three of them, which included mountains of sauerkraut. Louie also went for sauerkraut, and Bill and I settled for mustard, ketchup and pickle relish toppings.

Bill itched to glue his eyeballs to famous paintings. I had told my friends about the completely groovy Guggenheim Art Museum that was designed by renowned architect, Frank Lloyd Wright. They were all eager to go there.

While we munched away, Louie got directions from someone else who was also enjoying a New York dog. "Hey, dude, do you know how to get to the Guggenheim?"

The man wore an expensive looking gray business suit and shiny shoes. "Sure, but are you asking for directions because you have a car? I mean, if you've got a parking spot now, it's probably the only one available in the whole city. Leave it there and take the subway. It's easier."

Suddenly, a teenage kid in a Yankees baseball cap stood next to me. I had seen him, out of the corner of my eye, edging closer and closer. Without any greeting he asked, "Are you Flower Children?"

"What makes you think that?" I said and inched closer to Bill.

"Well, duh," he pointed to Louie, "he's got holes in his pants, and his hair is huge (he waved his hand at Louie's loose, waving curls)." Then he pointed to Brent. "He's wearing a Rolling Stones' tee shirt and sandals." Next he nodded towards Bill. "He's wearing a funny cap, and you're barefoot with flowers stuck in your long hair."

I glanced down at my feet. I had no need for sandals in Vermont. But I had grabbed them and tucked them under my arm when we got out of my car. I knew I needed to readjust to the big city.

My 'body guards' all declared, "Not me."

"She is."

"Ask her. She'll know."

Well, that response totally jolted me. "Hey, what happened to "You've got three bodyguards, and you're safe with us?"

My so-called bodyguards didn't say a word. But the kid sure did. For the next few minutes he bombarded me with all sorts of questions. I answered as truthfully as I could, since I was lousy at lying. "Yes, I've been to San Francisco. Yes, I believe in free love. Yes, I smoke pot. No, I have not been in jail, but I have friends there. No, I am definitely not doing it with all these guys. Bill is my boyfriend." I shifted my stance to nestle up next to him and turned away from the kid.

With bulging tummies, we separated ourselves from the crowd and headed to the subway. A totally groovy experience awaited us. Zipping along underground like that introduced me to the future, like going into outer space, especially when the inside lights flickered one time.

Being in the Guggenheim again relaxed me. The audacity of the upside down, eight layered, round building, with the spiraling ramp and glass topped dome felt solid and exhilarating to me. I appreciated its uniqueness this time much more than when I came here with Michael. I had a sense of what it all represented. The bold, break all the rules for the sake of art, thrilled me. I suspected Bill was totally enthralled.

"What do you think, Bill? We can ride the elevator to the top and mosey on down. Or vice versa."

Bill didn't respond. He had already immersed himself in his world. The three of us just backed away and turned him loose. Then we each went in our own directions until we rejoined two hours later. The guys and I were gathered together, outside in the sunshine, when Bill found us. He glowed.

We agreed that it had been a full day. A seven hour drive, plus a ride on the subway, and then the stroll around the art museum depleted our energy. Louie's never-fail internal guidance system, pointed us to the subway and the return trip to my car.

We found it unmolested. It even retained all the hubcaps. *Am I really in New York City?*

After checking our food supply, generously donated by Alex and Jason, we decided there was enough for dinner and a bit for breakfast. So, with a harried passerby giving Louie vague directions to Central Park, our navigator and pilot realigned his radar and off we went to find a camping spot.

The stars weren't as bright in the park due to the city lights, but we settled into our sleeping bags in the middle of a forest in the middle of the biggest city in the USA. We were all too exhausted from our very full day of adventure to do anything more than climb into our sleeping bags. We all had an undisturbed, good night's sleep with full stomachs and a plan for tomorrow.

Excitement came with the dawn. We were going to the Empire State Building and then take a ferry boat to the Statue of Liberty. That turned out to be as simple as it sounded. Louie's unfailing knack for getting us places and acquiring safe parking was fully operating. The day beamed with sunshine and good cheer.

I don't know how to adequately describe the view from the top of the Empire State Building. It reached one hundred and two floors above the ground. The top floors were not even visible from the sidewalk. The elevator ride felt like time being compressed as we slowly inched upward. The view took my breath away. I finally saw the immensity of the city. I couldn't move. My throat tried to clamp shut and my stomach knotted. Even though I recognized that I didn't have to live here ever again, the jarring noise, the constant frantic movement, the conniving non-spaces with the rude people, all this repelled me. But I would not perish here. I told myself, *I'm not trapped here. I'm just passing through. This city no longer has its grip on me.*

"Hey, Kimmy. Have you seen enough?" Bill whispered in my

ear. "Let's find lunch and then see the famous lady who welcomes all the immigrants who are looking for a better life." Bill gently pulled me away from the window and the daze I was in. He nudged me toward the elevator where Louie and Brent waited. My friends. My bodyguards.

Brent was the food connoisseur of our group. When we reached street level, he licked his lips, stood on tiptoes to look over the swarm of people walking by, and swiveled his head in search of a dining place. "I smell something really good. Do you dudes smell it? It's coming from that direction. C'mon."

We entered a softly lit, crowded restaurant and dined on some kind of Asian food. We each ordered something different and shared. I have no idea what kind of meat presented itself to me..

Louie sampled each of our choices. Washing down a giant sized mouthful, he offered his thoughts on the subject, "Probably, octopus, or snake, or maybe dog. I've heard that eating dog is very common in that part of the world."

" Whatever, dudes." Brent exclaimed. "Chow down."

I ate the rice and vegetables.

Next came the Statue of Liberty. That was so cool. We left the car, once again, and found our way to the ferry boat. From offshore, surrounded by ocean smells and lots of gray, I saw her the way people, who traveled across the ocean, saw her. She symbolized their hope for a better life. I think my mom may have been one of those people when she was a very little girl. Or her mother was, and she and her twin sister were born in the city. Anyway, I was impressed and humbled by the courage of those immigrants.

Climbing to the top of the Statue was a challenge for me because it was 162 steps (I counted), or twenty floors, up a skinny, metal, spiral staircase. I led the way with Bill right on my heels. We arrived about a minute before Brent and Louie.

The platform to view through the Statue's crown barely provided enough room for the four of us. We were the only ones there, and Louie lit up a joint. The smoke wafted through the portals of the crown to spread far and wide.

We were four young people from California in the crown of the Statue of Liberty. The symbol of hope and freedom. Louie was Jewish. Brent was a street musician. Bill was a Negro. I was a "proper girl" from Southern California who had gone astray. Ha! Ha! Ha!

I practically floated down the stairs. The ferry boat ride back to the mainland felt like being on a magic carpet. Gentle waves kissed the side of the ferry. Tug boats tooted. Seagulls swooped and cried out their strange calls. Brooklyn Bridge loomed in the near distance. Skyscrapers banded together in a wall of hostility.

"When we land, let's go back to my car and leave. Please. That's what I want to do."

My friends did not argue.

Brent's big smile reassured me. "No worries, Kimmy. We'll be outta here."

And we were. Henry (that's what I had named my car) perked right up when he saw us coming. At least according to my very stoned viewpoint he did. His doors opened to greet us warmly. I sat in the passenger seat for a change. A precise witnessing of leaving New York City bolstered my need to escape its confinement and drudgery. I had no idea why it was nick-named the Big Apple. It was not juicy and delicious to me.

Brent held a different opinion. He rubbed his hands together. "I bet I could make so much money here playing on the streets and busking for tips, especially from tourists. That gives them stories to tell about what they saw and how they were a part of it. And I could pick up different rhythms and styles. Wow. And with so many hip chicks to choose from. So groovy."

The drive south to our nation's capitol lasted five hours. We smoked more on the way there. I was totally stoned. To the max. All I remember about being there was racing Bill to the top of Washington's monument.

"Well, where do we go now?" Louie asked, as we sat on the broad stone steps that rose to the Lincoln Memorial.

We pondered the question.

I told my friends about New Orleans. I thought Brent would really dig the music there. I shared seeing all the battlefields and graveyards along the way. "Pure history."

Louie spoke up, "I'm glad you saw that part of the south, Kimmy. I'm sure I'd really like getting to dig it too. But," he paused and took a deep breath. "It is definitely not a good idea to drive through the South. Bill would not be safe. Remember the Civil War? The freeing of the slaves? The southern people were not happy about losing. In fact they're still up tight about it."

Brent added to that thought," We wouldn't be able to protect him."

Louie continued, "And you and him being together would only make it worse."

We held this conversation while sitting on the steps of the Lincoln Memorial, in the middle of our nation's Capitol, the place of "the home of the brave and the land of the free." The reality of Bill's skin color always shocked me. Since I'd never been exposed to racial injustice, except for my father's disapproval, I didn't know how to visualize what could happen to us if we drove through the southern states. I trusted my friends' advice.

So we took the northern route back to the West Coast. We drove through the Big Sky country of Montana. Open spaces, giant mountain ranges, lots more green. Brent and Louie said their 'goodbyes' in San Francisco.

Bill and I looked forward to the familiarity of our little home on the hill. He itched to draw his experience. I wanted to sit on the bluff above the Pacific Ocean, hoping to see the condors. I wanted to sort through all that I had seen and experienced. I felt that I had a clearer picture of what I wanted to do with my life, which definitely included Bill.

33

DEVIL IN DISGUISE

Coming home felt really good. Pat had stayed in our little house while we were away, to safeguard our stuff. I called her from a pay phone in Eugene, Oregon to let her know that Bill and I would be back soon. A bouquet of wildflowers on the kitchen table welcomed us. Everything was neat and tidy. What a treasure to have friends I could count on.

Bill headed to the university to find out if anyone was hanging around the art department. He wanted to share his experience at the Guggenheim with other artists. He also was eager to sketch out some new ideas.

I thought about getting a job. Maybe they would hire me at the ice cream parlor. I certainly knew a lot about the flavors. Or I could check out the bookstore in Isla Vista. Most of the community residents there were students at UCSB, who went home for the summer. Business would be slow. Still it would probably be smart for me to inquire.

Obviously I was not in a hurry to engage in forty hours a week of mind numbing employment. What did I want to do?

Bill was setting up his drawing table in our tiny bedroom. I was outside looking for avocados under the two trees in front of the house.

That's when Howard drove up and stepped out of his car. He was Eddy's first roommate. In Isla Vista. Being quiet, with nothing interesting about him, I never paid him much attention. It had been at least two years since I had seen him.

After Eddy and I got back from our winter hitchhiking trip to Colorado, we went home to visit our parents. When I returned to Isla Vista looking for him, it was Howard who answered my knock on the door. He leaned against the jamb looking me up and down.

Why do men so often do that to me?

He said, " Eddy's not here. He moved to Goleta. He's shacking up with a girl from his music classes."

This same Howard now walked down our sidewalk. I didn't know how he found me. He just suddenly appeared and said, "Hi, Kimmy, how're ya doing?"

I had left the front door open when I came outside, to let fresh air into the house. Bill must have heard our voices, because he came outside and stood next to me.

I shifted my attention from avocados to wondering why a person that I had barely ever talked to would be at my home. "Hi, Howard, what brings you here? This is my boyfriend, Bill." I wrapped my arm around Bill's arm and drew close to him.

Bill gave Howard a slight nod.

Howard stuck his hands in his pockets as he looked back and forth at each of us. "I've got some extra tabs of LSD. I thought you might like to join me for a little trip."

Bill glanced at me, then at Howard, and quietly said, "No, thanks."

The next thing I knew was that I had a voice in my head talking to me. *You don't have to do what Bill wants. You are an inde-*

pendent woman. You can drop acid with a guy who is not your boyfriend. Go for it. Pulling away from Bill I said, "OK. Sure. Why not? That sounds good to me." I jutted out my chin and swept my hair off my shoulders.

Bill stared at me, then stepped back. He didn't say a word, nor try to stop me. He just turned and went into the house.

I was so proud of my boldness. With the arrogance of my independence, I brushed my boyfriend aside. I willingly got into a car with a man I barely knew, because he offered me LSD.

After a short drive I was once again in the home where Eddy and I had made love behind the curtain that hung from the ceiling to surround his bed. That had been the only privacy from his roommate, Howard, who shared the space.

Eagerly I accepted the pill that would take me to new psychic dimensions. It had been several months since my last 'trip.' Those trips altered my concept of time, my vision, and my sense of reality. My mind expanded into a new awareness of possibilities for living and understanding life.

As I waited for the effects to take hold, Howard and I talked about 'old times.'

"You and Eddy listened to a lot of music, people I never heard of, or classical shit."

"Yeah, I liked Joan Baez and he liked Stravinsky's 'Firebird.' We both liked the Beatles. I mean, who didn't?"

"You two were always goin' places together. You never invited me to go with you." He leaned forward on the couch.

I shifted my weight on the kitchen chair. "Well, he was my boyfriend."

"Yeah, but he's not now. Why don't ya come over here and sit by me?" He patted the couch.

I sat up straighter. "I'm with Bill now. He's my boyfriend."

Howard licked his lips. "Yer always with some guy. Aren't ya?" He rubbed his hands on his thighs. " You know, I could hear what you and Ed were doin' behind that curtain. I bet you liked me hearing your moans and calling out his name. Didn't you? You've been with lots of guys. Haven't ya? And now yer with a nigger."

He stood up and came towards me. I didn't know what he wanted, but I didn't like him coming that close to me. I pressed my back against my chair. When I'd taken LSD a few times before, I mostly sat quietly and watched the patterns and colors that magically appeared before my eyes. If I moved around, or danced, the friends I was with made sure I was safe and happy. That's not how I felt with Howard. I felt closed in and threatened.

Vaguely aware that he grabbed my arms and pulled me from the chair I was sitting on, I stumbled and slumped in his grasp. He stripped my clothes from me and shoved me onto a bed. Sunlight streamed in through a closed, curtainless window.

I tried to fight. To stop him. I struggled to form the word "No. No." But he didn't stop. With one hand around my neck to immobilize me, he slowly unbuckled his belt and twisted out of his jeans, as he kicked off his shoes. He released his hold on me long enough to squirm out of his tee shirt.

I rubbed my neck, coughing to relax those muscles, and rolled onto my side. Everything moved around me. The floor and ceiling slipped in and out of each other. Sparks flew in between. Shadows swam around my head and I tried to bat them away. I squeezed my eyes shut, trying to make this mistake go away. I must have whimpered.

"Shut up, Kimmy. You know ya want this. Why else did ya come wid me? Yer boyfriend knew what I was after. He didn't try to stop me. Probably relieved that he didn't have to service you for a little while. Glad for the break. Worthless nigger."

He pulled on himself, then fell on top of me and pinned my arms above my head. I twisted and squirmed and tried to bite him, or somehow break his grip, but the drug had robbed me of my strength.

Howard forced my legs apart and penetrated me. He pounded his body against me again and again. "That's it Sweetheart. Thrash, bite, try to get loose. Pretend ya don't want it. But I know ya do because yer nothin' but a whore, a nigger lover. C'mon. Give it to me like ya gave it to all them others. That's it. That's it."

After he finished, this man rested his full weight on me. Then he released my arms and rolled off me. He stood and grabbed a pack of cigarettes from the dresser. "Don't go anywhere. I'll be back for more. Hahaha."

My mind swirled in and out of darkness as I shut out my reality. Shadows weaved on the perimeter of my vision. LSD episodes could last for twelve hours. I don't know how many times he 'came back for more.'

Howard blew his cigarette smoke into my face. " Well now, Kimmy, I'm bored. You didn't really give me the good time I was lookin' for. It's time to go bye bye, back to yer nigger." He threw my clothes at me and told me to get dressed.

Shaking with exhaustion I struggled into my clothes. Not waiting for me to put on my shoes, Howard grabbed my arm, dragged me to his car, and shoved me into the passenger's seat. He threw my shoes at me.

I slumped against the passenger door. The LSD was fading. I was weak and groggy. The rushing air from the open window helped to clear my thinking. I knew that I was in a moving car. I watched the world stream by in its continuous beauty and senselessness.

When we arrived back at my home, Howard parked the car and walked around to my side. Bill ran up the sidewalk and opened my door before Howard had the chance. Gently he helped me to my feet.

Howard's smug voice soiled the air. "Thanks, Bill. That was fun. She's all yers now."

Without a word, or a glance at the man who ravaged me, my boyfriend helped me down the sidewalk and into our home. I heard the car door slam, then Howard drove away.

I think Bill had completely understood Howard's intention, but he felt helpless to protect me and to oppose this dangerous white man. He had compassion for me. Yet, at the same time, why would I betray him and dishonor our relationship? Why would I leave him and go off with some man whom I barely knew?

I had been so determined to not be locked into the stereotypical role of 'a proper girl' raised in white middle class America during the Fifties. The new Spirit of the Sixties allowed me to break that mold. I wasn't alone. Other women argued and spoke up for their perceived rights. There were marches to the White House against the stupidity and horribleness of the Vietnam War. There was marching in the streets to set the Negroes free and to stop segregation. I wanted my freedom to make my own choices about who I was, what I did and where I went. However, foolishness and arrogance were my downfall. They led me to be raped and jeopardizing my relationship with my boyfriend.

Later in the evening after Bill had cooked our meal, which I barely touched, and washed the dishes, he finally spoke to me. "I don't want to go to bed yet. Sleep is a waste of my creative time. I have to learn, and do, all that I can now, because when we get old we slow down and our lives become dulled." He asked for my car keys so he could visit friends in Santa Barbara. I was in no healthy state of mind to go with him.

After he left, I walked through my little home, where I had known joy, friendships, and kindness, and access to a path that wandered the nearby hillside, with a distant view of the ocean. Now I walked with my arms clasped tightly around me, holding myself together. For the first time in my life I was terrified of the dark. My mind was in turmoil with reeling glimpses and sounds from my all too recent struggle with a man, or maybe he was a demon. When I looked at the windows, which didn't have curtains, I saw hideous faces on the other side, leering back at me. They altered their appearances, but mostly they resembled some kind of monstrous animals that screamed at me. I knew they wanted to come in. They wanted to rip me apart. Even when I closed my eyes, the frightening visions of those diabolical creatures appeared behind my eyelids, like the shadows that swarmed me during Howard's attack.

Perhaps a hot bath will soothe me. I ran the water to fill the tub. When I took off my clothes and felt the air touch my body, I shivered, then cringed. There were no visible bruises that I could see. I stepped into the hot water and submerged as much of me as I could. I needed to wash away the filth of my selfish actions and the reaction it had caused. I thought I was to blame for Howard's behavior because I had stepped outside of my proper girl upbringing. From that moment, I blocked the event from my conscious mind. I never told anyone, nor talked with Bill about what happened. And he didn't ask. Instead, I allowed shame, guilt and self loathing to take hold of me. That was the punishment I felt I deserved.

Until Bill returned later that evening, I kept the lights on, and avoided looking at the windows. I sought the oblivion of sleep, but it only mocked me. The next night as he preparedto leave, I begged to go with him. I did not want to be alone.

He drove us to the home of a family that we knew. They were 'society' people in Santa Barbara, an established family from a high income bracket. When their three daughters turned eighteen they were formally presented to society as debutants, meaning they were now eligible for marriage. This was the family that had sponsored Bill's first year at UCSB. He had lived with them. They were nice people and I felt safe.

I found a quiet place to sit in the living room, relieved that I wasn't bothered, because I was in no condition to interact with anyone. Bill came for me sometime after midnight. "C'mon Kimmy. It's time to go back to the house."

That was the only time I went with him at night. I understood that it wasn't OK. He didn't want to drag me around with him. I could see that he was making changes in his life. The next few nights he said, "I won't be gone long. You know where I'm going. You're safe here."

But that was the point. I didn't feel safe in my own home. I didn't feel safe anywhere. When I closed my eye lids, the monsters appeared behind them. So I was afraid to sleep. Although, during the day, I made myself act normal, like nothing bothered me, like I had not been raped.

"What kind of dreams did you have last night?" were now the only words Bill spoke to me daily. "You moaned a lot." We didn't make love. He began sleeping in the living room. Then he moved out and quietly slipped away.

34

SQUASHED BEDROOM

I still had a wrapped kilo of really good weed, from my smuggling trips with Bob, buried in the backyard. I had no intention of selling it, because it was meant for my smoking pleasure. But I needed money for gas, food and rent. I got myself hired at the Isla Vista bookstore. It was busy enough to appreciate my help. Two months was all I could handle there because I worried that Eddy, or Bill, might show up and throw my shame at me, even though I believed Bill wouldn't tell anyone that I cheated on him. However, I feared that Howard would go looking for Eddy to boast to him of his conquest. So I quit my job, having earned enough to move to San Francisco.

I asked Ruth if she and Pat would like to rent my little house. That way I could store whatever I didn't take with me in the garage. She and her sister excitedly said "Yes" to my offer. Ruth had plans for a little garden in the backyard. She even hoped to grow grapes for wine. (I marked where I had buried the pot so she wouldn't disturb it.)I introduced her to the landlord and the switchover happened easily .

It had been several months since I had any contact with my

dear friend, Brent. We had a mutually agreed upon platonic relationship. He was my buddy, the musical dude who could play almost any instrument. It took several tries of calling different people to track him down. When he called me three nights after I had sent out word, he told me, "Come on up. Little Sister. You can crash on our couch."

"Will your roommates be cool with that?"

"Absolutely. And it's roommate, singular. Her name is Doris."

I was happy to learn that Brent had a girlfriend. I looked forward to meeting her. If she was anything like him, she probably had multiple talents.

I didn't take much with me besides two baggies of grass. In fact, all I took were a few changes of clothes and some bedding. Any books, LPs, or pots and pans that I had acquired, plus my art portfolio, went into the garage at 'Ruth's Place.'

Brent lived somewhere in the middle of San Francisco in the tiniest apartment I had ever been in. It emerged from the adjacent house like a pimple. I didn't mean it was ugly. Just really small. The bedroom was wall to wall bed, while the kitchen and bathroom looked like renovated closets. At least the living room had two sunny windows filled with potted plants, a tiny dining table and the comfy couch.

Brent's sweet lady, Doris, was an amazing cook, especially with bread and stir fry dishes. She was the epitome of knowing "the way to a man's heart is through his stomach." Five feet tall with auburn curls, all sorts of bangles and beads, and shaking a tambourine, she was his true love.

Brent let Louie know I was visiting. It was good to see him too. He fired up a joint and passed it around our little circle. I breathed freely for the first time in what seemed like forever. I didn't explain to my friends why Bill and I had gone separate ways, and they thankfully didn't ask. Instead I said, "I want to hang out here in the city for a while. Do any of you know of a room for rent?"

Louie spoke up immediately, "I do, actually. You'd be welcomed where I am. We're mostly guys and your feminine presence would be appreciated. In fact, if you want, we can go there now and I can introduce you to Andy. He's in charge of running things there. What do you say, Kimmy?"

"Should I grab my stuff?"

Louie nodded.

I gave Brent and Doris hugs and fetched my toothbrush from the bathroom. I wrapped it and my clothes in my blanket and set off with Louie, handing him the keys to my car. It would be easier to let him drive, rather than have him direct me though the rush hour traffic.

We ended up across from Fisherman's Wharf. The house he lived in was an old Victorian that had not been divided into apartments. I left my stuff in the car and Louie led me inside. We stood in the foyer.

"Hey, Andy. Are you here? I want you to meet a friend of mine."

Andy emerged from an adjoining room. Blond curls cascaded down his back. Bits of chest hair poked through a holey black t-shirt. Frayed Levi's shorts and bare feet completed his ensemble. Smoke rose from the doobie stuck between his pouty lips. An open-faced bagel with cream cheese, tomato and green olives rested on his raised palm. "Hmmm, who's this you dragged in, Louie?"

"Andy, meet Kimmy. She's the groovy chick who took Brent, me and her boyfriend on the road trip across country. She just got into town and she's looking for a new pad."

Andy unabashedly looked me up and down. He took a big hit off his doobie, a bite of bagel, and grinned, "Well, the smaller cave beneath the penthouse is available."

A cave? A penthouse? What on earth are they talking about?

We walked into what had once been a high ceilinged living room.Windows along one side looked out onto a backyard filled with rose bushes and tangles of weeds. Turning around, I expected to see furniture. Instead I faced a floor to ceiling structure created from various old boards. It appeared to be two stories. There was a regular door three feet above the floor for the upper level. A step stool allowed entrance.

Louie spoke up while Andy munched away. "That's the penthouse. Spider lives there. We rarely see or hear from him."

Andy swallowed, wiped a bit of tomato juice from his chin. "But he pays rent at the beginning of each month, so the dude must be breathing."

I squared my shoulders and pointed to the two lower openings. "I'm guessing those are the caves?"

"Right on, sweetheart. Tony occupies the one on the right. The left one is waiting for your approval. The mattress comes with it."

I was being offered a four by eight by three foot high space with a twin sized mattress and the bottom half of a window. It reminded me of pictures I had seen of igloos with the low entrance tunnel. I would have to crawl into it.

Louie and Andy each had a bedroom at the back of the house. Nothing was upstairs. It went unused due to the rotten flooring. The downstairs mini bathroom had been rigged up with a shower. The kitchen was the biggest room. In fact it was the substitute living room with two couches and a rug, besides a big table and large pantry.

"How much," I asked, "do you want for the cave?" Andy stated a price I could afford and I moved in. I liked the challenge of the cramped quarters because that meant it was definitely my space. No room for anyone else. That gave me a safe feeling living with so many men. And there was another girl there, Billy Jean,

Andy's girlfriend who shared his room. She read a lot and giggled.

Christmas and New Year came and went. I walked in wider and wider circles exploring the neighborhood. My favorite place was Fisherman's Wharf with its open air market crammed with freshly caught fish, crabs, lobsters, and things I didn't recognize. The hot foods from different sellers tempted me with their delicious aromas. So yummy.

Across the bay stood the rock that was Alcatraz Island, with its federal prison. Its presence caused me to feel sadness tinged with fear. The men inside were convicted murderers who were kept in prison, on a rock in the ocean, surrounded by sharks.

I rode the trolley cars just for the fun of it, and was fondly reminded of the trollies in New Orleans. I visited with the few friends I knew. Time passed. I slept better. The monsters outside my windows in the little house on the hill didn't follow me to San Francisco. But they still lurked behind my closed eyelids.

At the beginning of February, Brent called me. "Kimmy, come see us tomorrow night. Be here by seven. Me and Doris want to show you something that is so totally outta sight. You will dig it to the max."

How could I resist? My curiosity was piqued. I drove there, found a parking spot. My friends and I walked to the Fillmore Music Hall that was a block away on Geary.

When I realized where we were going I grabbed Brent's arm and jumped up and down. "The Fillmore? We're going to the Fillmore?"

The very best musicians played there. Groups like Jefferson Airplane, Santana, Big Brother and the Holding Company rocked our souls. And I was going there!

Brent paid for us. "This is my payback for the far out cross country trip you took us on. Dig it, Little Sister."

We climbed the stairs to the balcony. We had a perfect view

of the stage. Brent sat between me and Doris. She could barely sit still with her anticipation. "In person, Kimmy. We're here in person. There is nobody like him......anywhere."

Then, all of a sudden, Jimi Hendrix stepped onto the stage and completely enraptured me. I knew his songs, "Foxy Lady" and "The Wind Cries Mary." And there he was, in person, just a few feet away from me. He didn't play any previously choreographed music. No way. The man just let the spirit move him. I had to hold onto my seat to keep from being sent into outer space. And the finale convinced me that anything was possible. This great, amazingly innovative musician ended his performance by smashing his guitar on the stage floor. I mean he swung it over his head with the full intention of destroying it. Brent and I looked at each other, wide eyed and speechless.

The thoughts galloped through my mind. *Why did he do that?.... Maybe because he was the creator of the music, and the guitar was just his tool.... He broke free from any and all restraints of what music was supposed to be.... The spirit of change that stormed through our culture demanding the breaking of a myriad of ideologies, rules and customs, spoke through this black man... But his audience was predominantly young white people like me , Brent and Doris... Holy Moly, he was sexy, fierce and authentic.*

Jimi Hendrix slaughtered the rule of a 'black man must be silent.' He told us what we yearned to hear. Jimi Hendrix played with the full strength of his being.

This man's passion accentuated my internal strife and dullness of spirit. San Francisco vibrated with new musical expression and outspoken ideology. Sexual nuances and preferences walked boldly down the streets.

But I had become bored with it, or disillusioned. Somehow I no longer fit it into the scene. No one expelled me. Instead, I dropped out of being a dropout. I packed up and drove back to Santa Barbara.

35

A SPECK OF LIGHT

The old hotel on lower State Street in Santa Barbara became my residence for the next month. The faded floral carpet in the second story hallway was worn and dingey. Paint flecked from the walls. During the night the ceiling light flickered. A pervading mixture of cigarette smoke and mustiness signaled the presence of old men, living behind closed doors.

I fit right in. Next month I would be twenty-six years old. Lonely and depressed, my life showed nothing of value. All of my adventures of riding the rails, hitchhiking, living in different cities, amazing road trips, pot smoking and smuggling, and experiencing the altered awareness from psychedelics, left me feeling drained.

The last eight years of my life, since I graduated high school, I had a sense of self empowerment. However, being able to break society's rule of being a 'proper girl', and emulating the freedom of men, was a false path, a rebellion. Where had all this adventure brought me? It apparently was not a true growth of inner self worth. This was a stark realization for me.

My deeper consciousness knew I was lonely. Afterall, I had lost contact with my true friends, the ones who cared about me and kept me safe. They had graduated UCSB and gone on with their lives. Some of them, like Don and Bob, had each married. Matt and Les were probably still in prison. I heard that Will had been released from county jail and moved back to his parents' home. I think Eddy moved to Colorado and Bill had a new girlfriend.

What was I doing? What did I want for my life?

I held that thought for a few days.

In the meantime I wandered down State Street all the way to Cabrillo, which was the fancy part of the coastal town, with its restaurants, shops and inns. None of that interested me. I had a passion for walking. It soothed me. A small paper sack in one hand always contained a PBJ sandwich, fruit and a candy bar. Solitude and movement guided me, while I struggled to understand what had happened to my exciting and carefree life.

Early one morning, after a lousy night's sleep, I exited that horrible hotel room and headed in the other direction, up State Street. After walking a couple of blocks I saw a man who reminded me of someone. It wasn't how he walked, with his head down. It wasn't his appearance because I only had his back view. He wore a dark suit coat and a cap like Bill always wore, soft tweed with a little brim. There was just something about him.

I hurried my steps until I circled in front of him. "Matt!" I cried out.

My dear friend had been released from prison. He stood in front of me. I leaned forward to hug him, but he jerked back.

His startled expression shifted slightly to a stare. "Kimmy." It was a flat statement. A few seconds passed and fuller recognition loosened his reaction. The stare softened to sadness, then molded to intent focus. His shoulders straightened and his chin rose. "I have to get to work." He pointed to the next office building.

"Matt, it's so good to see you. I'm glad you're here. I'm staying just down the street in the old hotel." I slowly reached out my hand to touch his arm. He didn't pull back. I told him my room number. "Please come see me." I hoped he would. He was my dear friend who had gone to prison for a few harmless joints of marijuana that I gave him. I could see he had suffered from the experience. The spark in him had gone out.

He nodded and walked into the building. I looked through the full length windows that covered the front. Several wall-high machines of some kind filled the space. They had lots of buttons, switches, and little lights. Later Matt explained that they were computers. I didn't really grasp what he told me, but I understood that his unique intelligence allowed him the capability of operating these new-fangled contraptions.

Matt visited me after work. One glance at my hotel room and he took me to dinner at a nearby Mexican restaurant. I babbled away about the places I had been while he had been locked up. He told me he worked mostly in the kitchen while in the Tehachapi State Prison. That passed the time for him. It was the only information he offered for his two years in the pen. It appeared he had learned to keep his feelings to himself.

When he walked me back to the hotel Matt said, "Kimmy, I don't know why you're living here, but you don't belong. I'm renting a tiny house a few blocks over. You're welcome to sleep on the couch." He gave me the address, and finally let me hug him.

So that's what I did. A week later I, and my meager belongings, moved in with Matt. While he was at work, I tidied up, although there wasn't really anything to tidy. My friend was very neat. Also, he was just my friend. I was safe with him and my loneliness abated for a short while.

I struggled to admit the thoughts that tried to get my attention. I paced through the tiny house, readjusting the pillow on the couch, making sure my blanket was out of sight underneath the cushions, pulling my finger across the windowsill testing for dust and straightening Matt's bath towel on its rack.

As I sat on a kitchen chair, with my hands clamped over my ears in an attempt to block the intrusive thoughts, I told myself to sit still. The thoughts whispered through my fingers. *You want a boyfriend. Someone who wants you and likes you. Someone to cuddle with and talk to. A strong man who likes the outdoors and understands what it's all about. He'll take you there and protect you. You can't do that on your own. You aren't smart enough. Look where you are now.*

My shoulders slumped. For all these years since high school I had trained myself to be independent and tough. To go where I wanted to go, and do what I wanted to do. I had amazing experiences. I regretted none of them. But one mistake. One mistake. Betraying my boyfriend. Thinking I didn't have to consider how my actions would affect him. And WHAM! Actually that happened to me twice. First with Eddy. Then with Bill.

How could this possibly be where I had come to? Exactly where my parents and society wanted me. Only desiring to be a wife who would honor and obey her husband. With no life of her own. Thinking I needed a man to take care of me.

I jumped up and shook my body like a wet dog would do. I went out the door and kept going. I needed to walk.

36
NIGHT CIRCLES

Darkness prevailed over me for the next year. Restlessness kept me moving in circles that grew smaller and smaller. I had left San Francisco because I became bored with its gay rights agenda and flower children fantasies. I spent most of my time there walking the streets alone, eating and sleeping alone. I had no goal, no objective. I hoped that moving back to Santa Barbara would alter that.

The grungy hotel on lower State Street that I moved into, did not help. I continued my isolation and long walks. My dear friend, Matt, rescued me by offering me his couch to sleep on. I felt safe in his tiny bungalow. As usual, he was kind to me and didn't question my comings and goings.

I knew something was not right with me. I felt dirty, spoiled, unworthy. Maybe I was depressed. I rarely sought out old friends. My human connection, other than Matt, consisted of parties and sex. Some of the men were casual acquaintances. Others, boyfriends of girls that I knew, eagerly offered their services. A close friend's husband gave up his fidelity to her, for a one time romp with me.

At a house party in the nearby countryside, I slipped through the backdoor with Lorenzo, who told his girlfriend, Kristin, "I'll be right back. I'm just going to take a look at Kimmy's car to see why it's making a noise." She knew what was up. I glanced her way long enough to register her seething scorn.

The smooth, tawny skinned Lorenzo and I weren't gone long. The full moon's glow led us past the parked cars that spread across the dirt driveway and onto the adjoining field. We wasted no time finding a place on the ground. I moved a few small, sharp rocks aside with my foot before this lover lowered me beneath him. I wore a short skirt, which made it easy for him to quickly pull my panties down. A twist of his foot slid them off so that my legs could spread. He unzipped his pants.

The encounter climaxed and ended quickly. The relief was appreciated by both of us. I imagined that his girlfriend would make sure this didn't happen again. I wadded up my panties and tossed them onto the backseat of my car as I drove away. There was no reason for me to return to the party.

Matt declined my invitations to go with me in the evening, as I dabbed on my gaudy blue eye shadow, too much mascara and very short skirts with no panties. I became aware that he was probably uncomfortable with my depressed attitude and out of control sexual activity. I learned to stop telling him about where I went, or what I did. He didn't reprimand me, except to say, "Be careful, Kimmy."

Recognizing that it would be better for my friend, if I moved, I drove to UCSB campus with the hope of bumping into someone who would know of a housing situation. My friends had all graduated by now and gone onto jobs and careers. Or married and started families. They had moved away from Isla Vista. Yet I decided to take a chance on finding someone familiar by walking through the student union.

As luck would have it, I spotted Pat. She sat in a booth with two other younger girls .

"Hi Pat, fancy seeing you here. You must be close to graduating. How are you?"

A big grin spread across her well scrubbed face. Pat was a natural girl. I never saw makeup on her which would have spoiled her wholesome appearance. Casual clothing of jeans and earth-toned sweaters complemented her rosy cheeks and bright eyes.

"Kimmy, it's so good to see you. Where have you been? Ruth and I have often hoped you'd come by sometime and see what we've done with the back yard and the front of the house. Flowers everywhere. Ruth found a bird bath from a secondhand store that now sits between the avocado trees." She motioned for me to sit down beside her. "These are my friends, Carol and June. We share a statistics class, which is unbearably hard. It's about the only thing that's keeping me from graduating." A pout replaced her smile.

I looked at her friends and said hello. The bangs of Carol's very short hair mostly hid a pixie shaped face. A dull green oversized army jacket buried her slight, flat-chested figure. Heavy chemistry books lay on the table in front of her over which she slumped.

June was almost her opposite in appearance and demeanor. Animated and boyish, she sat with an erect posture and a roving eye that took in every detail. Dark hair pulled into a ponytail spilled down the back of her spotless white t-shirt.

While Carol listened, Pat, June and I chatted about the events on campus and the upcoming track meet, which caused me to think of Eddy, the love of my life, who won all of his high hurdle events.

My fleeting memory was released when Pat asked me, "Where are you living now? Have you settled down yet?" She looked at her girlfriends. "Kimmy's been everywhere. She's the girl who took me hitchhiking to Idaho a few summers ago. Wow, was that ever a trip." Her laughter cascaded forth. Her friends' eyes widened as their mouths fell open.

"Well, truthfully speaking, I'm looking for a place right now. I came here hoping to bump into someone who could point me in that direction."

"Golly, Kimmy, you know you're always welcome to our couch."

"Thanks, Pat. I know that. I'm hoping for something to show up in Santa Barbara."

June took a quick glance at Carol, who met her eyes and gave an almost imperceptible nod."You could live with us," June offered. She spread her hands towards me, then back to herself. " I mean, we want you to. We have to ask Chuck, of course. It's his house. But just last night he said he wanted someone who could cook and maybe clean. Right Carol?" She beamed at her room-mate. "Carol and I aren't very good with cooking. Lately the laundry's been piling up because of this darn statistics class. The homework takes up so much time."

While June caught her breath, Carol nudged her in the ribs and tilted her head slightly towards the other side of the room. June wiggled and slapped the table top. "Yes. Of course. Chuck's right over there. Let's go ask him now." Without hesitation she and Carol slid out and motioned me to follow. Pat stayed in the booth, but swiveled around to watch us.

As we approached a booth on the other side of the room full of milling students, I saw an older man, about thirty. He wore a faded grey t-shirt and dark rimmed glasses. A book lay open in front of him. The girl he talked to looked to be barely out of high school. With long blond hair, blue eyes, frilly soft pink blouse, she leaned into him and listened raptly.

We stopped beside their booth and remained standing, waiting to be noticed.

June straightened her shoulders and cleared her throat, "Hey Chuck. We want you to meet Kimmy."

Chuck separated from his close connection with the girl and turned to face us.

Rubbing her palms together, June continued her introduction. "Kimmy's an old friend of Pat's." June turned and pointed back to Pat, who smiled and waved. "I remembered that you were looking for a cook and she's looking for a place to stay." Two bounces on her toes for emphasis. "Carol and I both really like her."

Chuck leaned back in the booth. He shifted his focus from the girls to me. Without smiling, he looked me up and down. I didn't budge. I'd been through this before. Let him get a good look.

"Is your cooking any good?"

"Yes it is."

"What can you cook?"

Something shifted deep within me. A rousing of my old self assurance surfaced as I rested my weight onto one foot and set my hand on my hip. With an assuredness that I didn't know I had, I took a deep breath. "I like casseroles with lots of creamy sauce, meatloaf and mashed potatoes are always good, sloppy Joes and French fries never fail, pork chops and stuffed bell peppers have their own appeal, omelets filled with mushrooms, onions, cheese and topped with salsa make a tasty breakfast, my pie crusts are especially flakey, I bake a variety of cookies, and have you ever tasted pancakes topped with sour cream, powdered sugar and strawberries?" Closing my mouth, I locked my eyes dead on his. I did not crack a smile.

Chuck had his own deadpan expression and ultra cool demeanor that vied for the upper hand. He put his elbows on the table and crossed his arms. "Would you be willing to do laundry and mop the kitchen floor?"

With that assuredness I didn't know I had, I cooly replied, "Certainly there would not be a daily need for that."

Chuck readjusted his thick lensed glasses and again looked me up and down. "I have my own room. The girls all bunk together. My friend, Roy, has a bedroom he uses when he's on leave from the Navy. He only shows up now and then for a day or two." Chuck paused to rub a hand across his chin. "I'll tell him to sleep on the couch. You can have that room." Another pause while he glanced at June and Carol. "I can't pay you anything. It's strictly room and board. Are you interested?" Again he leaned back.

Although I was relieved to be able to move out of Matt's home, I needed to be cautious about what I could be getting into. This older guy with these young girls didn't seem right to me. Yet I felt buoyant with the surge of energy from standing my ground against such a conceited man. I pulled back my shoulders and let my arms relax at my sides. "Yeah, I'm interested."

Chuck nodded his approval. He scribbled on a bit of paper from the notebook of the girl cuddled next to him. "OK. Here's the address. Come by in time to make dinner."

The girls and I walked back to the table where Pat waited.

Carol slid back into the booth and tucked her arms around her books.

June followed her, bounced around a bit to settle herself and smiled at Pat. "Kimmy's going to live with us. We'll be able to hear all about her adventures, and maybe even learn to cook."

Pat looked up at me. "I hope that works out for you, but please come visit Ruth and me soon."

"Thanks, Pat. Tell Ruth 'hello' for me." I turned to go, paused, looked back over my shoulder at the girls. "Darn, I forgot to tell him about my homemade bread."

37
CHUCK'S HAREM

Carol, June and Olivia, the girls who lived at the house I moved into, I thought of as Chuck's harem. From their willingness to do his bidding, I assumed they previously had little experience with an intimate relationship, or dating. Probably they were virgins before encountering Chuck. Just a year, or two, graduated from high school, receiving attention from this older man seemed to captivate them.

I could see that he made each of them feel special. Carol was assured that small breasts were desirable. June received praise for her courage to skydive with her father. Olivia cuddled next to him or sat on his lap. They responded to his every request without hesitation. I saw them clean his room, do his laundry, and wash his dishes. Homework was often spontaneously set aside to rub his shoulders, bring a cold beer from the refrigerator, or sit at his feet while he expounded on a new theory. Never did I hear them argue or offer any resistance. They all took turns spending nights with him.

Cleverly, Chuck had the girls share a room, so when one was

with him, the other two were together. They never felt alone, or excluded. Sister bonds were created.

I was given a separate bedroom. Chuck never tried to seduce me. He adhered to our arrangement of me doing the cooking and a bit of housekeeping. I could come and go as I pleased, as long as I provided breakfast and dinner daily, and sometimes lunch on the weekends.

Besides cooking and cleaning, maybe my role was to be a big sister, or confidant, like a house mother in a college dorm. Chuck seemed relieved that I was able to handle the monthly emotions the girls displayed. Cramps and tears annoyed him, especially if all the girls were upset at the same time. In that case, he stayed in his room with a 'do not disturb sign' on his door.

On the other hand, Chuck had something else in mind for me. I was to learn that he set me aside for his Navy buddy, Roy, who was stationed in San Diego, and sometimes came to visit. He was expected soon.

The girls were all a twitter to make a good impression. Olivia tried on different clothes, hairstyles and makeup. She wanted to shine, to make Chuck proud of her captured beauty. Carol huddled at one end of the couch in her army jacket. "Do you think Roy will be offended because it's not a Navy peacoat?" June brushed her ponytail and put on a fresh white tee shirt.

Since I had been living at Chuck's, my need for partying and impressing men had fizzled out. Paying attention to the girls, helping with some school assignments, and being creative with cooking shifted my attention to more wholesome endeavors. Besides, having had sex with other girls' boyfriends, or husbands, gnawed at me. I felt like trash. Being stoned hadn't dulled my awareness of those episodes. I still knew what I was doing, although I didn't know why. I needed to face my behavior and change. I doubted that I would ever be the 'proper girl' my parents and society raised me to be. I just wanted to feel good about myself. So I shut down my pot intake to face myself with a clear mind. I only took a toke now and then in the backyard, under the oak tree. Sitting quietly, I enjoyed the sunshine and watched little birds come and go, as I recalled the monarch butterflies on the bluff and the condors soaring above.

Roy's visit to Chuck's home offered the needed break in his regimented navy life. Weekend leave did not apparently provide him with enough travel time to visit his fiance, who lived in Stockton, which was north of Santa Barbara. I didn't know if his up-coming marriage would be one of fidelity, but it turned out that his prenuptial zone stood wide open. However, Roy knew better than to touch Chuck's girls.

Although they were the same height, an even six feet, these buddies had different bodies. Roy's Navy life kept him slim and trim with tight muscles. Whereas Chuck's love for food and beer produced an expanding belly that stretched his tee shirt. No obvious exercise, other than bed maneuvers and turning pages in a book, kept him soft.

Chuck declared that Roy's arrival called for a sumptuous dinner, lip smacking dessert and extra booze. " Kimmy, get a move on. Here's extra money. Hustle to the market for special dinner makings. Now."

I got the message. Roy was royalty.

I leaned on my mother's cooking for inspiration. Pot roast with vegetables, a savory sauce and homemade rolls for dinner. Cheesecake for dessert. Both would be winners. Two six packs of beer for the menfolk. Root beer floats for the girls. Otherwise I would muster up omelets stuffed with chopped onions, bell peppers and mushrooms, and hash browns on the side for break-fast. Sandwiches for lunch with fruit for snacks should be good enough. At least, that's what I would be serving. I pulled together the cheesecake early so it had time to set in the refrigerator.

Chuck and his buddy left the house soon after Roy's arrival. Patting him on the back with one hand, Chuck cradled a six pack under his other arm and announced, "We're heading out for a while. Probably cruise the town a bit. Maybe check out the babes on the beach."

Roy was talking and pointing at his parked car as they walked through the door. "Wait 'til you feel this baby's power. Mustangs were made to haul ass."

Two hours later when the buddies returned, half of the six pack came back with them. According to Roy, "I do not drink and drive. If I got stopped the Navy would find out and I'd be in a world of hurt."

That statement caught my attention. Maybe this Navy guy had common sense, or a decent morality after all. Maybe I assumed wrongly that he desired sex with someone other than his fiance. Of course I noticed Roy running his eyes over me when he first arrived. And I wondered what he would be like in bed. Then abruptly I wiped that thought out of my mind. He had a fiance, and I intended to curb my sexual impulses.

After 'thanks' for the meal I served, the others settled in the living room where Chuck let the girls tell Roy a bit about themselves. I remained in the kitchen cleaning up.

When we had all gone to our rooms for the night, and Chuck had decided who got to join him, Roy quietly slipped into my room.

I was already in bed. I pretended to be asleep, because I didn't want him there. But I didn't say anything. I just hoped he would leave. I didn't want a confrontation.

Without a word, and without hesitation, Roy undressed, drew the covers back and lay down beside me. I still pretended to sleep. That didn't stop him. He mounted me, fully aroused. He was gentle enough and quite thorough. My body responded. I moaned at the appropriate times. After he climaxed, he again didn't say a word. He simply lifted off me, pulled on his pants, and closed the door behind him on the way out.

I rolled onto my side. I didn't even bother to wash myself. *Why didn't he say anything? Why didn't I stop him? What have I become? Am I a housemother to Chuck's harem and a quick screw for his pals? This has got to stop!* I screamed into my pillow and fell into a restless sleep.

The next morning I awoke knowing that Chuck expected me to make breakfast and another outstanding dinner. I dressed quickly and went downstairs before anyone else stirred. Roy was asleep on the couch with his back to the living room. I closed the door to the kitchen and hurriedly assembled a lasagna which I put in the refrigerator. I taped a note with baking and salad instructions on the door.

With my car keys, two sandwiches, and my sketchbook, I walked out the front door. June sat on the porch steps lacing up her running shoes. I told her, "Read the note on the frig. I'm gone for the day."

I drove north through Santa Barbara, stopping at a market for bananas, Milky Ways, and a bottle of apple juice. There I bumped into a former, short time, lover. Paul was a good guy, but not really my type. He had filled in between Eddy and Bill. Safe and gentle, I trusted him.

"Paul, wow, fancy seeing you here. How's it going?"

He spun around, took a step back and grinned. " Well, far out! " Brief pause while he took a gallon of milk from the cooler. "Same ol', same ol'. Wow, Kimmy, it's good to see you." He leaned in and gave me a kiss on my cheek. His arms encircled three boxes of cereal.

I couldn't help but chuckle. Paul and a bowl of cereal were synonymous. Seeing him lightened my mood.

I told him I was back in the area. He told me where he lived.

"Drop in sometime. You'll be welcome. My roommate, Rod, makes trips to Tijuana, if you know what I mean?'' He gave me a wink.

"Sounds good to me, Paul. You might even see me soon. Stay cool, daddy-o."

I was gone for two days. I had no intention of returning until Roy had left, which would be tomorrow evening when he went back to the base. In the meantime I drove up the coast to the bluff where I had good memories. My sleeping bag still nestled under the hood of my VW Bug. I pulled it out and laid it under the eucalyptus trees, my guardians. I didn't need anything else but the solitude and the beauty of being outdoors.

Alone on the bluff, overlooking the Pacific Ocean was just what I needed. I walked barefoot in the warm powdered dirt beneath the stately trees, taking in their wonderful lemony pine aroma. Rustling leaves sang to me. A few tokes on a joint loosened my troubled thoughts. Memories of my friends flashed in and out of my awareness. Eddy, Bill, Nancy, Bob, Matt, Les, Gil, Ruth. *I wonder where they are? Are they all safe and happy? When will I be safe, and happy?* Memories floated through my mind.

I reached for my sketchbook, but I didn't need pictures to ease the turmoil of the dark path I had been on for too long. Instead, words caught my attention...hitchhiking, riding the rails, pot, peyote, proper girl, free love, sex, freak, loser. I released my troubled soul onto the paper.

> *I haven't the slightest idea*
> *Who I am.*
> *But the Grey Ghost rides in the afterdark*
> *Of my thoughts*
> *And clamors and hammers*
> *To know what I mean,*

Or what seems.
So I struggle and sigh,
And grasp and groan,
And scream for the alone
Of my awakening.

Late Sunday night I returned to Chuck's house. Roy's Mustang was not parked in the driveway. He was gone. I just had to reckon with Chuck.

He accosted me as soon as I walked in, like a coyote on a rabbit. He blocked me from going up stairs to my room. "Where have you been? Our agreement was for you to be here." He spoke with apparent agitation. His fists clenched and unclenched at his sides. His sneer mocked me. His chin jutted towards my face. Disheveled hair gave him a wild man appearance.

My voice remained calm, as my guts tightened into a knot. "We agreed that I would cook two meals daily with occasional housework such as mopping the floors." I wasn't interested in anything he had to say. I refused to kowtow to him. The proper girl attitude no longer worked for me. I took a step forward to go up the stairs.

But Chuck had more to say. He stepped closer to me. He leaned into my face. "Hah! You haven't been here for the last two days. You slunk away yesterday morning."

I stood my ground and steadied my breathing. "I noticed."

"Don't you smart mouth me. Who do you think you are? Do you think you're too good for my friends?" He threw back his shoulders and puffed out his chest.

I didn't respond. I shifted my gaze to the top of the stairs rather than at this hunk of lard who thought he was God's gift to women and had the right to control my life.

Chuck sputtered, working his fists open and closed, open and closed. "I give you room and board here. I don't expect any more from your used up self except preparing two meals a day. The least you could do to repay my generosity was be nice to my friend while he was here." His face burned red. The cords in his neck bulged.

I looked over my shoulder at the girls who had been huddled together in the background of the living room. Huddled together in obvious fear and confusion, Carol's face was buried in June's back. I saw the tears that streamed down Olivia's face. What had Chuck told them to frighten them so much?

This wasn't the time to give them comfort. I needed to take care of myself. Looking directly at each girl I said, "Chuck wants to know why I didn't stick around to let his buddy fuck me some more."

Collectively the girls gasped.

Before he gathered his wits to respond, I moved around him and went up stairs. I closed the door to my room and shoved the desk chair under the doorknob.

Chuck did not pursue me, and the girls also kept their distance. I assumed he told them to avoid me. The next day none of them spoke to me. It was Monday so the girls went to campus and Chuck stayed in his room.

My pent up energy begged release so I could think straight. I made up for my absence by mopping the kitchen floor and vacuuming the living room. I washed my sheets and the bedding used by Roy. Planning meals for the week and baking a two layer chocolate cake with a cherry filling occupied my mind. Between chores I walked around the neighborhood, or over to the high-school to use its track to run.

That evening I served the dinner I had made, but I ate alone at the little table in the kitchen. After washing and putting away the dishes, I left the house to catch the cool night air with a jog to the beach and back. When I returned, I headed to the kitchen for a glass of water. Chuck sat at the dining table with the girls standing, clustered around him. I felt Carol shudder as I passed by, and Olivia leaned in closer to him. June didn't twitch a muscle.

They had all ignored me for the past two days, and I wasn't curious about what held their interest this time. As I rinsed off my glass and set it on the drainboard, I turned to go to my room. That's when I saw the gun.

I pushed the girls aside and stood between them and Chuck. With my heart pounding, I yelled at him, "Is that loaded?"

Chuck leaned back in his chair, elevating its front legs. He beamed. His smile spread from ear to ear. He licked his lips to catch the drool that formed. "Of course it is, Kimmy."

I slammed my hands on the table and leaned towards him. "How dare you endanger these girls with your arrogance! Unload it now and give me the bullets." My voice shook and I felt adrenaline surge through my body.

Chuck's chair thudded back to the floor and then overturned as he jerked to his feet. I stood tall facing him, breathing hard. In one swift move he stepped towards me, and slugged me in the face with his fist. I heard myself groan as I slumped to the floor.

My attacker's voice bounced off the walls. "Leave her be. She doesn't deserve any pity from you. She's no more than a used up whore."

June, Carol and Olivia awkwardly stepped over me as they rushed upstairs.

When I rose from the floor, Chuck too had left the room. The gun was gone from the table. I felt my face for blood. There was none. The pain in my cheekbone and the profound dizziness kept me from moving, until I could gather my wits together. Then I made myself stand up and stumbled upstairs to my room. Gathering my belongings, I threw everything into the backseat of my car and drove to the parking lot on the Embarcadero. The lot there was well lit to protect the nearby expensive stores. I felt safe for the night. I had left that house of madness. My head pounded from the blow. I tossed and turned as I sought the shelter of sleep.

38

BACK TO THE BEGINNING

The next day I parked my car in front of the address Paul gave me. Slowly I walked to his front porch and knocked on the door.

He was home. He opened the door and gawked at me before he stammered, "Kimmy, what happened to you?"

I guessed that my black eye was obvious. "I was in the wrong place at the wrong time."

"Come in. Come in." Paul reached out and gently pulled me into his home. "You are safe here."

His two roommates said the same thing to me. They didn't ask for an explanation. Instead, they fed me breakfast and let me spread my sleeping bag out on the couch.

I crawled inside and slept for two days. When I woke up, I took a shower, put on clean clothes and washed the dishes.

The guys went about their own business and allowed me a quiet space. The first two weeks in my new home, I feared Chuck would find me. I stayed indoors. The demon visions, from my encounter with Howard, reappeared when I closed my eyes, so I had trouble sleeping for a while.

When my mind and nerves finally calmed down, I found that living with Paul and his roommates, Rod and Larry, was a relief and a pleasure. They each had their own agenda, and all of them were students at the city college. Quiet, unassuming Larry went full time, going for an AA degree in general studies so he could transfer to UCSB. I rarely saw him without a book. Paul and Rod took one, or two, classes, just enough to allow them on campus to meet girls. They also had part time jobs to cover their expenses, and Rod made periodic trips to Tijuana to score marijuana.

Because these three guys were like brothers to me, rather than boyfriend material, I decided to go celibate. I got off the birth control pills and was no longer on the prowl for sexual interactions. Instead, I wanted a completely different viewpoint than what I had experienced for the past nine years, or so. *Wow, it has been that long since I graduated from high school?*

My starting point for change took me to the city college. The guys' involvement there indicated possibilities for learning a variety of subjects, and perhaps meeting interesting people. While sitting on a bench in the campus sunshine, and considering possibilities, two girls walked by chatting merrily about their drawing assignment. *Really? Just like that I can maybe get myself into an art class?*

"Hey, wait up." I almost dove at them in my eagerness. I tried to act casual, but I'd already blown that. Even so, they guided me to the admissions office where I became enrolled in a painting class with an older male instructor, who turned out to be a groovy dude who played Beatles and Rolling Stones music during class.

I also found an old upright piano at Goodwill that was delivered to Paul's home. I tried to teach myself to read music but the lower keys, and the black keys confused me. I banged away mostly on the white ones. As long as I was stoned, it sounded to me like music from heaven.

Another way to keep me out of trouble, or even thinking about it, was to visit my parents. First I visited my father, who was still in Downey. He was relieved that I had returned to college, and he gave me enough money to cover my expenses there, plus extra for gas.

My mother had moved to an apartment in Seal Beach to be near my brother and away from my father. After visiting my mom for two days, I finally understood that she cared about me. She just didn't approve of my lifestyle. She wanted me to accept my place in society, as she best understood it. That meant marriage to a decent, hardworking man, like my brother. She wanted me to be a homemaker, because she wanted me to be safe and to do good with my life. That was my parents' real plan for me.

Letting them see that I was all in one piece and pursuing a reasonable direction, I returned to Santa Barbara. Domesticity became my grounding focus. Cooking and cleaning were my fortes. I baked almost every day, so the house held competing aromas of yummy food and marijuana smoke. Also I painted the bathroom floor and made curtains for its window. My roommates were startled by the makeover, but they were appreciative. In essence I had become a homemaker, and that felt OK. It came easily to me even though my mom hardly taught me anything. I guessed I had observed more than I realized. Then I found myself smiling when I pulled a sheet full of lemon bar cookies out of the oven, knowing that my roommates would fight over the very last one.

Time passed easily for me. The art class was cool. During my leisure moments, I chose to be outdoors. The beach, and especially my favorite spot on the bluff, overlooking the ocean, gave me the most comfort. Walking and running released tension and troublesome thoughts. Fresh air and the beauty of nature restored my spirit. My longing to understand, and to be a part of the natural world, with its majesty and mysteries tugged at my heart.

When I wasn't cooking, drawing, playing the piano, or going for walks, I visited Matt, who was emerging from his incarceration trauma. "Guess what, Kimmy. I've been accepted to a culinary school!" He was radiant. I didn't catch the school's location, but I understood my dear friend would be moving. That was our goodbye moment.

In the days to come I struggled with the sadness of failing to recognise the drifting away of friends. I had been too busy living my rambunctious and all consuming life to stay connected. Ruth and Pat remained in the little house on the hill. Don and his wife, Bonnie, were snuggled into their home at Painted Cave. That was it. The whereabouts of other dear friends were unknown to me. My present roommates were my human lifeline, but what did they connect me to? They had their own interests and paths to follow.

I was lonely. Probably that's why I seduced Rod. I needed to be held and rocked into a rhythm of togetherness. It was just that one time. I wanted a lasting relationship.

My actions, and their results, began to add up for me. Since high school I had taken so many crazy ass risks to break the mold of being a proper girl. Most of the time I had no clue what I was doing. Fortunately I had friends who cared about me and gave me some kind of grounding. At least they tried, especially Nancy, who told me that I needed a plan for my life. But after Eddy dumped me, I screwed up time and time again, until Ruth bailed me out of New Orleans with a bus ticket back to Santa Barbara. And I screwed up even more, with Bill. It just kept going like that until Chuck slugged me in the face.

Hopefully I'd received enough punishment to have paid the

price for so many wrong choices. *Now how do I come up with that plan that Nancy talked about?* All that I knew was that I really liked being outdoors. If I could have anything that I wanted it would be to live in some wilderness where I could learn to survive in it, like a pioneer. And mostly, I guessed, I wanted a man who loved me, and we could do that together. *Does that make a plan?*

39

THE PLAN ARRIVES

A week after the first of the New Year in 1970, I raked leaves along the grassy edge of our driveway. A car pulled in and left the motor running. The passenger door opened and out stepped a handsome man with an odd haircut, that was flat on top with long sides swept back. A beautiful, long haired, black dog stood beside him. The car drove away and left my future standing there looking directly at me.

It wasn't just the steady gaze that captured my attention, nor the fact that, like most men I had encountered, he didn't look me up and down. No. It was the clear blueness of his eyes, like the shore of a distant sea that beckoned me to sail away, that caused the rake to fall from my hands and my heart skip a beat

"Hey, it's about time you showed up here, " Rod's voice rang out from the open front door as he leaned out and motioned for the stranger to come on in. " It's been too long since I've heard one of your tall tales."

The man gave me a gentle smile as he, and the dog, turned and went into the house.

After I put the rake back into the garage, I slipped through the back door and listened from the kitchen as Rod and his friend talked about a place called Steele Ranch, which was in Southern Oregon. Apparently it was a gathering place for people who had dropped out of the American Dream of how life should be lived (according to the dominant, white male ideology of 'grab all the money and power you can'). Instead, this little enclave in the middle of the woods was a retreat for deeper thinking individuals who wanted to live a simpler, healthier lifestyle. Also, it wasn't a place just for men. I heard this intriguing man tell Rod, "Women are there too, chopping wood, going barefoot, letting their hair hang loose."

Quietly I ventured into the living room and sat on the arm of the couch. The man was sitting on the floor, with his back against the couch, and the dog's head resting on his lap. Rod faced them from the old stuffed chair. A lit joint went back and forth between them. Rod offered it to me, but I shook my head. That's when the man turned to look at me, and again gave me a gentle smile.

He revealed that he was only visiting for a couple of days, while he delivered the Belgian Shepherd to its new home, and then caught a ride with friends returning to their cabin, which was next door to the Ranch. He continued talking about Oregon and its Kalmiopsis Wilderness. He knew old timers who lived along its mountain road, and the clear running river filled with steelhead trout and otters. He also talked about the rugged coast and backpacking.

I listened intently, until I smelled the savory aroma of the stew that I had simmering on the stove for the past two hours. "Is anyone hungry?"

After the silence of attending to a satisfying lunch, the blue eyed man turned directly to me. "Tell me, Kimmy, what do you like to do?"

That was not an easy question for me to answer. So instead, I said, "Well, I've heard that 'a picture is worth a thousand words.' So let me show you," I said, as I motioned for him to come with me.

I drove us north, then up the road past the little house, to the nearby Painted Cave community. I wanted him to see the view that the condors had. From there, while the black dog sniffed and claimed several bushes and small boulders, I told him about my hitchhiking adventures, and the camping-out road trip. I didn't emphasize the guys who shared those times with me. Instead I talked about the places I had seen and what that all meant to me.

Later that night, back at the house, he told me more about Oregon having so many places to explore, and the freedom that it held.

I told him about riding the rails and smuggling pot across the Mexican border. Again, I didn't so much mention the people I was with. It was the experiences, the novelty and excitement of those events that I wanted him to know about me. I didn't mention boyfriends, nor the men who hurt me, nor my time in the cities. Those were memories I buried deeply within myself.

The next day I gave him, and the dog, a ride to the hills outside of Montecito, where the beautiful animal met its new family. The man and I continued driving on the mountain ridge road. It was so easy to be with him, his quiet manner and gentle smile. The blue eyes that seemed to notice so much. We could be quiet together, just seeing and breathing in the good air.

A day later, early in the morning when his friends arrived, he approached me. "Come to Steele Ranch with me. Meet more of my friends. We can hitchhike to the coast and back. You'll be able to see for yourself what Oregon's like. I know of a hollowed out giant redwood tree we can sleep in. The acres of Easter Lilies will be in bloom."

Nancy's words filled my mind." Know what you want Kimmy, and make a plan."

"I'll bring you back whenever you want…. What do you say, Kimmy?" His gaze upon me was steady. I felt he looked deep within me, and he liked what he saw.

It was then I realized that all my risk-taking adventures had brought me here, to this moment. The plan I had been wanting was being offered to me. I could explore the wilderness with this man as he taught me how to live in its unique story. We could share a remarkable life together. My heart pounded. I slowed my breathing. "Yes. I'll go to Oregon with you."

Acknowledgments

This story, which has remained in my memory in technicolor, has been brought to the surface, and released, through the encouragement of others. A dozen conscientious family members and friends read my first draft. They offered excellent suggestions for improvement. Most of them let me know that they wanted a sequel to find out, "What happens next?" Thank you for your honesty, insights and support.

A member of our critique group, Tona McFall, earns my respect as an aspiring editor. She taught me to recognize the ordering of my words, sentences and paragraphs to enable the flow and understanding of what I was trying to convey. "1,2,3." Thank you Tona.

My deepest appreciation for guidance goes to Judy Howard, self-published author of eight books. She is my writing guru, patiently and wisely coaxing me with the biggest challenge of all —to "go deep" within myself to find and tell the real story. I have profound appreciation for Judy.

Writing is both a thrilling and a humbling experience.

ABOUT THE AUTHOR

Kimmy is Zoë West's childhood name. She is a mother, who earned a degree in psychology, which helped to make a bit more sense out of life, both professionally and personally. In her spare time, she paints and displays her art in various galleries and shows in Oregon, where she now resides, on its southern coast. This is her first book.